Teresa Solana has a degree in Philosophy from the University of Barcelona where she also studied Classics. She has worked as a literary translator and directed the Spanish National Translation Centre in Tarazona. She has published many essays and articles on translation and written several novels she preferred to keep in her drawer. Her first published novel, *A Not So Perfect Crime*, won the 2007 Brigada 21 Prize for the best crime novel written in Catalan and has also been translated into French, German, Italian, Romanian and Spanish.

A NOT SO PERFECT

CRIME

Teresa Solana

Translated from the Catalan
by Peter Bush

BITTER LEMON PRESS
LONDON

BITTER LEMON PRESS

First published in the United Kingdom in 2008 by
Bitter Lemon Press, 37 Arundel Gardens, London W11 2LW

www.bitterlemonpress.com

First published in Catalan as *Un crim imperfecte* by
Edicions 62, Barcelona, 2006

Bitter Lemon Press gratefully acknowledges
the financial assistance of the
Institut Ramon Llull and the Arts Council of England

A CIP record for this book is available
from the British Library

ISBN 978–1–904738–34-3

Typeset by Alma Books Ltd
Printed and bound by
CPI Cox & Wyman, Reading, RG1 8EX

**institut
ramon llull**
Catalan Language and Culture

For Peter Bush

PART ONE

1

My brother Borja's name isn't Borja. It's Pep (or Josep). And his surname isn't Masdéu-Canals Sáez de Astorga. We're both Martínez on our father's side and Estivill on our mother's.

Unlike Borja, (I mean, Pep), I've kept the name and surnames my parents gave me: a humble Eduard (though still a Spanish Eduardo on my ID card) Martínez Estivill. My brother's name (or at least the one he prefers to flaunt) is Borja Masdéu-Canals Sáez de Astorga, notwithstanding an identity card he should have renewed years ago that proclaims him *José Martínez Estivill, born in Barcelona, son of Rosa and Francisco*. Naturally nobody knows that Pep, (I mean, Borja) and I are brothers. Twins, to boot. No one, not even my wife.

Our parents were born in Barcelona, although on my father's side our grandparents and great-grandparents hailed from Soria, in deepest Castile. As for Borja-Pep's imaginary family, as he himself likes to expatiate, his father was from Lleida, the youngest in a family owning large stretches of arable land and herds of cows in the region of Alt Urgell, while his mother was a rich heiress from Santander, the coastal resort where Borja's invented parents had decided to settle down after they married, and where he claims he was born.

This canny family tree enables my brother Borja to justify the fact that, despite his spectacularly blue-blooded surnames and the handsome family fortune he should logically have inherited (he presents himself as an only child, so as not to over-complicate matters), nobody in Barcelona has ever heard of the Masdéu-Canals Sáez de Astorgas. My brother is also quick to explain, when referring to his precarious financial state, that he comes from one of those ancient families which inevitably fell on hard times and whose genealogical roots are mired in a silt of aristocratic surnames of obscure medieval origin.

"Papa," Borja usually explains (from here on I'll refer to him using the name everyone knows him by, the one I'm now used to), "was unable to adapt to modern times and lost his entire inheritance. He invested everything in the family business in Santander, and managed to make a fortune. But the times were changing . . . The famous industrial reorganization of the shipyards came along, and, as if that weren't enough, papa fell foul of the Revenue, which wasn't his fault, of course, but down to a wretched accountant who lost him a heap of money," he concludes in hushed tones with a shake of the head as he embroiders his tale with pride, fatalistic resignation and always with the utmost conviction.

Though we are twins, my brother Borja and I are not at all alike physically. I mean we don't *look* like brothers. He takes more after our mother's family, who were rather carefree and slim, while I take after our father's, always on the sullen and chubby side. In fact, having left the womb a couple of minutes after me, Borja is the younger fledgling: nonetheless every so often it amuses my twin to remind me that, if we'd been a king's sons (the legitimate variety, naturally), he, not I, would have been the rightful heir to the throne. I tell him not to worry, I'm sure we wouldn't have fought each other for the honour. As far as I'm concerned, this peculiar idiosyncrasy of monarchies struggling to preserve vestiges of ignorance from past eras – namely, first spliced, last out – takes a weight off my mind. Perhaps because I'm a hesitant, shrinking violet, and Borja's the capricious, daring type.

We are twins and will both be forty-five in May, but I have to admit that my brother seems somewhat younger. He's still single, although for a long time he's had a sort of more or less steady girlfriend who likes to have him on her arm at Barcelona's most select venues. Maybe the only drawback in this arrangement – depending on your point of view, obviously – is that she is married.

Clearly, the husband of this girl (who is hardly a girl any more) is a guy with lots of money and no time to spend with his family. However, I deduce from stories Borja sometimes tells that she's not what you'd call a downtrodden spouse. The woman, Mercedes by name and Merche for short, belongs to that cohort of successful female lawyers who graduate from the Abat Oliva University to work in Barcelona's most select law practices. She devotes herself to the kind of work that brings in the bacon for graduates of expensive, prestigious institutions favoured by well-heeled Catholics who dedicate their talents to ensuring that the rich don't pay too much tax. Borja and Merche usually meet up on the odd evening and spend weekends together, when her husband goes on his travels. Apparently, this happens quite often, since he's an entrepreneur who owns factories in China (or something of the kind), and one of those successful men who revel in the ancient tradition of more than a little slap and tickle with their secretaries and other deserving causes, usually on business junkets to destinations never very far from a sweep of tropical beach.

They constitute, so Borja informs me (the fount of all my knowledge on the affairs of Barcelona's upper classes) a modern couple typical of this social background, sharing children and social activities but separating out lives and bank accounts. Merche has a teenage son who's overly fond of snorting coke (like his mother I suspect), whereas Borja, to the best of his knowledge, has no offspring. The only worrying vice I associate with him is Cardhu, and he can't drink that in excess because he's perpetually broke. I know next to nothing of Borja's love life before Merche.

In fact, despite the close relationship we enjoy now, the last twenty years of my twin brother's life are a mystery that only receives sporadic illumination when, under the influence of Cardhu, Borja makes the occasional, apparently sincere revelation. I clutch at such straws in order to painstakingly reconstruct periods of his life, and it's thanks to this Scottish beverage that I've found out he set foot in Australia, starved in Germany and would never work again as cook on an oil tanker. And also that he lived in Paris for several years, but more of this anon.

I'm still married to the same woman, my darling Montse, and we have three children: two fourteen year-old girls, also twins, and a terrible two who will soon be three. My brother Borja still boasts a splendid head of brown hair (to which I am sure Iranzo, his stylist, adds blonde highlights once a month), and loves silk ties, English pin-stripe suits and Italian casuals. I prefer corduroy and jeans, checked shirts and lace-ups. Although we are more or less the same height, just below six feet, I weigh in at twenty-six pounds more – not that I'm what you'd call fat. I'll admit I might be developing a paunch, and, like our father, a receding hairline that I do my best to conceal. My remaining hair, of which luckily there is a lot, is unaccountably greying in a way that doesn't give me a more distinguished air – not even when I imitate Borja and pile on the gel and comb it back. His skin is always an enviable golden brown thanks to a sun-tanning salon next door to his block, while mine stays milky white most of the year. Borja works out at a gym at least three times a week, but I get more than enough exercise with my contribution to the general house-clean every Saturday, and by playing with the kid every day while Montse's getting dinner. Borja is rightwing (for aesthetic reasons, he claims) and I soldier on as a non-voting, disillusioned left-winger.

I must confess that I blush easily when forced to tell even the most innocent of fibs, whereas Borja only goes red when he blabs something that sounds as if it's really true. In restaurants he is able to select wine not simply as a function of price and knows how to wield the appropriate utensils when dissecting a lobster, while I always end up ordering meat and giving the nod to whatever wine I'm asked to taste.

We are both partners (and the only employees) in a kind of consultancy, as we call it, which on our cards and letterhead proclaims itself *Frau Consultants, Ltd.* The name Borja chose initially was the Greek letter *Tau*, invoking Taurus, the sign of the Zodiac we share; it is not a word in Catalan or Spanish, and we felt that to be opportune considering the strange things that occur with language questions in our country, particularly on the Upper North Side of this city. However, someone made a mistake at the printers, and Borja, who is a touch superstitious, read it as an omen, decided to take the error on board and renamed our newly created company. *Frau* brings the word "fraud" to my mind, reasonably enough, and perhaps there is some of that lurking behind my brother's new moniker and his permanent state of bankruptcy. Borja appreciates the finer things in life and likes to splash out – which, given his circumstances, is not very often.

The truth of the matter is that Frau Consultants is not a real firm because it has no legal existence at the company registry and, in any case, the activities we undertake generate little in the way of invoices and paperwork. The consultancy we offer, and which our clients require, is too confidential in nature to allow for written contracts, let alone reports and invoices; but it is quite another matter to run to a decent office where we can see clients and hand out elegant, expensive cards embossed with our names and telephone numbers. As Borja says, they lend an air of respectability that leads important people to trust us, and at the end of the day trust is what it's all about. In terms of hierarchy, he's the company director and I'm his deputy. In practice, to make it crystal-clear, he provides the clients, class and personal charm, and I perform the bloodhound routines.

As we don't have a secretary (our current budget won't stretch to a blonde goddess manicuring her nails all day in the office, though she'd be one of the improvements Borja would like to introduce into the company), we are forced to give our clients the numbers of our blasted mobile phones. These are the very latest models thanks to an acquaintance of Borja who works around the shops in the port area and gets them on the cheap (I suspect that backstreet dealing in mobiles off the backs of lorries is one of the scams Borja resorts to when we aren't on a case). What we *do* have is a small, very chic office – top end as they say – on carrer

Balmes, very close to the plaça Bonanova, because we pay a peppercorn rent that was fixed years ago. Borja says this rent, ridiculously low considering we work in one of those districts in Barcelona where the nakedness of the graffiti-free walls verges on the obscene, is a favour granted by a grateful friend. I imagine it's a friend who's very grateful because my brother has kept the lid on various items of compromising information. There's a reception area, a small sink and 400 square feet of space containing our non-existent secretary's desk. Since it is so roomy, we've equipped it with two armchairs and a small sofa from the Ikea sales, together with two standard lamps and a brightly coloured carpet, a longish second-hand glass table, one side of which is slightly cracked, and six leather-upholstered chairs Borja bought on the cheap (a job-lot from a removal van, I guess). This is where we meet our clients, who are not exactly queuing up. With characteristic cunning Borja has had very flash imitation-mahogany doors set in one of the walls (the carpenter has yet to be paid, I fear), mounted with a couple of gilt plaques that proclaim our names and respective posts in italics:

Borja Masdéu-Canals Sáez de Astorga
Director
and
Eduardo Martínez Estivill
Deputy Director

When we see clients, our secretary is invariably on holiday or out on an errand. Nonetheless, there is always a little bottle of red *Chanel* nail varnish and other small items on her desk that supposedly betray a feminine presence: a

15

Liberty foulard draped casually over the back of her chair (which, one festive night, after a couple of generous measures of Cardhu, Borja confessed he'd requisitioned from a restaurant coat-stand), a copy of *Hello!* (inevitably a very out-of-date copy purloined from my brother's sun-tanning salon) and a plant that doesn't require much water. He reckons such anodyne objects lend credibility to the idea that a woman is at work there. We also keep a filched bottle of *L'Air du Temps* in one of the drawers of the desk, whereon rests a *Mac* that doesn't work, and occasionally when we are expecting a visit, we squirt the scent around and perfume the atmosphere with the high-class secretarial touch Borja believes to be so vital. As for our non-existent offices behind fake doors, they are always being painted or redecorated.

After all my setting of the scene, it must be apparent that our customers almost always belong to the upper classes, and that what we can offer them is absolute discretion in the matters they confide to us. "Eduard, lie under an oak tree and your acorns will prosper," Borja likes to repeat. It's one of his favourite sayings. The other is the one about God and dice.

"Eduard, God doesn't play dice . . ." he likes to quip when we find ourselves up a blind alley or enjoy a sudden stroke of good luck.

In fact, Borja and I play the role of intermediary in the kinds of negotiations the rich don't like to conduct them-selves, such as buying or selling whatever comes their way and pawning jewels and art objects. We sometimes get involved in collecting information on rival firms or disloyal partners, and occasionally we've even checked out the veracity of a prolonged absence from work brought about

16

by a pleasant, highly dubious depression. Unfortunately, as we have to earn our crust one way or another, we must also occasionally get to grips with cases of infidelity. We aren't detectives or anything like that, and that's precisely why our clientele decides to place itself at our mercy. It's not like contracting an agency of professionals to tail your wife (or mistress, which is usually what it amounts to), and then facing up to a grizzly individual who hands over a fat file and an even fatter invoice confirming your irksome suspicions – it's more like asking a friend to find out what he can in exchange for a generously filled envelope. We provide this friendly service: we don't bug, don't take photos, don't hoard files or write long reports. We work by word of mouth, and frequently relay our findings to clients comfortably ensconced together in one of the few decent cocktail bars that, according to Borja, are still left in Barcelona. We're not anonymous employees of a sordid private detective agency advertised on balcony hoardings, but two understanding friends who, if needs be, can find a word of consolation and offer a shoulder to cry on when one of our clients decides to divulge all. "Be prepared" is our motto, salvaged by Borja from our wretched time as obedient boy scouts. As he says, it reflects the professional skills we offer, not to mention the over-the-top fees we try to command.

You can take it as read that when I accepted Borja's partnership proposal I never imagined things would take off and that we'd find ourselves embroiled in trying to solve a murder case. I must confess neither of us had the slightest idea about how to tackle such a situation, either then or now. In fact all our knowledge of the criminal underworld originates exclusively – I kid you not – from reading crime fiction on childhood holidays spent in Premià de Mar with our parents and grandparents, when Premià was still a small village sufficiently distant from Barcelona to perform as a summer holiday resort. As far as I'm concerned, this bookish experience was supplemented on the beach at Caldetes, where Montse, the children and I still spend the summer: the main aim of such page-turning being to keep in check the tortured testosterone of a young man prostrate on the sand and surrounded by splendidly curvaceous flesh as naked as the day God brought it into this world. Frankly, our sources never went beyond Conan Doyle, Agatha Christie, G.K. Chesterton, Georges Simenon, Vázquez Montalbán and, recently, Mrs Jessica Fletcher and Colombo (the series shown repeatedly on television, of which Borja never missed a single episode). You can also take it for granted that the nearest we've ever got to pistols, and firearms in general, was the front row of the cinema stalls. As we are orphans, we enjoyed the privilege of never being conscripted, so neither of us has ever held a CETME, that Spanish army-issue rifle with a life of its own, characterized by a tendency to backfire at will. As for our knowledge of matters legal and forensic, they add up to a combined total of zilch, if not less.

Borja, and Einstein, may be right that God doesn't play dice, but I'm fairly sceptical when it comes to identifying coincidence and causality; I must, however, accept that in the case I'm about to relate, there were far too many coincidences for comfort. In the first place, how else would we have been drawn into the investigation of a tricky murder case in which leading figures from high society were key players? Given our total lack of know-how, the job was clearly beyond us, to put it mildly, but the strange

18

circumstances surrounding the case (and the fact we ourselves got embroiled), put us in the position of having to take the case on. I won't deny there were circumstances to inspire all our detective heroes, because the crime we confronted was the stuff films are made of. If newscasters tell us day-in day-out of crimes that are sordid, vicious and eminently predictable, the majority perpetrated by head cases on drugs or poor wretches who commit suicide or give themselves up to the police, tails between legs, it was our lot to investigate a case that lacked any such spice. It was at once refined and unnerving. To tell the truth, given our day and age's fondness for blood, guts and cheap sex, the planning and execution of "our" murder suggested that a minor, yet truly macabre, masterpiece had been staged.

2

It all began one morning early in December when we were breakfasting on coffee and croissants in the San Marcos café in the High Street in Sarrià. We hadn't anything better to do and it was too cold in the office. I had just opened the newspaper when Borja's mobile rang.

"He didn't say who he was, but he repeated the word 'confidential' at least eight times. I made an appointment for half-past four at the office," Borja explained after he'd rung off, then added "You'd better smarten yourself up a bit. I smell a big fish."

"That would do us very nicely. Christmas is coming and Montse's starting to kick up . . ."

"I told you not to worry. You'll get your double bonus. When did I ever let you down?"

It's true. Ever since we became partners, some three years ago, Borja has never let me down. It's as if he, not I, were the elder brother, even if there were only a couple of minutes in it. I don't know how he manages but I always end up being paid something before the fifth of every month when our mortgage payment is due. I suspect that when he's really at his wits' end he gets money from Merche, his girlfriend, or from Doña Mariona Castany, who has become a kind of aunt to him, but I don't dare ask. There are five mouths to feed at home, two belong to teenagers, and we can't make it to the end of the month on what Montse brings in. I can't allow myself the luxury of refusing Borja's handouts, wherever they come from, usually a brown envelope stuffed with dog-eared notes.

"You heard me, make yourself presentable."

"But I am really quite . . ."

"For the nth time, please wear your uniform."

What he calls "my uniform" is a dark grey Armani suit he forced me to buy (he was paying), a white shirt, also an Armani (I did the honours) and a tastefully striped silk tie my mother-in-law gave me for a birthday present, and which he approves of. It's what I wear when we see clients or take a dip in the world of the wealthy.

"And what will *you* wear?" I asked a touch sarcastically. "Will you dress up to the nines or say you've just come from the nineteenth hole?"

Borja sometimes turns up to our appointments in sports gear (not tracksuits, you understand, but designer polo shirts, cotton trousers and deck shoes), his hair still wet, as if he'd just taken a shower, a big bag of golf clubs or tennis gear slung over his shoulder. I've never seen him in action (in fact, as far as I recall, when we were kids my brother detested sport) and I've never discovered if he really plays or it's all a pose.

"I'm still undecided," he smiled. I knew he had something else on his mind right then: the advance we might extract. We finished our coffee, which had gone cold after so much chattering, and went our separate ways. It was almost midday and early, so I went home to eat, shower and change my clothes.

My wife, Montse, is usually very busy at this time of day and never comes home for lunch. She used to work as a professional psychologist, in a state school in the suburbs of Barcelona. When Borja suddenly appeared and our life took a 360 degree turn for the better, Montse soon abandoned her post, which she was sick to death of after years of bureaucracy, threats and disillusion. She and two friends opened an *Alternative Centre for Natural Wellbeing* in the district of Gràcia, just by the plaça de la Virreina. My wife and her friends were lucky enough to find roomy but decrepit ground-floor premises at a rock-bottom rent since the floor above was home to two dozen or so squatters and their dogs. The trio spent thousands transforming what had been a rag-and-bone man's shop into a space with the requisite New Age ambience, and I must admit they made it look nice and are doing pretty well. Against a backcloth of pastel shades, subdued lighting, ethnic music and scented candles, Montse and partners offer their female clientele a plethora of alternative therapies, from massages with unpronounceable eastern names and ecologically sound beauty treatments to techniques for defeating insomnia or flab. They also put on courses in yoga, Sanskrit and vegetarian cuisine and over the last few months have organized therapy sessions for smokers who want to give up (which Montse leads, though she herself is not yet an entirely nicotine-free zone). On Thursdays they put on literary get-togethers which usually involve performances by bards who self-publish with the help of a photocopier or by scraping together a public grant thanks to an uncle who works for the Generalitat, the Catalan government, and the gigs extend into the early hours once they transfer to one of the excellent *tapas* bars in the vicinity. At lunchtime, the Centre is usually going full tilt, so I grab a bite wherever I happen to be, often with my brother. On this occasion I had to come home to change my clothes. There was time enough to prepare myself a salad and a double-egg omelette, which I gobbled down with a couple of slices of bread smeared with tomato and a glass of beer, and have a short siesta and even read the Catalan version of *El Periódico*. (Borja expressly forbids me to carry this radical rag under my arm in the districts we normally frequent).

I left home still feeling drowsy at three thirty. The sky was completely overcast and everything pointed to a storm, and that meant the streets would soon be clogged with cars and traffic lights would mysteriously break down. I'd forgotten my umbrella, but as it was getting late I resigned myself to getting soaked if there was a downpour. I had to wait almost fifteen minutes for a bus, but by a quarter past four I was nervously carrying out my duties in our office.

I proceeded with our customary ritual and squirted around the secretarial perfume, knowing full well that later on Montse would smell the perfume, frown and interrogate me. Montse had become quite jealous, especially as I sometimes had to go out at night and didn't get back till daybreak. Fortunately, by that time she'd also turned Buddhist and was being more laidback about life. Nevertheless, whenever she felt the need, Montse would swallow a couple of valiums to bolster her worldview.

It was more than probable that Borja would show up a quarter of an hour late. Making clients wait, impatient people who were themselves usually very punctual, was his way of making them understand we had work coming out of our ears. In effect, at four thirty on the dot, the bell rang, and, as usual, I hurried to open the door. The door to the street was unlocked, as we have a concierge. The first thing I saw was our mysterious client's sunglasses, which were obviously intended to hide his identity given that the sky was pitch-black and the stairs were a mass of shadows. When he took them off, I realized I'd failed to disguise my startled reaction. You bet he was a big fish; my clever brother's nose had been on target! I had before me an MP, but not a second or third-rate backbencher, the kind who only warms his seat in parliament while his main contribution to democratic life is propping up the parliamentary bar and keeping liver disease specialists in clover. This man was one who liked to hold forth, hog the headlines and appear in football chat shows on television and radio. I recognized him immediately and prayed Borja would soon put in an appearance.

"Good afternoon. Mr Masdéu, I presume?" he asked most politely.

"Eduard Martínez, his partner, at your disposition," I replied, holding out a hand and ushering him in.

At first he hesitated, but then he crossed our threshold with considerable determination. Although I'm beginning to get used to such men of power, they still put me on edge, even when they're the ones with the problem. When faced with their preening, overbearing manner I always feel like a fish out of water.

"I had an appointment with Mr Masdéu," he said rather uneasily, seeing I wasn't the person he was expecting to meet.

"Yes, but I'm *au courant*. Please do take a seat. My partner will be here shortly. He had an out-of-office meeting . . ."

At that precise moment the telephone rang on our non-existent secretary's desk. I was expecting the call and picked up the receiver.

"Oh, hello. That you? (. . .) Don't worry, Mariajo isn't here. If you remember, she had to take those documents to the lawyers (. . .) Yes, fine (. . .) OK. We'll be waiting for you."

25

"That was him," I explained. "He'll be here in five minutes. He's held up in a traffic jam . . ."

"Better if the secretary's not here."

"She won't be in this afternoon. We usually send her off on errands when we know we're seeing someone who will prefer complete discretion," I said without a single blush.

It's a lie I've rehearsed so often I'm beginning to believe it myself. Sometimes I have the eerie feeling this Mariajo really does exist.

"What an excellent idea! Secretaries often say more than they should. Though, of course, there are always papers they can peek at . . ." he said glancing quickly around.

I assumed that was a subtle hint as to our methods of working and I reassured him immediately: "Oh don't worry on that count! Mariajo never finds out anything that's gossip-worthy. We in fact only employ her to see to the telephone and run the office . . . Besides, I suppose you know we prefer paper-free procedures. Believe me, nobody will ever find anything of interest in this office." Nothing could have been nearer the truth.

I'd suggested he should sit on the sofa and could now see him looking out of the corner of his eye at our office doors. The moment had come to explain why I didn't take him into more secluded surroundings rather than keep him in reception like a door-to-door encyclopaedia salesman.

"I do apologize. It's all topsy-turvy in there. We're painting and redecorating, and you know how these . . ."

"Oh absolutely. One knows when they will start but not when they will finish . . ." he agreed half-heartedly, trying to respond politely to my small talk.

"What's more, it's so cold . . . and so damp . . . The paint's taking ages to dry."

"Yes, it is rather cold this December. Perhaps we might even have a white Christmas . . ."

"And Barcelona can't cope with snow . . ."

"Oh absolutely. The city generates so much heat, the snow will never harden and is going to turn to dirty slush . . ."

It was clear the only conversation the man was prepared to pursue with me was weather-related. If Borja delayed much longer, we might get on to the latest Barça gossip, always a good time-filler. I suppose a professional sleuth would have used the time to make a few deductions to nonplus the new client, but I could think only of the obvious, that I was in the presence of an elegant, rather shy, high-society gentleman who was in a foul mood despite all his efforts to look the contrary. But, of course, this didn't help. I was in no position to admit I'd recognized him, although I suspect that was precisely what he was thinking, and I didn't dare talk politics or broach the reasons for his visit before Borja showed up. Thank God the telephone rang again to interrupt that derisory dialogue that was enhancing neither of our lives. This time it was my mobile.

"I'm sorry," I said taking it from my pocket.

"Please feel free," he replied visibly relieved.

I switched it on and put the tiny apparatus next to my ear.

"Yes? (. . .) How's it going? (. . .) Seven point twenty-two? (. . .) Agreed, buy. (. . .) Fifteen thousand, right. No, our client agrees. (. . .) Yes, we've cleaned up this time. (. . .) Give me a ring tomorrow, won't you? Goodbye."

These staged calls were also Borja's idea. After hearing such an exchange, some customers would ask if we also dealt in investments and, occasionally, we'd extract another bundle of *bin ladens*, as people call them, those ever elusive thousand euro notes we invested on the Stock Exchange. Nothing too risky, to be sure: all very confidential and never any contracts or paperwork. We let them think that for a small commission they'd get a higher return on their money, particularly on the cash they kept undeclared in their desk drawers. It wasn't true, but in worst-case scenarios the client didn't earn anything. He recovered most of his investment, made no profit and asked no questions. When a gamble worked, we kept the crumbs.

However, this time, our client didn't bite. He was nervous, though it wasn't undeclared funds that were apparently making him so edgy. I was about to initiate a conversation on Ronaldinho's virtues and Puyol's dedication when I heard the sound of keys being poked in the door. The room soon filled with a smell I found only too familiar.

3

"I am so sorry I'm late . . ." Borja apologized (in Spanish, to be on the safe side), after he opened the door with his own key. "I had a meeting in San Cugat and the traffic on the ring road was as impossible as ever . . ."

He was looking very distinguished in his stylish navy blue overcoat that would soon reveal a blue pin-stripe suit, a shirt with a thin blue stripe, the kind that comes with white collars and cuffs (the sort I really hate) and a buff yellow tie where ponies pranced.

Before taking his overcoat off, he went over and vigorously shook our visitor's hand. I felt he had somewhat overdone the eau de cologne. "Well? Have they finished yet?" he asked looking at me as he went to open the door to his office.

"No, of course not. The painters aren't done."

"Bloody painters!"

"Perhaps you already know who I am," interjected our client, showing signs of wanting to get down to business.

"Of course," I responded hastily before Borja put his foot in it. "Mr Lluís Font, Right Honourable Member of the Parliament of Catalonia. And who knows," I added, trying to flatter, "perhaps one day President of . . ."

I only said that so Borja would understand the class of person we were dealing with. As he only takes the odd glance at conservative papers like *El Mundo* and *ABC*, he's not very *au fait* with the ins-and-outs of the Catalan political scene, though I suspect he's no better informed about the Spanish right. My brother justifies his zero interest by saying he finds politics boring and politicians much of a muchness, whether they claim to be on the left or right. On the other hand, if you ask him where Julio Iglesias is holidaying or what stage the Infanta Cristina's pregnancy is at, Borja will give you chapter and verse.

While Lluís Font MP and I were exchanging meaningless pleasantries about the weather, I had mentally tried to remember what I knew about the character now perching on our smartish Ikea sofa. The Right Honourable Lluís Font was one of two political leaders battling for the leadership of his party (I won't say which, only that its Members of Parliament and councillors go to register their votes on the exclusive Avenida Pearson). It was very likely he would soon be put forward as a candidate for the Presidency of the Generalitat, although, the way things were going for his party in this neck of the woods, it was doubtful he would ever win the coveted title. He belonged to his party's moderate wing and was reputed to be a prudent, judicious man. From what I'd been able to glean from the Spanish press, he wasn't particularly popular with his own kind. It didn't help him that he was a Barça fan, but it was common knowledge he had a first-class brain when it came to football despite the fact he'd never dabbled in real estate, unlike the Presidents of most top football clubs.

He was slim, medium height and extremely refined. The dark grey bespoke suit he wore fitted him like a glove. His hair was on the fair side, and his skin displayed the same suspiciously dark sheen Borja was so proud of. He spoke reasonably correct Catalan, although clearly it wasn't the language he felt most comfortable with. His eyes were brown, almost honeyed and stared out rather vacantly, but

I suppose he wasn't the fool some people liked to think. He didn't wear prescription glasses and he reeked of one of those expensive, unmistakably male perfumes advertised on television when the holidays are upon us. He also reeked of money. He sported a gold Rolex, cufflinks and tiepin. Given the *tout ensemble*, I expect a lot of women would rate him a rather handsome middle-aged man.

"In our telephone conversation," he looked solemnly at Borja, "I mentioned that the matter bringing me here is strictly confidential. Some people have spoken most highly of you, Mr Masdéu, particularly of your discretion. I hope I can rely on you in this respect."

I noticed he was observing me out of the corner of one eye.

"You can rely on me. And on Eduard, my partner. I suppose you've gathered we work together. I may be the more visible face of our firm, but you can trust my partner as if he were myself. In fact, Eduard and I are like brothers." He smiled knowingly: "Don't worry. Nothing we discuss here will go beyond these walls. Do tell us what the problem is."

"It is a painting," Mr Font replied laconically.

"One you want to buy or sell?" asked Borja matter-of-factly.

"Well, neither, really. It is . . ." he hesitated before continuing, ". . . a picture I now have in my office that I bought a few days ago."

"Is it an antique? A collector's item?" Borja was warming to the chase.

"No, the painter is still with us."

"Then you think it's a fake, perhaps stolen . . ." ventured Borja, raising his eyebrows. The same question was on the tip of my tongue.

"No, nothing of that sort . . ." the MP cleared his throat. "The painting is genuine and I purchased it legally through a dealer."

It was obvious he found it difficult to explain himself and was getting really agitated. We needed get to the point as soon as possible, because our office heating didn't work. The wrought-iron radiators looked a treat but they are also part of our act and my feet were freezing. I guess his were too.

"Well, then? What *is* your problem?" asked Borja in that mellifluous tone he sometimes uses.

"What is at issue is that the portrait . . ." the MP wavered once more. "I mean to say the woman modelling is my wife," he drawled, measuring his words and trying to conceal his unease at his confession.

"Ah! . . ." we both exclaimed in unison.

Borja and I looked at each other askance. From the way our client was behaving, there was every possibility we had another case of infidelity on our hands. That I find particularly distasteful.

"Are you suggesting the portrait of your wife in the painting isn't what you were expecting? That you're not happy with it?" asked Borja egging him on.

"No, in fact . . . do you see," the MP finally decided to get to the point, "I had no idea my wife had been modelling." He paused. "I mean I was very shocked when I came across a portrait of my wife in an exhibition," he finally confessed.

"Perhaps there's nothing more to it, and your wife just wanted to give you a surprise . . ." Borja suggested warily. "Perhaps she had it in mind as a Christmas present."

"I don't think so," he said shaking his head. "I discovered the painting by chance in a catalogue I receive through the post (fine art is a hobby of mine and I subscribe to some gallery publications). It seems the portrait in question was shown in an art-show held in Paris, and indeed the painting merited a whole-page reproduction in the exhibition catalogue."

"You don't say!" whispered my brother.

"The artist," the politician added, ignoring his reaction, "is a Catalan painter who is well-known to connoisseurs. From what I have read, apparently he now lives in Barcelona, but that is all I do know. I don't think he is exhibited much here . . . But of course," he shifted uneasily on the sofa and caught his breath, "you can imagine how astonished I was to discover Lídia in one of his paintings . . ."

And then he added: "Worst of all, the paintings went on show in a very famous Paris art gallery!"

The MP was furious and his face gradually reddened beneath the fake brown veneer. With good reason. There are many ways you can find out about your partner's infidelities, but this had to be one of the most original. Borja saw I was making every effort not to laugh and directed one of his thunderous looks at me.

"I expect it isn't her. There's probably just a great similarity between that model and your wife," my brother suggested very plausibly.

That seemed like good common sense. I'd also thought we might be dealing with a husband who was at once jealous and paranoid. It wouldn't be the first time.

"No, and no again," the politician shook his head. "Apart from the fact that I recognize the shoes (my wife likes to wear the most expensive, extravagant shoes) the woman in the painting is also wearing a gold necklace she is very fond of. Also," he explained, "Lídia happens to have a small scar on her neck, from an operation she underwent when she was young, and this necklace is the one she puts on every day by way of camouflage. Naturally, she owns more expensive necklaces, but that's beside the point. It is true that the dress the woman in the painting is wearing is quite unfamiliar. It is dark-coloured and must be from a year or two back, because Lídia never wears a dress more than once or twice . . . So do you see," he sighed, "I am not in the slightest doubt but that it is her."

"Yes, the shoes could be a coincidence, but the necklace would be taking it too far," I agreed. "Are you sure it is the same one?"

"Absolutely. There are three fine gold threads that intertwine. The clasp is a flower of turquoise stones with a small ruby set in its centre. It is a very special necklace her father commissioned from a famous jeweller. An exclusive design, you understand."

"Naturally. Have you spoken to your wife about the painting?" Borja enquired.

"No, I have said nothing as yet. I didn't dare, in case it turned out to be a simple misunderstanding," he said rather nervously. "The painting is in my office. Lídia doesn't even know that I know of its existence. What really concerns me is whether she is having an affair with the painter . . ." he touched his chin. "I expect you are aware of the position I hold in my party and my responsibilities in parliament . . . I mean, apart from any personal upset it would cause, you must understand it will not do me any favours at all if the story starts to leak out that Lídia . . . Not that someone has painted a portrait of her, do you see, but that . . ."

"I understand," Borja nodded understandingly, so Mr Font MP realized there was no need to linger on details that might be most humiliating.

What passed through both our minds was what anyone might have concluded: no doubt his wife was finding an outlet for her frustrations with a younger man, an artist who devoted time to appealing to her vanity by painting intimate portraits like the one in question for who knows what in return. The worst of it was that she hadn't found a way to be sufficiently discreet in order to keep her husband in the dark about her little affair.

It was plain that what most terrified the politician was the possibility of scandal. If it emerged that the wife of a future candidate to the Presidency of the Generalitat was carrying on with another man, and what's more that there was an incriminating work of art out there, it would soon signal curtains for his political ambitions. Being the leader and public face of a long-established conservative Catholic party didn't marry too well with having a spouse who was unfaithful. In the event, the scandal would no doubt be hushed up. It is still possible in this country, in some cases and under certain circumstances, to prevent such incidents from surfacing, but the final result would be no different. Perhaps there wouldn't be any big newspaper splashes, but there would be a steady drip feed of gossip and rumour leading to telephone calls and pressure behind the scenes. And that wouldn't stop till the cuckolded husband ceased to be the visible face of a party that was inspired in equal parts by Vatican ideology and the most vicious variety of neo-cons.

Mr Lluís Font MP asked us whether we minded if he smoked, lit a cigarette and continued with his tale.

"A couple of weeks ago I sent my secretary to Paris and got him to buy the painting discreetly. The offending object cost me 18,000 euros . . ." he remarked visibly annoyed.

"Take a look at this. I have bought you the exhibition catalogue. You will find all the details of the painting here," he explained as he opened the catalogue and showed us the portrait. "Of course, if you want a closer view, you can come to my office on the Diagonal, by Via Augusta," he added.

Borja and I glanced at the catalogue and stopped at the page with the portrait of our new and distinguished client's wife. The painting in question was an oil on canvas, signed by one Pau Ferrer and measured twenty inches by twenty-eight. It portrayed a woman between thirty-five and forty-five years of age, in my estimation, who was contentedly sprawled over a dark red armchair. She wore a dark, possibly black dress, with a generously low-cut, seductive neckline above which the aforementioned necklace glittered. You could see the clasp, a flower of turquoise stones set with a small ruby. Her shoes certainly caught your attention. They were bright red, low-heeled with ankle-straps and very fetching. They would have had pride of place in any shoe fetishist's wardrobe and it suddenly struck me that perhaps our honourable member of parliament was one such. At least, I thought rather enviously, he had the wallet for it and a wife ready to comply. I'd never be able to persuade my Montse to wear heels, let alone see her spend a month's wages on shoes like that.

I revisited the portrait. The woman was on the blonde side, and, although it had possibly seen the inside of an operating theatre, her nose displayed a degree of distinction. Dark, almost black eyes appealed languorously and seductively to the onlooker. Long, slightly unkempt hair fell over the dipping neckline. Her lips pouted, a dark, dark red, though not vulgarly so. It was a mouth inviting a kiss.

There was no landscape or interior you could identify. The background to the scene was a mass of shades of grey splashed with a few brushstrokes of blue. I don't know much about painting, and although I thought the portrait was pretty good, I found it quite disturbing. The woman was extraordinarily beautiful, I had to admit, but the expression on her face was strange in a way I couldn't explain and it made me feel uneasy. The way she looked out, intense and distant, was the central focus of the painting. I've no idea why but I could only think it was a blank look, as if no real life inhabited those eyes when the artist painted them. They seemed – and I sensed that immediately – like the eyes of a dead woman. Montse would have called it a kind of premonition. I'm still not sure whether the chill running down my spine was triggered by looking at the portrait I found quite sinister, or by the frozen polar climate engulfing our office.

"Your wife is very beautiful," Borja murmured politely.

"Yes, Lídia is still a very splendid woman. Perhaps too much so . . ." Lluís Font MP paused and extinguished his cigarette. "Look, I just want you to find out what the hell is going on. And I need to know as soon as possible."

"Leave it with us," suggested Borja. "What's your wife's name? She's Lídia? . . ."

"Lídia Font, of course. Her maiden name is Vilalta, if that is what you mean."

I was quite familiar with the surname of Vilalta. If I made an effort I'd surely remember why.

"How does your wife fill her time?" I started on my routine questioning. "Does she work? Travel a lot? Belong to any association? Follow a set time-table?"

"Lídia is an interior designer. She spends her day visiting furniture and design shops. She also belongs to a club that's close to home, where she spends a lot of her time . . ." And, after a moment's reflection, he added, "She also likes to do charity work and that kind of thing. She says it's good for my career . . . I mean," he said hurriedly correcting himself, "that is what people in our position should do to help others."

And he added: "She is ambitious. Perhaps even more so than me. That's why I am surprised she has got mixed up in an affair that might ruin my career. Lídia knows that whatever damages my prospects, will also damage hers. We have always prided ourselves on working as a team!" he declared forcefully.

"I need to put a question to you, but I'm not sure how . . ." Borja hesitated. It was always a touchy issue, but one you had to broach in certain circles. "Does your wife belong to the Opus Dei? Does she belong to one of those religious groups? . . . I mean do the two of you . . ."

The question concerned the activities and connections of the said Lídia as much as her husband's. We knew from experience that it's better not to tangle with Opus members (or even worse with the whats-its of Christ). They are powerful and, since they have faith, they have no scruples, the one clearly cancelling out the other. Although Borja is rightwing, he particularly loathes this kind of fanatic.

"We do not belong to the Opus and are not *Legionaries of Christ* . . ." our MP shook his head, somewhat offended. "Of course, we are Catholic, but not *that* kind. I suppose," he allowed, " it is one of the reasons I'm still not our party's official candidate."

"But everything points to you being selected this time round. They don't seem to have many options," I said, remembering what I'd read a few days ago in the press.

"When does the committee meet to vote on the candidate? Soon, I expect? The elections are almost upon us . . ."

"After the holidays," he confirmed. "Pressure has been brought to bear from some quarters, but I expect I shall be elected." And then added, remembering why he'd come to see us. "If all this doesn't get in the way, naturally . . ."

"No reason it should," my brother pronounced. "I must thank you for being so frank. It makes our life so much easier. We'll set to work immediately and will keep you informed." Borja paused and cleared his throat. "Well, we shall need a modest . . ."

"Of course, of course, I had anticipated paying you an advance," the MP took a chequebook and a gold Parker from his topcoat pocket. "Will 3,000 cover it?"

"Our advance is always 5,000," lied Borja.

"Not bad . . . that's more than half a million pesetas! . . ." spluttered our putative client. No matter he was a rich man. Filthy lucre is always filthy lucre.

"If it's not convenient . . . We can settle later," waxed a seemingly indifferent Borja. "We're in no rush."

Our client seemed slightly put out and I felt a small surge of panic. Of course we were in a rush: we were both broke! Borja had surpassed his own arrogance by asking for so much, though I'd got used to my brother's swagger many moons ago. I've never understood how he can uphold the notion he has no money worries when he's without a cent to his name, and I'm still surprised how his insouciant manner always gets him his way. I sweat, stammer and go red in the face, and that's why I prefer to keep my mouth shut when it's time to talk money.

"Who do I make the cheque out to? In your name, Mr Masdéu?"

"No, 'to the bearer'. In confidential matters, 'no names, no traces' is always my line . . ."

"I hadn't thought of that," came the reply. You could see from a mile off that he was lying. "Of course I can settle in cash, if you prefer . . ."

"Even better."

Lluís Font took an envelope from his topcoat pocket and placed on the table, one on top of another, 100 and 500 notes to a grand total of 5,000 euros. It still left a good wad in his envelope.

"Don't imagine I always carry so much money on me," he explained. "I just happened to collect in an old debt today . . ."

"Of course, of course," nodded Borja following his drift.

For the last three years the only money my brother and I had ever seen was what lawyers, notaries and banks like to call "black" money. We don't worry because it saves us the bother of having to justify to the Revenue income from an enterprise that doesn't exist.

"I expect results soon," he said returning the envelope to his topcoat pocket.

"And I expect, sir, to have something for you in a couple weeks," Borja reassured him, and I noted how, perhaps because he was an MP, my brother didn't dare speak to him in a more familiar tone as he usually would. "I suppose it would best if we called you on your mobile, as soon as we find something?"

"If I don't answer, it will be because I am in committee or in a debate. Leave a message and I will return your call as soon as I can." And he added, half-heartedly: "It may all be a misunderstanding . . ."

"I'm almost sure that's right," nodded Borja. "But you'll

feel much better when we've got to the bottom of it all. Sometimes women do strange things to draw attention . . ."

"Very strange things indeed!" I corroborated, knowing full well what he was referring to.

"Have you any more questions for me?" it was obvious the MP was keen to leave our office.

"What's your wife's schedule like?" I asked. "I mean when does she usually leave home and so on? . . ."

I'm generally the one who sees to the more prosaic questions, because my brother Borja forgets the small details the moment he's pocketed the readies.

"She usually leaves the house at around ten to go and see her shops and suppliers. It's another matter in the afternoons. She goes to the hairdressers, the gym, meets with friends . . . At least, that is what she tells me. As I divide my day between Parliament, the party and my office, I'm never at home . . ."

"Very well, very well we'll see what we can find out about the portrait painter and from Monday will start trailing her." Borja concluded.

"Do whatever is necessary, but don't feel you have to inform me of every step you take. The fact is I am not overjoyed by the idea that I'm arranging for you to spy on my wife. Above all," he said emphatically, looking down, "be discreet."

"Don't worry on that front," Borja assured him. "We know what we have to do and how we have to do it."

Even after he'd related the embarrassing story of his wife's likely infidelities and the lethal impact they might have on his career, Lluís Font MP didn't seem any less powerful. He had no doubt found it a struggle to take this step and put his fate in the hands of complete strangers, but I couldn't decide

41

whether he was merely worried by the prospect of a scandal or was genuinely jealous. Did the MP love his wife or was it just one more marriage of convenience? He had possessed the necessary cool or sang-froid not to put his wife on the spot and demand she explain the painting, which would have been his most obvious option. At least, that's what *I* would do with Montse if I ever found myself, improbably I hope, in similar circumstances. But there is no doubt, as Borja keeps telling me, that life north of the Diagonal is very different to the life that most of us mortals lead.

We bid the MP farewell like the competent professionals we are not, as we tried simultaneously to suppress the glee sparked by the sight of the small bundle which Borja had hurriedly tucked into his pocket: what was an annoying hiccup for Lluís Font MP brought salvation to our domestic economies. Such is life. When I shook his hand, I noted how cold his hands were. Mine were frozen.

Wow, 5,000 euros, more than 800,000 pesetas of old! Borja's eyes gleamed with that special shine buffed by sight of a pile of banknotes. Borja has a really good nose for money; I can't think where he gets it from.

"Well, kid, that's Christmas sorted!" he exclaimed euphorically when we were finally left by ourselves. And added, "And there'll be more to come."

"Thanks. But for the moment, half will do me fine," Borja had been so kind as to slip me the envelope with its full contents. " You don't have a cent either . . . If you don't mind, tomorrow morning, after I've been to the bank, I'll go and buy Montse the earrings we saw. You know she hits forty the day after tomorrow."

"Of course! I've got a present for my leftist sister-in-law too . . ." he laughed. "And if I were you, I wouldn't keep

42

going on about her hitting forty, particularly in front of her."

"Well, you know I think she's delighted. You know how pig-headed she is. She's determined not to be depressed now she's in her forties, and ever since she's been a Buddhist and spends her days eating soya to fend off whatever . . ."

"I'll probably go Buddhist too," he said, turning serious as he pulled on his overcoat. "A lot of folk around here," he was referring to the well-heeled part of town where our office was, "have gone Buddhist recently. Eduard, you've just given me an idea." And he added, as if plotting some thing, "I expect it's a good way to make contacts without spending a cent . . ."

"That's your business. But remember we're expecting you on Saturday night for the party."

"Don't worry. I'll be there."

It was almost six o'clock and we decided to take the rest of the day off. Borja had a date with Merche, his girlfriend, and I was so cheered up I decided to give Montse a surprise by getting home early. Then I remembered it was Thursday, the day of her literary soirée, and that she wouldn't get back till the early hours. Nevertheless, I resolved I'd be there to welcome her with the good news. I knew that my lack of work had been worrying her recently.

Borja announced he would call up his friend Doña Mariona Castany and try to arrange to see her in the morning. If there was any decent gossip on Lídia Font, Mariona Castany was sure to be in the know.

Although it was out of his way, because I live in Gràcia and our office is, on the contrary, very close to where Borja rents his little bachelor pad, my brother drove me in the Smart to our front door. It had started raining again some time ago.

43

"I'm still waiting," I reminded him as I got out of the car.

"What? Oh, yes, too true! . . ." he exclaimed, elated. "You know what, Eduard? God doesn't play dice."

"And when he does, they're loaded!" I riposted.

4

"You mean Borja-Mari's coming to the party tomorrow . . ." Montse quipped.

The kids were still in bed and we were having breakfast in the kitchen. It was early and we'd just switched the heating on. It was cold.

"For Christ's sake, Montse, one of these days the girls will hear you and repeat that to his face," I protest whenever my wife cracks this particular joke. "And don't complain so. Knowing him, I bet he'll bring you a nice present."

Montse likes to make gentle fun of Borja and in private calls him Borja-Mari. If Borja is in itself a snobby name, then Borja-Mari sounds even posher, although obviously there are flesh-and-blood people who are really called that. Nevertheless, Montse's fond of Borja, even if in her presence (perhaps simply because she is there) my brother over-eggs his pose as an elegant, charming, blasé man of the world. He soon won over our kids, who love him like an uncle though they don't know that's what he is really. I'd like to be able to tell my wife Borja is Pep and that he's my twin brother. But that day is still far off.

"He's very peculiar," said Montse pouring out her second cup of coffee. "I don't understand how you two managed to pair up . . . He's so different to us! The way he dresses, the stories he tells . . . Although I get the impression he's one of those with the gift of the gab and never a cent to his name."

"Darling, in his position and with his contacts, he's forced to lead a certain life style . . ."

"On his uppers, like you and me," she retorted. "Even so, he's not what you'd call evil."

"Of course he isn't. In his way, Borja has a heart of gold," I tried to defend him, as ever.

Montse had sussed Borja out a long time ago, but I don't think she suspects for a moment he is my brother. It's strange she's not noticed the similarity that exists between Borja and the portrait of my mother hanging in our dining room, particularly after she immediately spotted how I resemble my father. I'm not looking forward to the day she realizes Borja and my mother are like two peas in a pod, because then we really will have a problem.

"I reckon I like him because he always makes me laugh. He says such silly things!"

"That's why you like him and because he lets you fill his head with all that esoteric nonsense," I replied, rather envious of my brother's charms.

When he comes to lunch or dinner, Borja listens more than politely to Montse's passionate harangues about how she earns her crust. The benefits of karma, I Ching, feng shui, or the Flowers of whatever . . . I think my brother also believes in all these things. Once a friend of Montse drew his astral chart and predicted a wonderful future for him. Now as Pep is no longer Pep but Borja, in his new identity it turns out my brother wasn't born on his actual birthday. His star as Borja is Aquarius, not Taurus, although Montse and her soulmates claim he's Aquarian from head to toe.

"I've told you a thousand times that natural medicine and Buddhism aren't at all esoteric!" insisted Montse, who'd got out of bed in fighting mood. "What's more, it's how I earn my living. And not so badly, as you may have noticed!"

"True enough," I had to demur. "You know, love, you can just ignore me."

At the end of the day Montse with her Alternative Centre earns a sight more than I do. And OK, what they get up to isn't in any way esoteric, as she never tires of telling me, but the place *does* happen to call itself Isis, which is pretty strange. That's what's advertised on the board over the doorway and on the pink and lilac promotional leaflets that she and her partners scatter around the neighbourhood: *The Isis Alternative Centre for Natural Wellbeing*. If they had to give it a woman's name, they could have chosen any Jill, Jane or Juliet. I think it's no coincidence she and her cronies went for the name of an Egyptian goddess who was the object of a rather idiosyncratic cult of the Romans (by the way, in the Sants district there's a clip-joint that boasts the same name, but I've been very careful not to mention that fact to Montse in case she gets the wrong idea).

Yes, Montse earns, but not that much. The two of us earn enough to get by, although she's right in one thing: we may not be millionaires now but our life now is infinitely superior to what it was before. There's no comparison and it's all down to Borja.

Now while I'm familiar with every fad followed in Montse's Centre, in too much gruesome detail for my liking, my wife has little clue as to my line of work. She thinks I prepare financial reports for big companies: feasibility studies, whether a business is profitable or needs an injection of capital, and such like. She also thinks I act as an investment consultant to individuals and entrepreneurs. She's aware that discretion is a basic aspect of my work, a condition imposed by my clients, and thus accepts I can never reveal very much about what I do that gets us to the end of the month. In fact, I could make up any old story without a worry in the world, and often do, since Montse, like most mortals, hasn't a clue about high finance. As far as I'm concerned, I've learned that when you have money it's easier to make more, and that to amass a fortune, as Borja tells me, you must pretend you're rich from day one.

"I'll have to spend the whole of tomorrow in the kitchen. Can you go to the Bolet bakery and buy the cake?" Montse asked. "Better make it a big one, right? And chocolate . . . While you're about it, get some cava."

Montse was born in Sarrià and we only ever buy cakes from Bolet's, the small bakery that competes with the patisserie that belonged to Foix the Catalan poet. My wife comes from a not very well-off family like mine, but as a loyal daughter of old Sarrià, she hankers after her old haunts.

Nowadays Sarrià is a neighbourhood for all sorts, where top executives rub shoulders with snobby ladies, university professors, South American maids and the usual grandmas and grandpas living on modest pensions, but the district retains a charm many other areas in Barcelona have lost or never had. The vicinity of the main square, with the church, town hall and market, retains that village aura of which the locals are so proud, with its old two-storey houses that have almost all been restored and the quiet, clean streets, some still adorned with exotic plants sprouting in big earthenware pots by house doorways. Joana, my mother-in-law, who's a widow, still lives in the same old, non-centrally heated flat where Montse and her sister were born and she refuses point blank to give it up. Although she calls it "her home", she in fact rents, and I'm well aware the children of the owners read the deaths column full of hope every morning and dream about how they'll spend their inheritance when they sell the building for a small fortune. The flat where my mother-in-law lives is "infested with a sitting tenant", as they say nowadays.

"Bolet's isn't exactly next door to the office," I retorted. "And I wasn't planning on going in tomorrow as it's Saturday . . ." I could see Montse wasn't about to relent, so I added: "All right, I'll ask Borja to drive me there. We could probably drop by at lunchtime or this afternoon."

"Even better."

"We'll be quite a crowd. I'll have to buy at least half a dozen bottles. I don't know whether there's room in the Smart . . ."

"More like a dozen I'd say," she added dryly. "As the day after's Sunday and nobody has to be up at the crack of dawn . . ."

"A dozen! So how many people have you invited?" I sighed. "I saw the pantry shelves were weighed down with bottles of wine. Are you sure we'll have enough chairs?"

In a word, Montse was going to celebrate in style on Saturday night. Who'd have thought she'd like the idea of hitting forty? The fact is she didn't look forty. She wore her age lightly, not like me. I sometimes look at her and can still see the same idealistic young girl I fell in love with all those years ago.

"Would *you* rather see to supper?" she asked, raising her eyebrows, and in a tone of voice that made it clear the question was purely rhetorical.

Sometimes Montse is implacable. I'm sure if she knew what I was really up to she'd not be at all amused. As Borja says, my wife is a lefty who's recycled herself into anything labelled *alternative*: *alternative* diets, *alternative* medicine, *alternative* cosmetics, *alternative* ecology and a good few other *alternative* options. Now she's taken up Buddhism, like most of her friends, because it's an *alternative* philosophy of life rather than a religion. She still gathers her hair into a single plait, wears flat shoes and ethnic clothes, and, for sure, always smells wonderful thanks to the concoctions they use at the Centre. Luckily, Montse has nothing in common with those lipo-suctioned, silicone-padded women my work often brings me into contact with. Though she sometimes gives you the impression she's a bit out of this world, Montse is real enough. Every single inch of her.

It's true I also often feel ill at ease in my new profession. Given my political ideas I can hardly feel proud of the way I now earn my living, but, as Borja usually reminds me, I used to work for vampires in white collars and not for an NGO. Naturally, my brother and I have never got involved in any off-limits business. We've never touched traffic in drugs, women or immigrants, or anything like that. We could say to a degree that we act as trustworthy stewards to the rich. Besides, I have to admit that the strange trade I now pursue is what saved my marriage. It's most likely that if Borja hadn't appeared so opportunely, Montse and I would now be separated – if not divorced – and my little son, Arnau, wouldn't even exist.

We had been going through a bad patch. Montse and I were fed up, bored with our respective jobs and the life we were leading, working long hours to pay the mortgage and the children's schooling, and with hardly any time for ourselves. Montse was earning her living as a counsellor in a secondary school, which meant she wiped noses for a wage that even the pupils reckoned was pathetic. After fifteen years as a school psychologist, she couldn't face any more juvenile delinquents, mafiosi fathers, sadistic adolescents, racist mothers, pregnant teenagers and skinheads, not to mention an acquiescent Authority too politically correct to even hear a mention of such things. Despite being a leftwing feminist, she'd concluded it was necessary to bring back uniforms, corporal punishment, iron discipline and rote learning. Naturally stubborn, she refused to take sick leave for her depression, and I could see her going downhill fast and was powerless to help. The Authority described the school where she had a permanent post as "challenging", and Laia and Aina, our identical twins, were also going through a difficult time. They were fighting at home and their teachers kept sending us silly notes blaming us for their bad behaviour. Personally, I didn't think things were *that* bad but Montse had become disturbingly paranoid and saw tragedies looming on every side. One day she spotted a tattoo on Laia's leg and went berserk. It was only a transfer but Laia got a good hiding. For a couple of months Montse felt remorse for the blows she'd given out, convinced she'd traumatized our daughter for life, and began to take Prozac. Unfortunately, the artificial improvement in her state of mind, relative to the quantity of pills she ingested, was accompanied by a gradual decrease in her libido, to put it politely. In other words, one side effect was to put me on bread and water.

As for me, I'd been working far too many years in a bank in the morning and as an accountant for a small computer firm in the afternoon, and couldn't take anymore. I'd become a respectable, timorous bank clerk whose only hope in terms of changing his life was to win the jackpot in the Christmas Lottery. To make things worse, the bank where I worked had been taken over by a bigger fish and the new bosses decided to reorganize the staff via a wave of redundancies and a canny restructuring of the workforce. In my case, thanks to the fact I'd worked there for twenty years and was still too young to take early retirement, the generous sods offered me two options: either to accept voluntary redundancy, with compensation that was hardly generous, or to go to work in Lleida. Monte refused point blank to change city, and I wasn't exactly grabbed by the prospect of spending a minimum of four hours a day risking my life in a train. But if that was not enough, there was another problem. A problem that went by the name of Raquel.

The fact is that quite unintentionally (at one of those office parties, after soaking every one of my neurons in a whisky whose name I'd rather not remember) I embarked on an affair with a married colleague, and didn't know how to extricate myself. What started as a straw I'd grasped when plastered turned into a nightmare. Raquel, for that was her name, was stricken and talked about separation, divorce and starting a new life together. I won't go so far as to say she was harassing me, but she came pretty close. She even threatened to show up at our place and tell Montse about our so-called relationship, as she dubbed it. This really shook me up, and what with Raquel and the reorganization at the bank I was at my wits' end.

I won't deny that initially I quite liked Raquel. She was good in bed, very hot in fact, though I don't understand why the hell she fancied me, given I'm quite run-of-the-mill between the sheets. I'm not trying to justify myself by saying she was the one to make the first move at the party, or the one who booked a hotel room a few days later, or the one ringing and texting me all the time, but this is what happened after Montse had been on Prozac for several weeks.

The fact is that the affair, for want of a better word, had taken a turn for the worse and I was scared. I was still in love with Montse and besides that there were my daughters. I fancied Raquel but wasn't in love with her. I'd not considered the possibility of separating from my wife for one second, and even less so for someone like Raquel. All things being equal, there are women you'd spend the night with (particularly if it's a freebie), but not necessarily the next day. Montse was for life, even though neither of us knew how to climb out of that black hole swallowing everything except our mortgage repayments and instalments on the car.

Borja appeared at that precise moment. My brother came back into my life the same way he'd left it, out of the blue, with no prior warning, as if it were the most natural thing in the world. One day, after fifteen years without a single sighting, he swanked elegantly outside the branch of the bank where I worked and suggested I should resign from my job and become a partner in this strange enterprise we now have on our hands and which legally doesn't exist.

He'd lived abroad, as I knew, and in all that time our only contact had been via the occasional postcards he wrote me and the letters I sent to a post box in Paris. One such letter had invited him to our wedding but he never came. What he did was to send me a set of very fine crystal goblets that arrived in equally fine fragments. I was tremendously upset and went round antique shops until I'd collected a dozen of something similar that cost me an arm and a leg. I said nothing to Montse. To justify the expenditure, I invented a couple of yobs who'd mugged me with a syringe when

I came out of the metro. It was the second lie I'd told her since we'd been going together.

"Hey, kid brother, how are you?" he rasped that day when I emerged from the bank. It was almost three clock and he'd obviously been waiting for me for some time. "Still working here? You've put on weight . . ." he said looking me up and down.

I hardly recognized him. His hair was cut short and he exuded the same elegantly sophisticated style he now assumes. I was so delighted and surprised I couldn't think what to say when I finally did react. I immediately invited him home for lunch.

"Fine but first we have to talk," he said, smiling enigmatically. "I'll come to your place, if you like, but you shouldn't tell your wife (Montse, isn't it?) or anyone I'm your brother." He paused while a bemused look spread over my face. "I must tell you that I'm not Pep anymore. I'm Borja from now on. Borja Masdéu-Canals Sáez de Astorga. Yes, you heard right! . . ." And he proudly showed me a high quality business card. My amazement increased in leaps and bounds.

"Fuck, things have changed in all this time!" I exclaimed. "Although you've obviously changed much more than your name . . ."

I was happy to see my brother again, but also rather hurt by all those years he dropped out of my life. Borja isn't just my only brother; he's also my twin. And fifteen years, I remember thinking, is a hell of a long time. Perhaps too long.

"Let's go for a beer and I'll tell all," he bounced back at me.

"No." I shook my head. "I'll ring Montse and tell her I

54

won't be home for lunch today. I'll think of some excuse and you and I can go and lunch elsewhere. You've got some explaining to do, Pep! . . ."

"Borja," he corrected me. "Remember I'm Borja now."

I took him to the Set Portes, a well-known restaurant not far from the bank. As it was Friday, I had a free afternoon, although Raquel kept texting me to say we should meet. I decided to take a risk and, before I had time to regret my decision, I switched off my mobile. I didn't want any lover inopportunely souring our meal.

The restaurant was packed with tourists and what looked like businessmen agreeing devious deals between courses, but we were lucky and got a table. It was next to a family of riotous Russians who ate and drank like Cossacks, and we agreed to emulate them. I ordered paella – one of the chef's specials – and a bottle of Rioja. After all that time, our fraternal reunion merited a celebration.

However, rather than letting him speak, I rushed into telling him about my affair with Raquel and the crisis in my marriage. I told him how I hated my work and the decision the new bosses were forcing me to take. We didn't notice we dispatched the bottle of Rioja and a plate of olives before engaging with the paella. Two more bottles soon hit the dust.

I don't think I could have come at a better time," he smiled very confidently. "You seem to have got yourself into a right state."

"I don't know what to do . . ."

"Eduard, God doesn't play dice . . ."

It was the first time I'd heard him pronounce the phrase that I'd end up hearing time and again. On that occasion, however, after all the wine I'd sunk, I almost asked him if the guy up there didn't play dice then what the hell was he doing the day our parents were killed in an accident. But I shut up and let him speak. It was his turn.

"So how are you?" I asked, switching tack. "What happened to you over all those years? Are you married? Do you have a girlfriend?"

Borja proceeded to tell me very little, indeed nothing in particular, about his life. He'd travelled, tried his hand at various trades and seen enough of the world to learn that the good guys always end up losing. His silences led me to deduce his love life hadn't been days of wine and roses.

"I'd rather not discuss that," he said looking down. "Better we talk about the future. About our future."

He explained his idea – the company where we now work – and suggested I should give up my job and enter into partnership with him. He'd been a rolling stone for too long and wanted to settle down, or so he said.

"I have a couple of matters to settle and can't carry them forward by myself," he said confidentially. "I need you, Eduard. And anyway, it's not as if your finances are booming."

"No, you're right," I had to agree. "We're still paying the mortgage off, and although Montse works and is a civil servant, we only just keep our heads above water. And the twins are a bottomless pit. You must meet them, Pep." I still hadn't got used to calling him Borja. "After all, they are your nieces!"

"All in due course. If everything turns out as it should, you'll pay off your mortgage before long and be able to take that trip round the world you wanted to do when we were kids." He paused. "You haven't done that yet, have you?"

No, I hadn't. When I succeeded in escaping from the hell that was life with my uncle and aunt at the age of twenty-three and set up on my own, I enrolled on a university course. I couldn't give up the bank job that fell into my lap at the age of nineteen thanks to mysterious strings pulled by uncle, yet at the same time I still dreamed of becoming a writer. Borja had been much more adventurous than me, had gone abroad and fled the miserable vision of the world with which our relatives soured our adolescence, and I was alone. Too alone to embark on an adventure I'd always dreamed I would share with my brother. I'll never cease to wonder how different our lives might have been if our parents hadn't crashed on the Garraf corniche when Borja and I were thirteen.

In any case I never managed to write a single novel or finish my degree course, and *Don Quixote* was partly to blame. To my great misfortune, I can't stand that book. In those heroic days when we students went on wildcat strikes and smoked joints in the Arts Faculty quad, I was a proud, naïve idealist, and that got me into the odd spot of bother. Including never taking my degree.

"I don't know what Montse will make of all this," I reflected aloud while I polished off the *crema catalana* I'd ordered for my dessert.

"So you ended up marrying your psychoanalyst! That's really funny!"

"No, I didn't, Montse isn't a psychoanalyst. She's a psychologist." I pointed out.

"Yes, but you did get involved with her," he smiled mischievously.

In fact, it was down to *Don Quixote* and my trauma that I met Montse. She had just finished her psychology degree and was the friend of a friend's girlfriend. After she'd worked out my problem she insisted on helping, and, although she failed in that, I did end up marrying her.

True, I have a trauma in relation to *Don Quixote*. I only have to hear the title mentioned to go all jittery. I can't help it, but I have a terrible complex about it, a sort of phobia, I've always thought it's because it is a novel everyone praises to the skies. Politicians, whatever their stripe, quote from memory some of its wittiest lines and praise its author, and suffer no outrages of fortune when it comes to spending our taxes on all manner of commemorations and homages, which, knowing the likes of them, just have to be extremely dubious. For my part, I'm convinced most of our parliamentarians have never bothered even to leaf through the book, although, to be honest, I should confess I've never been able to get past the first forty pages, and it's not for want of trying.

To be frank, not to have read *Don Quixote* is not such a serious problem, unless you happen to be a student in a Department of Spanish Literature. Naturally I'd have behaved much more intelligently if I'd imitated most of my companions and pretended I'd read it. It would have been sufficient to repeat pompously and authoritatively a handful of ill-digested critics. Rather than this, let's be quite clear, I behaved remarkably stupidly.

I had only a year to go and couldn't think of any better topic for my final dissertation than a study that would show how almost nobody in this country (in this city, really) had read from beginning to end the sacred text of Spanish letters. I wasted my time getting 500 questionnaires distributed – yes, five hundred – in and outside the faculty, a sample that included every social class, from patrician

Pedralbes to proletarian Santa Coloma de Gramenet. Of the 500 surveyed, eighteen were emphatic they'd read it from cover to cover and had really enjoyed the experience (needless to say, not a single one belonged to the faculty or had passed through its halls). The remaining 482 confessed they hadn't even tried to read *Don Quixote* or hadn't got beyond the first fifty pages. Always for the same reason: as a novel it was too long and too full of words they didn't understand, not to mention the miles of footnotes that some demented sadist had decided to concoct with the clear aim of demoralising the long-suffering readers. These 482 en masse answered "no" to section "D" of the survey which asked if they would be prepared to confess to their sin in public.

Predictably, I felt relieved after seeing those results and a little less lonely. It turned out I wasn't the only person in the world who'd not read that masterpiece of world literature! Unfortunately, the staff in the department didn't rate my original contribution to the study of Golden Age literature and muttered that rather than wasting my time so dreadfully I should have immersed myself in the tome and forgotten all that nonsense. They swore they'd never give me a degree, whether in that faculty or any other, and also declared *if you attempt to go all quixotic and make this survey public* (verbatim) *someone will ensure you get a facelift* (also verbatim). As I wasn't at all sure what going all quixotic entailed, I decided to drop it and deliver myself unto Montse.

"My only condition is that you don't tell your wife I'm your brother," Borja pressed me while we were still in the restaurant. "If she knew, she'd put her foot in it sooner or later. Eduard, this business will only prosper if we can persuade our clients I am Borja and belong to their social circle. Believe me, it's the only way they'll confide in us. Just think of it as your second chance in life."

"I don't intend to change my name," I objected.

"That won't be necessary," he hurriedly explained. "You can go on being Eduard Martínez and who you are now. Well, no need to go around proclaiming you're leftwing and all that . . . I expect you're still waving the red flag, aren't you?"

"And what about you?" I asked, although by this stage I could imagine his reply.

"Bah, I don't believe in politics any more!" he said, making a gesture that suggested he'd given all that up: "You know, if you have to make a choice, I prefer the good life."

I decided not keep prodding, afraid he'd come out with some really outrageous comment. On the other hand, the decision I faced was too important to take on the spur of the moment, particularly after we'd landed ourselves with a skinful of three bottles of Rioja and a couple of glasses of cognac. I asked him for time to think the offer over.

"Goes without saying! Take as long as you like. But remember what mother used to say: 'If you want to catch fish . . .'"

"'. . . you've got to get your arse wet.' Yes, I remember. Course I do!"

Thoughts of our mother made us sad, and we fell silent for a while. I could see Borja's eyes glinting and I was about to burst into tears. Then I remembered I'd not taken any flowers to the cemetery for at least two years.

Borja insisted on paying, then suggested we went for a stroll to clear our heads. We zigzagged up the Ramblas and when we reached the plaça de Catalunya, he pushed me into a taxi. He said he wanted to show me something.

He took me to the office on Muntaner, where Borja had yet to install the fake doors. For a time he even fooled me into thinking a secretary existed who was eternally absent. He adopted a professional tone I didn't recognize and explained he was dealing with a case related to valuable jewels from a legacy that had disappeared. He had to scrutinize every move made by the relative who had allegedly put his hand in the jewel box, in case he showed them in public or tried to sell them on the sly. The person compromised by the affair, a public figure, preferred not to tell the police or contract a professional detective agency. He wanted the matter resolved with the utmost discretion.

I sat on Borja's suggestion for a week. As things were in such a bad stew at home with Montse, and I couldn't sort out the situation with Raquel, I thought I'd hit rock bottom and things couldn't possibly get worse. "From lost to the river", I told myself in good old Spanglish as a preamble to one of my few courageous acts ever. I agreed to accept the redundancy package and my brother's offer: the time had come to escape from a life that had ground to a halt. We invested the money in Montse's business and the situation began to pick up. At the age of forty-two, thanks to my kid brother, I could make a new start with my wife, and despite all the upsets and difficulties we faced at times, I've never regretted my decision.

As for Raquel, Borja guaranteed he'd get her off my back. I don't know how he managed it, but the fact is that, overnight, my lover stopped besieging me and disappeared mysteriously from my life. Apparently, she and Borja had a conversation, but I haven't the slightest idea what my brother said to her. I only know that the day I bumped into her in one of the city's big department stores she looked daggers at me and screamed I shouldn't go near her.

"Don't even look at me!" she cried, grimacing in disgust.

I took her at her word, fled the scene and ran to tell Borja what had happened.

"Do what she says," was all he said, grinning like a Cheshire cat.

As I know my brother and I have always been on the cowardly side, I decided to let things be and not probe further.

5

"You want candles on your cake?" I asked timidly while I was still putting my coat on.

"Of course!" Montse seemed shocked I should ask. "I want forty. Not one less!"

It was almost nine o'clock and Montse had to hurry so as not to be late. Thanks to the advance we'd extracted from the MP, she was in a good mood and didn't protest at all when I told her I couldn't take Arnau to school. I'd agreed to meet Borja to plan our approach to our new case, after I'd put the money in our bank account and bought her birthday present. My brother and I might be able to buy the cake and cava after we'd spoken to Mariona Castany. I was relying on him to bring the Smart.

I don't drive. I expect it's part of the fall out from the accident that killed our parents. Although I did try to get my driving licence for a time, I suffer panic attacks whenever I sit behind a steering wheel, even when the engine isn't switched on. Luckily Montse is an excellent driver, but I can't expect her to spend the day chauffeuring me around. Whether I like it or not, I have to see to myself and use public transport, which is very ecological but not what you'd call practical.

Borja doesn't own a car, though he usually drives Merche's two-tone Smart. I imagine it seems rather absurd for two men like us, in our particular line of business, to move around Barcelona in a tiny red and white car that catches the eye and is really quite girly, but we don't have any choice. Merche also owns a silver Audi that's really stylish but she rarely lets Borja drive it.

My brother's girlfriend is one of these tax lawyers who earns an annual salary that shouldn't be allowed and always wears a fortune in clothes and jewels alone. Not to mention her hair-dos and various beauty treatments, what with anti-wrinkle and cellulite treatments and work-outs in the gym . . . Merche is four years older than us, and despite her efforts she looks her age. From what Borja has told me, I reckon she spends what I earn in a month on skincare.

It's not that she's a particularly beautiful woman; you could say she's a self-made woman by dint of her credit card. A reshaped nose (and from what I can make out, tits and bum as well), a permanent tan, immaculately peroxide blonde hair, dresses from Chanel at the very least . . . Merche's hair always looks as if she's just left the salon, too stiff for my liking, and I've never seen her not made up. She usually trails a strong scent of perfume in her wake, no doubt a very expensive brand that makes me feel queasy. Everything about her is excessive, like the mink she flaunts to work even when it's not cold. She's always in a hurry and the smile permanently set on her face is more of a grimace. However, her eyes seem sad and I've never seen her laugh spontaneously.

"I can't think why you don't make an honest woman of her," I once told Borja. "She appears to be in love with you."

"Because she'd find out I'm Pep, not Borja. Besides, she's already married. We're fine as we are."

"You know, if she really loves you, she'll understand why you use a pseudonym . . ." I went on in good faith. "It must be really hard for you!"

I don't know if I'm a romantic or just get into a state over complicated love affairs. It doesn't mean I don't like looking at girls, particularly in the fateful summer months when I can imagine things that even make me blush. But I've been living with Montse so long I don't how I'd survive without her.

"I can't see what your problem is, I mean with leading a more normal life," I sometimes blurt out.

"Forget it", he invariably retorts.

There was a queue at the bank that cold December morning and I reached the office half an hour late. Borja was in excellent form.

"I phoned Mariona and we'll drop by her house for a drink at one," he announced. "Let's see if we can find out what the latest gossip is on the high-falutin' Mrs Font!"

"We'll have to tread carefully, because if Mariona suspects we . . ."

"You leave it to me," he grunted. "And not a word about Pau Ferrer! Mariona is very clever. If it all turns out to be a misunderstanding . . ."

"This case is giving me bad vibes. The painting's got a strange feel to it, you know? Sinister even."

"Bah, that's normal in modern art! . . . The gloomier, uglier and nastier it is, the more it fetches," he pronounced like an expert. "Hey, time for a coffee, it's bloody freezing!"

"It wouldn't be a bad idea if they came to sort out the heating," I suggested. "One of these days a client will get frost-bite."

"You know that's not on."

No, it wasn't on, down to some issue over the rent for the flat. I preferred not to ask.

"By the way, before I forget", I said changing the subject.

"The shoes Lídia Font's wearing in the painting are red. A very bright red."

"I'm glad you told me. Did you notice anything else?"

"Well, her lips are red as well. Like the ruby in the necklace. But you know rubies are red."

Borja is colour-blind. Really colour-blind. It's not that he gets red and green mixed up, which is what people think is the case with people who suffer from this complaint, but he sees them as the same colour. Our mother discovered this when we were seven, and ever since my brother's had a complex about it. Perhaps because of the jokes he had to put up with at school, or maybe it upsets him to think he sees the world differently to most of humanity. Personally I think he's being silly, but Borja doesn't want anyone to know he's colour-blind, as if it were a defect or slur that, if it were public knowledge, would destroy the sophisticated socialite image he's created for himself. As he's so preoccupied with his appearance, he has banned both colours from his wardrobe so he doesn't mix them up when he gets dressed, or so he says. The only exception I'm aware of is a crimson tie Merche gave him as a present and which he hardly ever wears.

From the moment Borja discovered he suffers from severe colour-blindness we agreed a secret code. When his disarray threatens to betray him, I scratch my nose discreetly if the colour he can't recognize is red, while if it's green, I ostentatiously put my hands in my pockets. I sometimes simply make an innocent remark to alert him, and, ever since we've been partners, this has worked a treat because nobody, not even Merche, has noticed his strange sight. On that occasion, it had gone completely from my mind and I'd not given him the agreed signal when we talked about Lídia Font's shoes.

"While we're about it," I added. "Montse said her sister is coming to the party. Unaccompanied."

"I feared as much. Will there be a big crowd?"

"A good few, apparently . . . Naturally lots of Montse's friends, from her Centre."

"So we'll end up plastered."

"More than likely. Lots of alternative this and that but they all like a good piss-up . . ."

"So be it," he said shrugging his shoulders, "I hope Lola doesn't have too many high hopes."

Montse had long been angling to pair off Dolors, Lola from the day she separated, with my business partner. Dolors, I mean Lola, is Montse's younger sister, and like us they don't at all look alike. Lola lives in the Born district near the church of Santa María del Mar and likes to design and produce jewellery, handbags and hats, although I don't imagine she earns enough to live from this activity. She prefers a very youngish, rather exotic style of designer gear, and I have to admit she's good-looking. Her hair is short, often dyed a different colour, and she wears square, paste spectacle frames. She rounds it all off with big necklaces and earrings she herself designs, and usually applies a deep red lipstick to her fleshy lips. She sometimes opts to dress in black and adopt airs from Greek tragedy that soon evaporate after a couple of drinks. She's a heavy smoker and often gives the impression she's a marble short.

"I'm sorry," Borja apologized, "I just can't stand her."

Lola had been divorced for four years (her former husband, who's an architect, left her for a nymphettish draughtswoman), and ever since she has drifted from one shoulder to another, or, to be more precise, from one bed to another and from one disappointment to another.

Fortunately, as her ex was well heeled, she got a hefty divorce settlement. She liked her brother-in-law Borja, and Monte was convinced they'd make a perfect item. I thought she was wrong.

"Why not bring Merche along?" I suggested half-heartedly. "You don't need to say anything about her being married."

If Lola saw him in other female company, she'd probably desist.

"No way," he cut me short. "Come on, put your coat on and let's get moving. I parked the Smart outside, and I don't know about you, but I need a coffee before I can look Mariona's martinis in the eye. Bugger this weather . . ."

We went to the bar on the corner to warm up and kill time smoking and drinking coffee. Borja used the time to flick through the society pages of the ABC and I got depressed reading about the disasters afflicting the universe. After a while, we got into the Smart and headed towards our friend's mansion. We had to drive round a while to find a parking space, but it was barely a couple of minutes past one when we strolled up to the front door of the hugely rich and most distinguished Doña Mariona Castany.

6

My brother's aristocratic friend lived alone in one the few modernist mansions still surviving intact on the Bonanova in the upper reaches of Barcelona, with a chatterbox Argentine butler and a shy Philippine maid who never said boo to a goose. It was a vast, tastefully and expensively decorated pile you reached via a splendid garden that extended behind the house into a small wood. An enormous bougainvillea spread over one of the walls of the house that, in summer and autumn, was covered in purple flowers that gave the small palace a fairy-tale aura. A thick vegetal tapestry of dark-leaved ivy, as old as the house, completely isolated the mansion and the garden from the outside world.

Doña Mariona Castany had inherited the house and the whole family fortune on the death of her father. The one and only heir to a patrimony that the next five generations of Castanys would be hard put to pare down – not for want of trying – she refused to contemplate the sale of her palatial abode, even though estate agents were continually knocking on her door and offering veritable fortunes. In another era, the exclusive parties and concerts she held there were the envy of her female friends and enemies, but, ever since her husband died, Mariona hadn't staged a single event. She'd say sadly she thought it would be in bad taste.

She'd been widowed seven years ago. Her three daughters, in their day excellent catches that every fortune-hunter in the city chanced their luck with, were now married and had given Mariona six grandchildren – two a-piece – and three less wealthy but quite arrogant sons-in-law she only tolerated in small doses. Apart from being incredibly wealthy herself, Mariona was intelligent and didn't suffer fools gladly.

When we were approaching the door, we passed a familiar face beating a quick retreat. He didn't look up but grunted a polite "Good day".

"I recognize that face," said Borja as the man walked off.

"Of coursed you do. It's Enrique Dalmau, the politician. You must have seen him on the telly." And I added, "He's an MP, and belongs, by the way, to the same party as our client."

"I see . . ."

Marcelo, the Argentine butler, greeted us as effusively as ever and accompanied us to a spacious drawing room adorned with art-deco lamps and furniture, every one an original. Mariona was waiting for us reclining on a kind of settee, in a rather theatrical pose. She was more or less the age our mother would have been, a well-preserved sixty-five year-old, and she'd adopted Borja as if he were a nephew. Borja would sometimes call her "Aunt Mariona" half affectionately, half in jest. I didn't dare, but Borja would not just peck her on the cheek (I limited myself to a respectful, firm handshake) but venture a gallant, sensual kiss to her hand too.

She was tall, thin and dynamic. Her silvery, almost white curly hair reached down to her shoulders and her blue eyes sparkled as she chain-smoked Winstons. Now and then she gave a little cough. Her narrow, pointed nose, accustomed to exquisite fragrances as well as to the two packets of cigarettes she polished off daily, supplied an aristocratic air that snub noses, for whatever reason, never do. She wore the latest fashions which made her look more youthful, although she had the good taste at her time of life not to attempt to wear anything low-cut. Mariona Castany had money and class. That day she'd donned stiletto-heeled black boots to highlight her long legs, tight-fitting leather trousers and a short-sleeved white T-shirt with the word "Chanel" splashed at breast level in letters of mother-of-pearl sequins that glinted like fish scales. Her dark skin contrasted with her pale pink lips and nails. It wasn't hard to imagine Mariona in her heyday driving men crazy.

"So Lídia is two-timing her MP . . ." she smiled as she served up our dry martinis, adding a few drops of gin and a slice of lemon peel.

"I never said we're working for her husband," replied Borja, winking at her after he'd sipped his martini. "I only asked you what you know about Lídia Font."

Doña Mariona Castany is the kind of woman who knows the low-down on everyone. She and my brother met by chance at the opening of a Tàpies Foundation exhibition and soon became friends. Mariona's positive that one of the girls at the exclusive Swiss finishing school where she studied was Borja's fictitious mother. It turned out that one of the Spanish pupils was from Santander. Mariona couldn't recall her surname. She was a María Eugenia and, from that day on, Borja's mother assumed that name.

"What a pity your mother died so young . . ." she sometimes tells him. "It's not as if we spent a lot of time together, because my parents soon brought me back to Barcelona, when they saw that living away from home didn't suit me, but obviously I knew her. She was so shy, such a shrink-ing . . ."

"Yes, she was ever so," Borja always replies, remorsefully but never blushing. "She didn't enjoy the school either and soon returned to Santander. She would reminisce about you . . ."

Mariona and my brother finally created the fiction that she and the so-called María Eugenia had been good friends. After a few martinis Borja will sometimes regale us with anecdotes about the finishing school Mariona had previously told him and she laughs her head off. I suppose she clings to her relationship with Borja because he reminds her of her childhood.

"This is Borja Másdeu, son of María Eugenia from Santander," she explains when doing her introductions. "We studied together in a private college in Switzerland. Poor dear, she died very young at the age of forty. Cancer . . ." And adds: "It's as if Borja were a nephew of mine. Look after him, won't you?"

Mariona has opened many doors for Borja and is an endless fount of information, though I'm not sure she doesn't smell a rat in relation to the tale of Borja's mother. I get the impression she's sufficiently intelligent, has the sense of humour and *savoir-faire* to follow his drift with a straight face and amuse herself into the bargain. We always have recourse to Mariona when we need to get the latest on the gossip circulating among Barcelona's upper classes that constitute the fulcrum of her intense social life. But far from being a gossipmonger, she's a past master in the art of chasing the latest news and putting two and two together. She's discreet, well informed and efficient. At any given moment she knows what to say, how to say it and to whom. She's up-to-speed on everyone's ups and downs, but never one to run and pick up the phone and gossip with her woman friends when she's just come across a juicy titbit. They say her discretion and advice have saved more than one marriage.

"Mariona, we'd like you to tell us what you know about Lídia Font," Borja asked her. "You *do* know her, don't you?"

"Do *you* know what you're getting into?"

Her question, expressed in a tone of voice that wasn't at all innocent, alarmed us. All we wanted to know was what people were saying about our client's wife on Barcelona's upper side. What kind of person she was, whether she'd a reputation for having affairs with other men, whether she got on well with her husband . . . If at the end of the day it was all down to infidelity and a jealous husband worried about his political future, as seemed to be the case, Mariona's comment seemed quite uncalled for.

"Yes, but do you know her?" Borja persisted.

"Of course, I know her!" She sighed. "Do I have any choice? She's one to look out for. Lídia is also a kind of second cousin of mine. Didn't *you* know that?"

We shook our heads and she sipped on her drink before launching into an explanation.

"Do you see, I had a cousin on my mother's side, who was older than me and rather dim-witted, and she had a daughter . . . My cousin, poor thing, died quite young – she died from a broken neck one winter skiing in Cortina – and her husband, Esteve Vilalta, we called him Estevet, remarried, this time to Ernest Pou's daughter, one of the Sabadell Pous, the textile manufacturers, when everyone thought she'd end up dressing saints in church – Rosa, I mean, the Pous' daughter, because she was so wet and without a spark . . . But who'd have thought it, she married

Estevet, who now looked at her as if she were a supermodel, and they had another daughter, Lídia, although Rosa was getting on by this stage . . . Obviously, in fact, Estevet and I aren't family, but Lídia is a kind of second cousin, don't you think?"

"I suppose so," I replied trying to digest the whole story.

"Properly speaking, there is no blood link, but given that Lídia is step-sister to my other niece, she is in a way, you know, what English people would call my second cousin-in-law . . ."

Borja interrupted her genealogical disquisition: "You must have things you can tell us," he insisted. "I believe Lídia is married to a politician who's now an MP. I bet she likes the busy social round."

Doña Mariona Castany smiled again, offered us a second martini and lifted a cigarette to her lips and waited for Borja to offer her a light. My brother was quick to show off the gold lighter Merche had given him for his birthday. After a couple of drags, Mariona settled down on the sofa, toyed with a cushion, and began holding forth.

"Dear old Lídia is a nasty piece of work. And you know how I hate to run anybody down, but . . ."

"You know that nothing you tell us will go beyond these walls," Borja assured her.

"Yes, though everyone knows whatever I can tell you. Let's see, where should I begin . . . You could say Lídia is the sort that mistreats her staff and looks down on all and sundry. She doesn't dare try that on with me, naturally . . . She's hoping one day she'll wheedle me into letting her redecorate this old house of mine. She's ambitious, much more so than her husband Lluís. And always has been." Then added, as if confidentially: "When she was a youngster, she played that dirty trick on her step-sister Sílvia. The poor girl even attempted to commit suicide . . ."

"Good heavens!"

"Lots of people are gunning for her, and lots try to keep out of her way. She has a vicious tongue on her . . ." She paused, as if pondering what to say next. "I can only say that when she has something in her sights she won't stop till she gets it. But you know what people are like. Everyone panders to her. Well, almost everyone . . ." she smiled.

"I see your cousin is not exactly your cup of tea," I countered politely. "And as I don't have the privilege of being your putative nephew, I'll not probe any further."

Mariona Castany directed a second withering look at me that translated into "You idiot, how dare you interrupt me." She'd aimed the first at my feet when she realized I was wearing dark shoes and light, though not white-coloured, socks. An unforgivable *faux pas.*

"I don't know what else I can tell you . . . She comes from a good family background obviously . . . Her husband as well, I mean, in their case, neither married for money . . . Of course they're not the wealthiest couple in Barcelona, by a long chalk," she added contemptuously.

"She's also clearly interested in politics," interjected Borja.

"Bah! She hasn't the slightest idea about politics," Mariona exclaimed, shrugging her shoulders. "It's the limelight, not politics she's after. She's dedicated tooth and nail to ensuring her husband makes it to the Presidency of the Generalitat one day. Poor Lluís! He's not what you'd call thick, but he's hardly a genius."

"Well, that's never been an obstacle to political success," I suggested not at all maliciously.

Both Mariona and Borja turned a deaf ear to my wit.

"I imagine," continued Mariona, "she already sees herself playing the role of first lady. Appearing in newspapers and magazines, organizing receptions, entertaining celebrities and bowing to the King and the Pope . . . She excelled herself trying to wangle an invitation to the Prince's wedding, because she apparently knows the Infanta Cristina. Failed in the attempt, obviously."

"Does she set her sights that high?" I enquired.

"She's not short of contacts. Her line of work – interior design – helps her to earn money and hobnob with the high society. She's no fool."

"It's clear she knows the design business and charges the earth," said Borja trying to dig more dirt. "They say she's got first-rate taste and knows a lot about painting."

"It would really be too, too much if she didn't, given the sums she's charging! With the budgets Lídia works with, anyone can have good taste," she riposted, pretending to be scandalized and ignoring the subtle comment connecting Lídia Font and the world of fine art.

"I've always thought good taste and elegance were at odds with money. That they're something innate," I said continuing on the same line that Borja had initiated. "Or so everybody says. Naturally artistic sensibility has to be cultivated, going to museums and art galleries . . ."

"Stuff and nonsense! Good taste depends on your pocket. It's a business, like any other. When they say that someone has good taste, it's either because he's rich or because he's trying to ape the rich." Our hostess still hadn't bitten on the hook we were casting in her direction.

It wasn't the first time the conversation had drifted on to such issues. My brother's friend liked to expatiate on her vision of the world and pontificate from her pedestal as the wealthiest of Catalan women. It is *very* simple according to her: the world is divided between rich and poor. The rich have enough money to follow their every whim, be it a Van Gogh, a house on the Riviera or a seat in Parliament. The rest of us are the poor. Mariona doesn't distinguish between those who live in a cardboard box in the metro and those inhabiting six hundred square feet of real estate south of the Diagonal.

"Look, Eduard," she added, as if clinching the issue, "the only thing elegance is at odds with is poverty." And instinctively, but this time not all maliciously, her eyes focussed back on my shoes.

Borja decided the time had come to take a risk and put his trust yet again in the discretion of this woman who was an institution in certain spheres of city life. He cut to the quick.

"But does your cousin have a reputation for acting like Mata Hari? I'm asking whether she's happy with her husband," he asked lowering his voice.

"Do you see, Borjita? I was right first time! I knew it had to do with bed-hopping!"

"So she does have her lovers," suggested Borja.

"Well, the fact is she's not famed as a man-hunter," Mariona admitted reluctantly. "A nasty upstart, certainly, but no affairs have been registered so far as I know. And that's quite odd . . . I'd always assumed her to be quite frigid," and then she whispered: "Poor Lluís always looks as if he gets poor service. In any case, if Lídia does have a lover out there, she's very discreet. But I've not seen her for some time. I can ask after her, out of casual curiosity, you know," she said condescendingly.

"Would you, Aunt Mariona? Would you please?" Borja begged in that half flattering, half seductive tone that served him so well with women like Mariona Castany.

"I will go to my club on Monday afternoon and ensure Lídia's name crops up in conversation. Don't you worry, I'll find out any gossip doing the rounds about her or her husband. But it's such a boring place! . . ."

The very wealthy Mariona belonged to an exclusive, expensive club near the Bonanova, but apparently didn't find it very entertaining and went very rarely. When we heard the chimes of one of the mansion's grandfather clocks we realized it was past two o'clock. Borja checked the time and went as if to get up.

"We won't bother you any more, Mariona. I'll ring you next week. I expect you're very busy now Christmas is upon us . . ."

"Humph, I'd almost forgotten! Wait a minute!" she exclaimed, imperiously forcing Borja and me to sit back down on the modernist sofa where we'd been sipping our martinis. "I have something for both of you."

And as she said this, she rang an invisible bell we couldn't hear.

"Did madam want something?"

Marcelo, the butler, appeared within half a minute. He was in uniform and looked immaculate.

"Indeed, Marcelo, would you be so kind as to bring the two parcels in my study, the ones in red wrapping paper?"

"Of course, those on your desk top? I think I saw them this morning, when I was tidying . . ."

"Just so. Thank you." And added: "It's my Christmas present."

A couple of minutes later Marcelo reappeared with his servile smile and two parcels exquisitely wrapped in red, shiny paper. The smaller one was for Borja, and mine was flat and long and surely contained a tie.

"Here you are. Open them at home."

"Madame, if that was all . . . I believe someone has knocked on the front door, and as the maid is in the kitchen preparing lunch . . ."

"Go to, Marcelo, see who it is. And while you're about it, accompany these gentlemen . . ."

"You shouldn't have gone to such trouble," said Borja courteously. "But I've something for you. I almost forgot too." And extracted from his pocket a rather more modestly wrapped present. "Happy Christmas, Mariona."

"How wonderful!" She smiled like a little girl. "I love surprises! Thank you, my dear. I will put it under the tree with my other presents and open it on Christmas Eve."

I blushed, because I'd not taken her anything. It hadn't even occurred to me that I should and Borja had never suggested I should. As usual, he came to my rescue. "It's from both of us. We saw it and thought it was made for you. I do hope you like it."

"You *are* such a darling," she said. "You too, my dear Eduard. My thanks to you both. Now, off you go, I have guests coming for lunch!"

Marcelo brought our coats and accompanied us to the door.

"I think that of late dear Madam hasn't been very well," he confided anxiously. "That cough worries me. She should see her doctor, but you know what's she's like . . ."

That's how Marcelo was. He would perform like a butler on celluloid and always overacted the part in relation to Mariona Castany. I think he'd missed his vocation as an actor; in fact I could swear I've seen him in a television ad.

"I think she looks fantastic, Marcelo," Borja replied. "Besides she's in superb form. Is there a problem we are unaware of?" My brother seemed alarmed.

"She shouldn't smoke so much. She sees off two packets a day . . . Perhaps you could persuade her to smoke less and sleep more. Madam has great respect for you . . ."

"I'll mention it to her the next time we meet. Take good care of her in the meantime, won't you, Marcelo?"

Marcelo had been in Mariona Castany's service for fifteen years ever since he left Argentina and I think he was really devoted to her. He must have been well into his fifties and retained an enviable shock of black hair. He lived in and did the honours as chauffeur, master of ceremonies and gardener. He must have been on a good salary (much more substantial than mine naturally), and since a goodly number of staff saw to the house during the day, his work wasn't particularly onerous. Physically, he looked a man who liked his sport and pampered himself. I've always thought he was gay, of the dandy variety, and absolutely the kind of butler that suited a lady like Doña Mariona Castany.

On the way out we walked past a well-known architect who was Mariona's age. Rumours had abounded for years that they were lovers, from long before she was widowed. He too was wealthy and led a respectable, married life. As far as we knew, like our friend, he'd never been involved in any scandals.

Once we were in the car, we couldn't resist the temptation to open our presents. Mine was a bold, if elegant, Hermès tie, and Borja's, gold cufflinks, also Hermès.

"Very stylish," I admitted. "At long last I've got a change of tie! But I'll only wear it in the office in case Montse starts getting jealous."

"Our Mariona is a real lady," said Borja delightedly, eyeing his cufflinks. "You know, the rich aren't known for their generosity."

"No, they're usually misers. That's why they're so rich."

"And Mariona is one of the filthy rich!"

"You know, I never thought to bring her a Christmas present. I mean I wasn't expecting a gift from her. It's assumed you're the nephew . . . It was lucky you had the forethought!"

"In fact I didn't," he smiled. "Such a dreadful oversight on my part. I gave her the present I'd bought for Montse. I don't know if she'll like it. I hope so."

"May we ask what it was?"

I was curious to know what kind of present could equally well do for my Montse and the wealthy Mariona Castany.

"It was a necklace from the Atlas mountains, from Morocco," he replied. "I know how much Montse likes ethnic baubles. I expect Mariona will consider it an exotic touch. But I must go back to the shop this afternoon!"

"Courtesy of the MP's advance."

"Right, better than pennies from heaven."

"And later on, if you don't mind, we could drive over to the Bolet bakery," I suggested. "It's too late now . . . I've got to buy the cava and cake for tomorrow, but if it's not convenient . . ."

I thought that, as it was Friday, he must have a date with his girlfriend.

"Merche's off skiing with her husband this afternoon and will be away the whole weekend." It was as if he'd read my thoughts. "You know, we can forget our investigations till Monday. We'll have to tail Lídia Font for a few weeks at least, to find out what's she's up to. Shit!" He paused to dodge a car that had just jumped the traffic lights. "In the meantime you can look on the internet and see what you can dig out on Mrs Font and that Pau Ferrer fellow. That might save us some time."

Borja picked up the computer we have in the office, a see-through designer Mac that doesn't work, from a skip. When we need to use the internet, I use my twin's cheapo PC which always does the job. It's incredible the amount of information you can get without budging from your chair, but you have to be careful. Borja is a case in point: he's uploaded his fake CV to the web.

"It's almost three o'clock," he said as he stopped the car in front of our front door. "All right to come for you at six?"

"You sure you don't want to come up and have a bite? I can rustle up something quickly . . ."

"I'm a bit sleepy after Mariona's martinis. I'd rather go to my flat and have a rest. I've got a game tonight."

"Whatever. What do you reckon then?"

"It's obvious the lady's up to something with the artist," my brother asserted. "Maybe they're still carrying on. I suspect it will be quite unpleasant."

"Particularly for her husband. It's incredible how a spot of infidelity still turns the world upside down!"

"What do you expect?" He smiled. "The institution of monogamy is to blame. Your entire life with the same woman . . ."

"I assure you that suits me down to the ground," I retaliated, remembering with some irritation how the previous night Montse had come home late and chirpier than usual after the post-gig drinks.

Montse was waiting for me. She'd decided to take the afternoon off to get the party ready, so we ate pasta and salad together. As we were by ourselves, I suggested a siesta. Although she was still a little hung-over, Montse was in excellent spirits.

"What then? Have you got my present?" she asked.

"Don't go looking for it because you won't find it," I replied, remembering it was still in my pocket and that I hadn't thought to offer it to Mariona as Borja had, although it would have been over the top as a Christmas trifle. I'd bought her antique white-gold pendants, set with sapphires, which I now hastily hid under my pants in my wardrobe where I imagined they'd be safe from Montse's prying hands.

We got up around five, in an even better temper. I showered and percolated some coffee. Montse said she was off to the market and I got ready to go out. Borja would soon be here in the Smart.

"Don't be late, will you?" begged Montse. "It's your turn to help out with Arnau tonight. The girls are sleeping over at a friend's house."

"Don't worry. Besides, Borja's got a bridge school tonight."

While I waited for my brother, I sat in front of the computer and typed in Lídia Font's name on Google, but didn't find anything to help us in our investigations. She was born in 1958 in Barcelona, forty-six years ago that is (I'd say she looked younger, to go by the photo). Her official biography informed me that she was married to politician Lluís Font and was a professional interior designer. She presided over a foundation dedicated to helping handicapped children and was an honorary member of an NGO that sponsored children in the Third World. She also held an important post in an animal protection society. She'd been given two awards for interior design and one or two more for her charity work with the less fortunate.

As for Pau Ferrer, the painter of her portrait, I was shocked to find he was born back in 1941, which meant that he had sixty-four summers under his belt. He was born in Barcelona but had lived in Paris for many years. According to one interview, he'd been living for the past few years in Sant Just Desvern, in a huge hangar that doubled as his house and studio. He'd mounted dozens of exhibitions (and, apparently, earned plenty of money from them), and more recently he'd concentrated on portraits. His work was on show in London, Paris and New York and some critics considered him to be a leading contemporary artist. Although no expert, I quite like his paintings, though I'm not sure I'd want them hanging in my dining room.

I printed out everything I found and put it in a folder.

"We'll start tailing her on Monday," Borja suggested as we drove towards Sarrià. "Sooner or later we'll find out if she's involved with the painter," he said pensively.

"You look worried. Anything wrong?"

"No, I was only wondering," he sighed, "how we can fix it so we extract another 5,000 from the MP before Christmas. "Shit," he added resigned, "Life has just become more and more expensive since we got into the euro!"

7

"Fucking hell!"

"Good morning, you mean?" said Borja driving off. He'd double-parked for a moment in front of the entrance to the downstairs lobby and I'd just got in the Smart and settled into the small seat. It was Monday and I'd been waiting for a quarter of an hour.

"Fucking hell!" I repeated.

"Hey, I'm only ten minutes late," he half-apologized. "I know we said nine o'clock, but I was just leaving when I noticed a coffee stain on my tie and I obviously had to go back up and change. Apart from that, the traffic's always nose to tail at this time of day. Don't worry, we'll be there in time. It's early still."

I didn't answer. I was in a bad mood. Borja was driving along Via Augusta and I tried to distract myself and postpone the inevitable row by looking out of the window. There was a traffic jam, as usual. When we stopped by a traffic light level with the North-American Institute, I couldn't hold back any more and exploded.

"You know, Pep, what the *hell* is going on in that head of yours? For fuck's sake! Do you realize the mess you've got us both into?" I felt the blood throbbing in my head and the vein swelling in my neck.

"Ah, so you've heard . . ." piped Borja, not daring to look me in the eye.

"Have I heard, you might well ask?! Would you like me to

sum it up for you? Let's see, yesterday morning I was happy in bed, sleeping off my hangover (because obviously with all the whooping it up at the party I didn't get to bed until well past seven) when the phone rang. Montse took it as she was up. After a while, when I'd finally managed to get back to sleep, Montse came in and asked me to look after Arnau because she had to speak urgently to her sister. She was on a high and had a big smile on her face. She even winked at me. Know why?"

"No . . ." but his *no* meant *yes*.

"It transpires," I went on, gathering my breath, "that Lola called to say that you two had finally got there!"

"Shit."

"Shit, indeed! Because they were at it more than an hour. And when I tried to lie down again for a bit of post-lunch siesta and escape the day's big news, my head was throbbing after all the cava and Montse's chatter, Lola rolls up ready to shoot the breeze."

"I'll look after it . . ." he said opening a window and lighting up. I asked for a cigarette, although I was trying to knock the habit. It wasn't the best of days to try.

"You've got no idea," I retaliated. "Do you know what you've done?"

"Come on, it can't be such a big deal . . ."

"Not such a big deal? Do you mind telling me why you decided to hop into bed with Lola? Do you know what that means, what she now expects from you, and worst of all, from me?"

"Come on, Eduard, Lola and I weren't born yesterday . . ."

"Right, you're old enough not to shit your pants!"

I left it at that. We were driving up Mandri and Borja was going more slowly than usual. It was only twenty to ten and

I was afraid we'd miss Lídia Font driving out of her garage. It would be the last straw if that happened on our first day tagging behind her.

While Borja drove and I bit my tongue, the sun had time to put in an appearance among the clouds and I noted it was a cold but magnificent day. Nonetheless, my bad temper was far from going away. Borja could see that and tried to justify himself.

"You know what happened when we left your place," he said keeping his eye on the road ahead, "Lola asked me to accompany her home in a taxi. I couldn't refuse. You know I'm a gentleman in such circumstances. And then she insisted I went up and insisted I had a drink. It was very late, as you can imagine. And one thing led to another . . ."

Borja looked rough. He didn't look as if he'd had a good night's sleep. For my part, what with my hangover, the restless night because of Arnau and the anxiety prompted by this romantic tangle, I'd hardly shut my eyes.

"Do you want to know what it's all led to?" I exclaimed in a rage. "Can you imagine? Well, Lola now has high hopes, and why? You may ask! She and Montse spent the whole of yesterday interrogating me. What did I know about your private life and your girlfriend, what did I think about all this, what's Merche like, should Lola take the initiative and ring you . . ."

"OK. So I'm fucked."

"Yes. Well and truly. Couldn't have put it better myself."

Lola had been eyeing up Borja for some time: you didn't have to be an Einstein to realize that. Not that I've anything against my sister-in-law, on the contrary, I like her, though I find her a bit scatty and there are days when her neuroses get me down. But she's a good sort, loves our children and Montse is very close to her. In the end I've come to appreciate her, but it's one thing to be her brother-in-law and quite another, God forbid, to be her partner.

In fact, I think what most bothered me about this business was the fact Borja had always said Lola was the kind of woman he detested: a resentful feminist, fodder for the analyst and a Prozac junkie. He wasn't far wrong but it hadn't stopped him from licking his lips and jumping between the sheets with her.

Lola was thirty-eight, divorced and on the unstable side. She went from depression to euphoria as eagerly as a manic depressive or people who are too well-read on the subject. She'd been psychoanalysing herself for four years and going to parties and soirées in pursuit of the love of her life, none of which stopped her from spending her time criticising men and proclaiming how much she'd like to be a lesbian in order to bypass male tyranny. Ever since she separated from her husband she'd lived alone in a small flat on Princesa, near the Born, that was sometimes neurotically clean and tidy and at others a chaotic mess. As she was childless, she spent hours at our place. In the summer she spent a fortune on adventure tourism, trekking through exotic countries and then had family holidays with us and regaled our evenings with tales of her amorous feats between one gin and tonic and the next. Those trips didn't seem to do her much good and she'd invariably come back more depressed than usual.

According to Montse, she'd liked Borja from day one. She slunk behind him the whole party, as everybody noticed, and I have to agree that Lola looked stunning that night. She wore black from head to toe, and despite the cold outside, made sure her generously low neckline showed off her nipples whenever she leaned forward. She also wore long, square tortoise-shell spectacles (though I don't think my sister-in-law needed them) with lime-green frames and lenses, a mini-skirt and black calf-length boots that gave her a rather martial air.

I couldn't understand how Borja had fallen into the trap. Maybe it was the bubbly, or perhaps he didn't in fact dislike her as much as he pretended. Behind that outlandish façade might there lurk a pretty but gauche woman? Despite her sophisticated pose, I find her quite naïve.

The fact is that between the Saturday night party, Sunday hangover and Monday's spot of bother, Borja and I had had little time to prepare the case we'd been contracted to solve. We still thought this was an investigation that would be as easy as pie. If Lídia Font did have a lover, we'd nail him sooner or later. Our strategy would be the one we always use in such cases, although on this occasion we might have to be more prudent since Lluís Font was a politician in the limelight and his pocket could provide our livelihood for a good while yet. We'd tail his wife, try to muster maximum info on one Pau Ferrer and subsequently, relaxing by three shots of Cardhu, (in the Dry Martini or Gimlet on Santaló, I expect), relate to the MP the results of our enquiries, before suggesting a new line of investigation to be accompanied by a similar brown envelope stuffed with the readies.

We parked the Smart a couple of streets up from where our client lived, and waited in silence. As it's a one-way street, if Lídia Font were driving, we'd see her pass by. If she came out and walked in the other direction we'd have time to drive round and catch her on Bonanova. We didn't wait very long. At five past ten, the garage door opened and out came a small, spotlessly white Mercedes. Although the windows were tinted, we knew that the striking Mrs Font was behind the wheel.

We followed her along the Diagonal as far as the plaça Francesc Macià. After leaving her car in a parking lot, Lídia Font walked towards carrer Calvet and went into a furniture and interior design shop. It was one of those expensive establishments typical of the area, brimming with objects I found to be in particularly bad taste. After parking our car, and in order not to catch her attention by standing and waiting for her in the middle of the street, we went into a small bar almost opposite the shop and ordered a couple of black coffees with a spot of milk.

"The woman's got class," said Borja referring to Lídia Font. "You can't deny that. Whatever Mariona says, it's something you either do or don't have."

"Yes, like an open cheque book in your handbag," I retorted. "That's what decides it."

"Hey, forget your prejudices." Borja knew only too well what my opinion was of most of our clients. "What's more, she's good-looking."

"I don't deny that. But I tell you she's not my sort."

Half a minute earlier, trailing her along the street, we'd been able to scrutinize her. It was the first time we'd seen her in the flesh and Borja was right: Lídia Font had class, or style, or God knows what. At any rate, qualities most women in her position didn't have. Being who she was and having what she had, I recognized she seemed fairly sober, at least as far as her dress-sense went.

She was of slender build and walked confidently, like someone who knows she is somebody. Beneath the three-quarter, off-white coat she wore unbuttoned we glimpsed a flecked dark grey trouser-suit and high-necked black sweater. She also wore black high-heeled bootees and was clutching one of those huge handbags that can hold half a lifetime. A mauve foulard reaching down to her knees and blonde hair added a touch of colour. It looked as if she was wearing everything for the first time. Borja and I agreed her appearance was both elegant and unobtrusive, as befits the wife of a future candidate for the Presidency. She had gathered her hair into a ponytail and wore enormous Hollywood-star style sunglasses.

She lingered more than an hour in this shop that sold expensive, horrific adornments. While we waited, neither Borja nor I mentioned the small matter of Lola. I'd no idea how I could fix things so as not to get on the wrong side of Montse and her sister. Apart from being my brother, Borja was my business partner, and I wanted to avoid at all costs having to suffer any fall-out from his fling with Lola.

Just after midday, Lídia Font left the shop with another woman and they both went into a cafeteria a few metres from the spot where we'd lodged. Borja and I left our bar, now immersed in a thick smoky haze, and found a table in the same cafeteria. When Lídia Font took her coat off, we both could testify that she wasn't a gram overweight and that Newton's law didn't seem to affect her. Everything was absolutely in its rightful place.

The woman accompanying her was in all probability the owner or manager of the interior design shop and she too wore expensive designer clothes, but her manner was more deferential. She ordered a coffee and gobbled down a croissant, while Lídia Font left her bottle of mineral water half-drunk and smoked a couple of cigarettes. They both talked about a wedding, we deduced of a mutual friend, and issues relating to some patterned cloth from a well-known

Italian company. Nothing caught our attention, although it was difficult to catch what they said when they started to whisper.

Just before one o'clock Lídia Font paid the bill and both women walked out of the cafeteria, kissed and bid farewell to each other. We were getting ready to fetch the Smart when Mrs Font passed by on her way to plaça Francesc Macià. At that time of day, the Diagonal was packed with cars, pedestrians and a few rash cyclists. Lídia Font made her way through the crowds and went into the Sandor that was just beginning to fill up. She took off her coat and sat at one of the small tables by the window. Apparently, she had a rendezvous.

The Sandor is an elegant bar that existed when the square was still named after the fascist Calvo Sotelo. It's the kind of establishment that posh folk frequent for aperitifs or pre-dinner drinks, and our client didn't stand out at all. As we were certain Mrs Font had yet to notice us, we went in engrossed in a discreet business conversation and stationed ourselves at one of the tables at the back. That corner gave us a good view of the whole place, and the bodies of the customers at the bar gave us cover. Lídia ordered a beer and, fed up of coffee, we followed suit.

Mrs Font removed her glasses and the slide holding her hair in place. We could gaze at her against the light and didn't have to worry about being noticed. We didn't need to speak, because both Borja and I then understood why her lover, if that is what he was, had tried to immortalize her in oils although, as we could now appreciate, he hadn't done her justice.

Lídia Font was much more beautiful and sensual than the woman the painter had captured on canvas. When she loosened her hair to remake her ponytail, the Sandor was transformed for a few seconds by her splendidly mature beauty. She was probably not a natural blonde, but her hair shone like gold, or at least I thought so. She was wearing pearl earrings and a diamond ring that would have served her well at the prince's wedding: I became convinced that what Mariona Castany had hinted about her cousin's would-be frigidity was the mischievous comment of a jealous female. Lídia Font emanated the kind of sensuality most women hate in another representative of their own sex: the one that drives men mad. All things considered, she had the feline air of a Fifties Hollywood goddess, the kind to whom I professed perpetual fidelity.

She had large, dark bright eyes, a gaze trained to seduce and a smile that could leave nobody untouched. That look was nothing like the dull expression the painter had created. She used make-up sparingly as befits naturally beautiful women, and didn't flaunt the sun-baked lizard shade of brown that is the fashion in these localities. She took an interior design magazine from her handbag and began to leaf through it and didn't bother to sip her drink.

A few minutes past one o'clock we saw a tall, slim woman come in who must have been in her fifties. She greeted Lídia Font aloofly (downright coldly, I thought) and sat down next to her. The newcomer took her coat off, a mink she'd just bought apparently, ordered a vermouth and glanced around. She seemed relieved to find no one who recognized her.

Her long smooth hair was dyed an unnatural bluish black, and she wore lots of make-up around her small, gimlet eyes and on her lips, which were a strident shade of pumpkin orange. She had a deep tan but the cardboard quality of her skin and grin was typical of women who've had a facelift. Her lips also looked as if they'd been modified, and though she was thin, her body wasn't exactly svelte. A short, tight-fitting dress emphasised her bony frame. She wore brown knee-length boots with a matching handbag embossed with the letters YSL. Her display of jewellery was far more ostentatious than anything the MP's wife wore. Despite the time she spent every morning in front of the mirror, she was ugly and doomed to wither prematurely.

From our vantage point, Borja and I could hear little of their conversation. They whispered very quietly in Spanish. The dark-haired woman seemed to get angrier and angrier and more distressed, and gesticulated as she spoke. In contrast, Lídia Font remained cold and aloof. My brother and I then began to understand what Mariona had told us about her cousin. She was a beautiful but scheming bitch and we saw how skilled she was at infuriating the other woman. Her attitude revealed a Mrs Font who wasn't the ingenuous goddess with golden tresses whose epiphany we'd just witnessed.

Borja and I deduced a negotiation was under way and that Mrs Font had the upper hand. The other woman gulped down her vermouth and asked for a second. Lídia Font had barely sipped the beer she had ordered when she sat down.

We thought we caught the stranger mouthing the words "party", "shitty" and "fuck", but, to tell the truth, neither Borja nor I are expert lip-readers, so that was all we could pick up from where we were sitting. Lídia Font continued unperturbed. We regretted not taking a table nearer to them, but we'd be trailing her for a good few days yet and didn't want to risk arousing her suspicions by bumping into her every five minutes.

While we tried to read those women's lips, Borja's mobile rang.

"Why don't you answer?" I asked.

Borja looked at the number and switched his phone off.

"No, I can deal with it later on."

"It might be another client," I responded sarcastically.

"I think not . . ." he replied, looking down and putting an act on.

"Ah, right you are."

I presumed it must be Lola and thought how Montse would give me the third-degree treatment that night when she got back. That is, if she'd not invited Lola to dinner as well. I was forced to interrupt the thread of my thoughts because the two women suddenly got up and exchanged icy goodbyes. The woman with the deep tan paid the bill and was the first to leave. She seemed upset and insulted. Her interlocutor, on the other hand, sat down again and stayed in the Sandor for a few minutes more. Whatever they'd been talking about, her barely concealed smile of satisfaction revealed that she'd got her way.

Finally, Lídia Font got up and decided to return to her modest mansion. Her husband had assured us that, when she had no other commitments, his wife always ate at home in order to maintain the spartan diet that enabled her to keep her size thirty-six. Then she'd have a siesta, watch some women's programme and wouldn't normally reappear in the world outside until well gone five.

For our part, we were tired and hungry and decided to eat. Of course it would have been much more professional to take turns to stand guard on the corner by their house, in case Mrs Font changed her mind and decided to invite her lover to lunch, but that way of working was tedious in the extreme. Besides, we knew from experience that the one left on watch inevitably dozed off. So we looked for a restaurant with a cheap set lunch and trusted what the MP had told us about his wife's eating habits.

After refuelling, though still drowsy, we parked ourselves back outside the Font mansion. At about half past four the MP's wife emerged, this time on foot and in a hurry. She'd changed and was dressed much more informally. She stopped a taxi on Bonanova and we followed her in our Smart: to a beauty parlour.

She spent almost four hours in that hairdresser's, while, squashed and stiff-necked, we got bored and froze to death in our tiny car. I curbed my tongue and made a real effort not to broach the subject of Lola. It was gone eight o'clock when she decided to leave the beautician's. Unfortunately, it was dark by this time and we were in no position to appreciate the results of so many hours of self-sacrifice. We followed her back to her house and waited there till nine o'clock when we saw our client drive his Audi into the garage, and so we decided to call it a day.

The next morning Mrs Font took a taxi to the Corte Inglés. We pursued her though the department store, in case she'd got a date there with her painter friend. She spent a couple of hours trying on blouses and trousers in the boutiques on the women's floor, but looked at lots and bought little. Then she went up to the cafeteria, had a coffee and spent almost an hour smoking while talking on her mobile. Just after one, she went down to the perfume section and purchased, amongst other lotions and liquids, a bottle of Chanel Number 5 (I've always wondered whatever happened to Numbers 2 and 8, say), and thus burdened by several packages, she finally got into a taxi.

As we'd left the Smart in the store car park, we decided to leave it there and hop in a taxi. We ended up outside a well-known restaurant in the carrer París in the heart of the Eixample. Lídia Font strode into the eatery, and Borja, a few seconds later, announced he would take a discreet look inside.

"If she's with a man, we'll try to get a table," he told me, "if not, we'll eat opposite."

"Sure, this restaurant doesn't look cheap."

"With all those bags, I expect she's meeting a lady friend. I'd bet my birthright on it."

"What makes you think that?" I asked intrigued.

"It's Bags' Law and it's infallible," he came back at me.

Thanks to my brother, over the last three years I've learned a whole lot of subtle insights that were news to me. For example, that when lunching with a lady friend, women from a certain social class first go shopping in order to appear in the restaurant laden with bags and, so much the better if they're the exclusive designer variety. It's a matter of quality rather than quantity. This way I've learned that a single Loewe or Vuitton bag beats any number from Bulevard Rosa or the Corte Inglés, that Armani and Chanel level peg and that Zara is a no-no. This is Borja's Bags' Law. And it's not the only unwritten code that reigns in particular zones of Barcelona's upper reaches.

Yet again my brother was right. Our client's wife was going to lunch with a lady friend, who also had her supporting cast of bags. Four Corte Inglés against two Bulevard Rosa could be rated as a technical draw, perhaps with the MP's wife getting a slight edge. On this occasion, the relationship between both women seemed much more relaxed. According to Borja, who'd spied on them from inside the restaurant, they'd greeted each other effusively and everything pointed to the other woman being one of her wealthy friends. Conversely, Lídia Font gave the impression she was too intelligent to commit an indiscretion in public with a man who wasn't her husband, particularly in that sort of top-class restaurant. So we left them to get on with it and went to our tapas in the rather more modest bar opposite.

When Lídia Font left the restaurant a couple of hours later, we trailed her on foot to another furniture shop where she stayed for half an hour until she decided to return home with us close on her heels. We waited in our car, which we'd recovered during her long post-lunch chit-chat, but decided to call it a day at seven thirty: Barça was playing and we didn't want to miss the opening minutes of the game.

There were no novelties over the next few days. Shops, lady friends, more shops and the odd social event, sometimes accompanied by her husband. On Thursday afternoon Mrs Font went shopping with her daughter, a pallid, skinny adolescent who didn't seem to have inherited her mother's seductive beauty, and on Friday we visited more interior design shops and dozed off in our tiny car near her elegant mansion. The monotony was beginning to exasperate and it all pointed to a complete lack of anything suspicious in the lady's behaviour. We were mistaken, because very late on Friday afternoon the exemplary Mrs Font had a surprise in store for us.

8

It was just seven o'clock and pitch black. Borja and I were tired, fed up of mounting guard by the MP's mansion, and wanted to go home. We also knew that the Fonts had people coming to dinner that night so imagined we could shut up shop and retire for the night. We were about to drive off when we saw Mrs Font emerge sheathed in luxurious mink, and in a rush. On this occasion, rather than taking the Mercedes, she walked to the Bonanova and hailed a taxi. The vehicle headed into the centre and we had no choice but to point our Smart in the same direction.

"I wonder where the fuck's she's off to at this time of night? With all this traffic!" Borja exclaimed.

The taxi turned down Balmes. We were on our way to the madding crowd.

"I don't know where the hell I'll park! It's nose-to-tail out there!" My brother hated driving in the city-centre. "When she gets out of the taxi, you follow her on foot while I try to park," he ordered, giving me no opportunity to protest.

"I'll call you on your mobile to let you know where we are. You'd better leave the car in a parking lot. I expect she's off shopping again . . ."

"I hope to God she's not!"

The taxi continued down Pelaio and Lídia got out in the plaça de Catalunya where the Ramblas start. She crossed the street and went into the Zurich, a café that once had a charm of its own but had been refurbished, sanitized and swallowed up by the controversial "golden triangle" alongside Habitat and FNAC. There was no trace of the old café, a meeting-point for left-wingers where the smell of marijuana mingled with the stench of urine from the lavatories. Gone was the old lady that looked after them, an old dear, always incredibly tarted up under a grotesque black wig, who never forgot to demand a tip.

Once inside, Lídia Font acted as if she were looking for someone. A man, in his late fifties, greeted her timidly. He was sitting at an unobtrusive table in a far corner, and I had to reconcile myself to a small table at the other end. The place was packed at that time in the evening, given it was freezing outside.

"Hurry up, Borja," I appealed into my mobile. "She's got a man with her!"

"Fuck! There's nowhere. Every little space's taken. Don't let her out of your sight! And take good note of what they say."

Deafened by the other customers' hubbub, I could catch none of their conversation from where I was sitting. All I could do was focus on the man's appearance and see whether what I'd learned from the detectives in the thrillers I'd read was any help.

What could I deduce from his appearance? In the first place, the man didn't seem to belong to the Fonts' circle of acquaintances. Although he was well dressed, suffice it to say he was more in my line than Borja's. He was wearing a dark green sweater over a white shirt, and sported bifocals. Their metal frames were very antiquated, the kind you rarely see nowadays. His was a traditional balding pate, not a shaven affair, and the scant hair he did have was neatly combed and he was clean-shaven. He seemed modest, polite and restrained. Ordinary looking, I'd have said, not someone wanting to attract attention, except for the fact he was rather dowdy. On the empty seat next to him I could see a brown blouson and a shabby black motor-cycle helmet. He was drinking an infusion of tea, and Lídia Font, as ever, had ordered mineral water.

They chatted for some twenty minutes. The man looked on intently as she explained something sourly. I felt he was getting angry and agitated. The MP's wife was steering the conversation and he seemed to be answering back in a way she found unsatisfactory. I wasn't sure what Borja would make of it – he understands more about these things than I do – but from my perspective, they weren't lovers. The stranger was clearly getting increasingly agitated and I also started to get anxious seeing that my brother wasn't putting in an appearance. I knew when we did finally meet up, Borja would give me a third-degree and I wasn't sure I was up to the task. I prayed he'd turn up quickly and take back the reins on this case.

It wasn't to be, because Lídia Font jumped to her feet and slipped on her mink coat with a minimum of fuss and in a manner that was an accomplished display of power. Haughty and overbearing, she said goodbye to the man while her face expressed her complete contempt. This time she didn't pay the bill and left the bar without looking over her shoulder.

The stranger looked worried and despondent. He sat there in dismay and I saw him ask the waiter for a cognac. I didn't know what to do. I had to decide whether to spy on him or follow her, and opted, rather rashly perhaps, to go after her while I tried desperately to communicate with

101

Borja. He must have been underground as there was no reaction from his mobile.

Mrs Font crossed the street and went into a perfume shop opposite the Zurich, on the other side of the square, and I did the same. She spent a quarter of an hour smelling and scrutinizing various little bottles. She bought some bath salts and brightly coloured soap using her credit card and finally took a taxi home.

I followed her in another taxi, and when I did manage to speak to my brother, I found he was still trying to park the Smart in the centre of the city. As it was still early we agreed to go for a drink. He was anxious and wanted to hear what had happened as soon as possible.

"You know driving in the centre of Barcelona the week before Christmas is a fool's game," he told me over the mobile. "I need a drop of Cardhu. Get into a taxi and see you in Harry's in twenty minutes."

Harry's is an old-fashioned cocktail bar in the Eixample. It's normally frequented by middle-aged couples that don't look as if they're married. The men are usually wearing ties, as they've just left the office, and the women are done up like secretaries or whores who own their own perfume shops. Long, yellowish hair, swooping necklines, mini-skirts and gold Duponts are the order of the day. But it's a pleasant, quiet enough place when nobody's playing boleros or Julio Iglesias songs on the piano. At that day at that time, it was agreeably dingy and low-key.

Three couples were there who were past the fifty mark and jazz was being played over the loudspeakers. Borja hadn't arrived. I sat down, ordered a gin and tonic and lit a cigarette while I started to put together mentally the report I'd give my brother. I wasn't feeling very bright. I was worried about other matters as well and the first sips of my G and T began to go to my head. Quite spontaneously I started to think about the marks the twins were getting at school, Montse's threat to become a vegetarian and the dinner Lola and my brother had planned for tomorrow night.

The fact is, Lídia's mysterious date wasn't the only surprise that afternoon. While we were parked by the MP's house, just before our client's wife went to her date in the Zurich, Borja had admitted he'd agreed to dine with Lola on Saturday night.

"I thought it was best to accept her invitation, have dinner with her and put the record straight . . ." he explained as if it weren't at all important. "Elegantly, of course," he sighed. "I don't want to throw it in her face but, you know, the other day I drank too much and really put my foot in it."

"Not just your foot, by all accounts . . ."

"You know what I mean. And please don't be so coarse," he rasped.

"Which restaurant do you have in mind? I don't expect you'll choose any thing too romantic . . ."

"Right . . . she said she'd cook. We're dining at her place," he confessed, head bowed.

"Shit."

My pursuit of Lídia Font had forced me to go from one end of the city to another, and the fact I was the only eye-witness to our putative adulteress's unexpected tryst had stressed me out even more. I was really enjoying it in Harry's, my feet had warmed up and I was relishing the cold taste of gin in my mouth. I liked the music they were playing – Miles Davis, I think – and the tune made me remember times past, before I met Montse, when I still lived with my aunt and uncle and was fully up for the revolution, drinking to the death of Franco and falling in love with girls with plaits and long skirts who were on the pill and wore no make-up. As I sank comfortably into one of Harry's leather sofas, letting my thoughts be led incoherently by the gin's soothing effects, my eyelids closed and quite unawares, I dropped off to sleep. That improvised truce was short-lived, because I soon heard Borja's voice ordering a Cardhu as he sat down next to me and excitedly started shooting questions at me. Reluctantly I came back to earth and packed my little collection of *madeleines* back into my trunk of memories. My brother was anxious to find out every last detail of the disconcerting scene I'd witnessed a while back.

9

Our client rang Borja on his mobile very early on Monday morning to summon us to a meeting. He called us to his office on the Diagonal, which he described as his private retreat. It had been a very quiet weekend at the Fonts' house because they'd decided to spend it in the family chalet in Cadaqués and my brother and I had taken advantage of their absence to rest and forget each other as best we could. The bad news was that Borja and Lola's dinner party had ended up in Lola's bedroom with chocolate croissants for breakfast.

"This will end in disaster!" I predicted in a foul mood as we drove to our meeting with the MP.

"It was the oysters and the cava . . ." he pleaded. "A blow below the belt from your sister-in-law."

"Nobody forced you to eat them. If Merche finds out you're shagging another . . ."

"I'm not. I just slipped . . ." he said lowering his eyes.

"Yes, into the wrong bed."

We got to the MP's office at almost one o'clock. It wasn't an especially large or luxurious place, which surprised me. I mean it didn't seem like the office of a lawyer who came into his profession through his family, although I recalled that the Font patriarch, the MP's father, had in his day made fruitless incursions into the world of politics. Everybody knew the MP didn't like to talk about this aspect of his father's life, given that not so long ago Lluís Font senior had been linked to the Falange and that was now a black mark.

Font and Associates' legal practice was on the Passeig de Gràcia and was still one of the most prestigious and expensive in Barcelona. Perhaps that's why I was really expecting something quite different. The office on the Diagonal where we'd been summoned comprised a lobby, a small meeting room and an office that looked on to the street. It was here that our client conducted all manner of business. Probably nothing to do with the law, though no doubt equally lucrative.

His desktop was a mess and strewn with papers. Five or six newspapers opened at the political pages were spread across it and heap of dossiers tottered perilously at one end. The MP was in his shirtsleeves and had loosened the knot of his tie, but still looked immaculate. A parcel wrapped in brown paper lurked in one corner behind the door and looked as if it must contain his wife's portrait.

"I'm grateful you were able to come here," he said shaking our hands. "It's been a very hectic day."

Apart from his secretary, no one else seemed to work there. I could see no flag, no institutional photograph, not even any election posters nor indeed anything to betray the fact we were in a very important politician's office. There were, however, two computers (one for his secretary and one for him), a fax, a telephone and mountains of books and reports piled higgledy-piggledy on a rather rickety unit that hadn't seen any changes rung since the Seventies. The MP invited us to sit down and offered us a cup of coffee.

"I know it's very early days, but I wanted to know whether you've uncovered anything," he said. "We're going to ski in

Baqueira early in the morning and won't be back till the 24th, in time to celebrate Christmas Eve. I will most probably have to come back to Barcelona for a party meeting," he signalled, "but I will return to Baqueira the same day."

It was 20th December, so only five days to go to Christmas. The truth is that in barely a week we'd managed to find out nothing significant.

"We have really only just started on the case," Borja apologized prudently. "But if you like, we'll explain what we've uncovered so far. Not very much . . ."

"Go ahead."

"We know," my brother breathed in, "that Pau Ferrer isn't currently in Barcelona."

We knew that because it's what the message on his answer-machine said. And he added: "He spends long periods in Paris, where he intends to pass this Christmas." This was pure invention on Borja's part.

Lluís Font listened in silence to my brother's explanations and kept shifting in his chair. He looked disappointed.

"These matters take time," Borja added, "particularly if you have to tread carefully. There is one thing though . . ."

"Oh, really?" the MP raised his eyebrows hopefully.

"Well, it's probably nothing. And perhaps nothing to do with the painting . . ."

"What is it? Have you uncovered something odd?"

I felt our client was overdoing his alarm.

Borja took a small black diary out of his coat pocket and ran through what had happened during the week we'd been trailing the man's wife. He lingered on the details of her exchanges with the dark-haired woman in the Sandor and the strained encounter with that stranger in the Zurich. The expression on his face made it plain he'd immediately identified the mysterious woman with the deep tan, although he said nothing. He was much more interested in the man in the Zurich. He seemed genuine when he admitted he had no idea who it might be.

"Are you sure he wasn't the painter? Perhaps he's pretending to be out of the country so you don't bother him . . ." he paused. "I sometimes make the same excuse myself."

"Absolutely impossible," I interjected. "That man was nothing like the photographs we found on the internet. The man in the Zurich was much younger."

"And what's he like? Physically?"

"The Zurich man?" I asked.

"No, the painter. You say you've seen photographs . . ."

"He's older —"

"Into his sixties," Borja interrupted, who always explains himself better than I do. "In fact," he consulted his diary again, "he was born in 1941, so is sixty-four years old, but he's pretty well preserved, one has to say. He looks like an artist and apparently is not without money."

"I'm not surprised. The amounts his paintings fetch! . . ." the MP added, arching his eyebrows.

"Well, he inherited money from his family, particularly from his mother, who was French," Borja continued. "At any rate he also seems to have made quite a lot of money from his paintings. He's lived in Paris for many years and is very well known there. According to our sources, he decided to establish himself in Barcelona at the beginning of the Nineties, but got very annoyed when he tried to set up an arts foundation and no institution would support him. He bought a studio years ago, a huge hangar in Sant Just Desvern, where he also lives apparently. Mr Ferrer is reputed to be something of a bohemian and on the extravagant side. And he's . . ." Borja paused, lowering his voice, "on the left. A pacifist and such like."

"That's all I needed!" the MP sighed as he looked at the ground. "Lídia in a liaison with one of that lot . . ."

"We really don't have any evidence . . ." I said to cheer him up.

The MP lit his cigarette. At that point his secretary came in with the three coffees and reminded him he had a long list of calls to answer.

"And the man in the Zurich?" he enquired, after the secretary shut the door. "Are you sure what you saw wasn't a lovers' tiff?" He aimed the question at me, the only eyewitness to that encounter. "Perhaps they're involved in some kind of love affair."

"No, absolutely not," I shook my head. "I'm sure there was no kind of . . . intimate relationship between that man and your wife. You know, I felt he wasn't the class of man to make an impression on a wife like yours. That's to say, he looked more like an office worker or a travelling salesman . . ."

"I'll try to take a look at Lídia's diary, to see if that helps. In the meantime, you should use the time we're in Baqueira to concentrate on finding more out about that painter. He's the only lead we have for the moment. I'd like to think that this portrait," and he pointed to the package behind the door, "is the only portrait he's made of Lídia. If there are others circulating . . ."

"Indeed, that's why we must go to Paris as soon as possible. We can take advantage of your stay in Baqueira and carry out an on-the-spot investigation. I am sure we'll uncover something there," Borja improvised.

I didn't know how the hell I'd explain to Montse that I had to be off and to Paris of all places just before Christmas. I'd have a mighty row on my hands at home. Montse had been talking for years about us spending a romantic weekend in the City of Light, but we kept postponing it, either because of lack of funds, or because of the children. I knew my wife wouldn't be amused one bit if I went to Paris without her.

"Very well, if you think it's indispensable . . ." said the MP. "I only ask you to be as discreet as possible. I mean I hope you won't turn up on the fellow's doorstep and ask him point blank whether he's carrying on with my wife."

"Of course not!" exclaimed Borja. "There are other means. Trust us."

"Given the circumstances, I fear I have little choice," he said before adding ruefully: "We politicians are used to not trusting anybody."

And nobody ever trusts a politician, I thought to myself. But now it was Borja's turn. He always looks after that side of things.

"Quite. We shall need funds set aside to cover our travel costs, the hotel . . ."

"Of what order, exactly?"

"Well . . . at least another 5,000," Borja replied very persuasively, as if he'd been asking for a light.

I couldn't help giving a start when I heard the sum mentioned. Lluís Font had handed over five grand less than a fortnight ago, and the only information we'd given him we found surfing on the internet. True, we had kept his wife under close surveillance for a week, but I still considered it excessive. Lluís Font didn't protest but opened a drawer and started counting notes until he'd got the five K Borja had requested.

"That makes ten all told," he said very seriously. "I hope you can tell me something rather more concrete on your return."

"Don't worry." Borja rushed to soothe the MP. "I am sure we'll get to the bottom of this mystery in Paris."

At that moment the telephone rang and he asked us to excuse him. There had been a meeting of party high-ups that afternoon and he still had lots of calls to make. We left his office as happy as cats who'd got the cream, and decided to celebrate that unexpected windfall with a juicy aperitif.

"We'll go to the travel agency this afternoon," Borja said chomping on a prawn. "Perhaps we should leave tomorrow morning . . . The man's obviously impatient. If it all turns out as it should, we can wrap this case up in a couple of weeks. Say . . . you wouldn't be prepared to go to Paris by yourself, would you?" he asked casually.

"No bloody way!" I protested. "I wouldn't know where to start by myself in Paris . . . Besides, it's years since I spoke any French. Not since secondary school, to be exact."

"Fine, but you can be sure Pau Ferrer speaks Catalan. With that name . . ." he insisted.

"What's up? I thought you'd fancy a trip to Paris, all expenses paid . . ." I was at a loss to understand my brother.

"The fact is I don't really like Paris that much." I thought I detected a sad tone in his voice.

"Well, you don't say!"

I didn't have the slightest intention of going to Paris by myself to converse with a rich, bohemian artist I didn't know from Adam in order to try to find out whether he was having an affair with the wife of a Catalan MP.

111

"Forget it, it was a passing thought. We'll both go," he sighed.

But we couldn't go to the travel agency that afternoon. After lunch, while I was lolling on our sofa, Borja rang me sounding much the worse for wear, to say he was in bed and his body felt totally exhausted. He had flu. I went to his place the next morning and found he wasn't feeling any better. He still had a temperature, was coughing and only felt up to sleeping. As he lives by himself, I took some provisions, but discovered someone had beaten me to it and that his fridge was full. I prayed it wasn't Lola.

Borja lives in a tiny attic in the upper part of Balmes that I think belongs to Merche. Although it's a small flat, it's decorated with expensive, exquisite good taste and a woman's hand is in evidence. My brother, who's a real fusspot, usually keeps everything spotlessly clean and tidy. I imagine he's not paying any rent, because this kind of flat in that lordly part of Barcelona costs an arm and a leg.

The flu kept him in bed for several days so we were forced to abandon any idea of going to Paris before Christmas. We decided to defer the trip to after the holidays as I refused to go by myself. All I'd do in Paris would be to have a miserable time and act the fool and that's exactly what I told Borja. He used his convalescence to rest and recoup his energies (something he really needed to do what with Merche, Lola and this case), and I made Montse happy by helping with the Christmas preparations and with Arnau. I can't deny that that year Montse and I were in very high spirits. Thanks to the MP, seasonal prospects looked better than we'd predicted, for the first time in many years. Moreover, Montse had decided against turning vegetarian, Lola had left us alone for a few days and the twins' school marks weren't as bad as we'd feared. Everything seemed to be going full steam ahead, so I allowed myself the luxury of relaxing a little and took advantage of Borja's flu and the Fonts' holidays in Baqueira to lose myself in a thriller Montse had given me as a St George's Day present and that I'd yet to open.

10

Christmas Day was almost over when the telephone rang. Although it was nine o'clock, I was still in bed trying to sleep off my lunch because, as happens every year, I'd wolfed down too much Catalan stew, capon, turrón, vermouth, wine and cava, not to mention the liqueurs. The girls were watching television and Montse, who'd just got up, was tidying the kitchen. Arnau was sleeping like an angel, oblivious to parental stomach upsets and hangovers. I couldn't remember how I'd made it to our bed. All I do know is that when my mother-in-law gave me the usual two farewell smackers to the cheek at around seven, the smell of cognac from her stale breath blotted out the wave of cheap perfume she'd been giving off since she arrived.

"It's Borja," announced a surprised Montse. "He's seems to be in a bit of a state. I think something's up."

I got up reluctantly, with a thick head and furry mouth. Borja would be coming to lunch tomorrow, as it was Boxing Day. Montse had insisted on inviting him, I expect Lola played a hand in that, and his call was most likely to be an advance apology to spare himself that squirming experience.

"Get ready. I'll be round in twenty minutes to pick you up," he muttered down the phone.

"What the hell do you mean? It's Christmas Day!" I protested. "Do you want Montse on my back? Besides, I've got a hangover . . ."

"Eduard, it's urgent," he said unabashed.

"There can't be anything that urgent today!" I repeated. "Get yourself to bed. See you tomorrow."

"It's Lídia Font. She's not with us any more," he said before I managed to hang up. "It looks like she's been murdered. In her own home."

"Good God!"

"The MP called me and asked us to come straight away. They're still waiting for the judge to arrive."

"And what the fuck are we supposed to do?" I started to get as alarmed as him. "I mean that painting is one thing: a murder is quite something else."

My wife, who was standing next to me, gave a start when she heard the word "murder" and listened hard. When I did hang up, I'd have some explaining to do. I needed to think of something credible.

"Get a move on," my brother insisted. "I'll be there in twenty minutes." And he hung up on me.

As I had no time to invent an explanation, I decided to tell Montse the truth. MP Lluís Font had contracted us to make some enquiries into a painting he'd bought in Paris, and, as my partner had just told me on the phone, his wife had been murdered and he wanted us go to his house as quickly as possible. I didn't tell her that the painting in question was a portrait of his wife.

"What kind of enquiry?" she asked. Her tone was half anxious, half curious. "I thought you and Borja were financial advisers?"

"That's right, but paintings and works of art are also investments, as you know . . ."

"Well I don't understand how the hell your line of business can involve a murder," she argued. "Was it a break

116

and entry? Or perhaps he did it? Yes, that must be it! . . . It's yet another case of domestic violence!"

"I really don't think so, love . . ." I responded as I started to get dressed. I was praying Borja would come quickly and spare me this interrogation. "It's probably a burglary, as you —"

"I don't know why you have to get involved in some thing like this . . ." she grumbled. "On Christmas Day! . . . You'd better go carefully, particularly if politicians are mixed up in it. We know what lengths they can . . ." She arched her eyebrows and looked dead serious. "Listen to me and keep your distance, Eduard. I've a funny feeling, a kind of presentiment here in my tummy."

"No, you've got a bad case of seasonal indigestion, like me. Besides, I can't leave Borja in the thick of it."

"You say it's to do with an MP?" she asked, her curiosity well and truly aroused. "Which party? Is he right wing or left wing?"

"It just so happens," I had to confess, "that he's on the right."

"So you work for *them* now . . ."

Montse made me feel as if I'd sold my soul to a group of extra-terrestrials set on exterminating the planet.

"So do *you* ask your customers which party they vote for?" I asked as if shocked. "Beggars can't be choosers nowadays, Montse. You know that only too well."

"I reckon this is all very strange."

And then, in that icy tone that only women can muster, she pronounced those terrible words that somebody should erase from the dictionary.

"We need to talk."

We were beginning to have a problem. Until now Montse

had swallowed the brief explanations I'd given her about my work, but it now looked like she'd be giving me the third-degree treatment. I'd be forced to tell more and more lies and, knowing my poor memory, would soon give myself away. A little red light started to flash in some corner of my brain.

"Come on, darling, they probably stole the painting as well . . ." I insisted. I knew, however, that Lluís Font had that safely tucked away in his office. "Borja said he'd tell me all on the way. Do me a favour and rustle up a coffee while I have a wash and finish getting dressed. My belly's about to explode . . ."

"I told you you were eating too much turrón. You lot scoffed every bit of the chocolate one."

"Your mother outdid me, she soaked up a bottle of Torres 10 single-handed."

"Don't exaggerate!" she smiled, putting the coffee on to heat up.

Fortunately, the girls as well as being glued to the telly, had their earphones in and didn't hear a thing. And if that wasn't enough, they were amusing themselves sending text messages on the mobiles we'd given them for Christmas. (Thanks to Borja, these had come at a bargain price.) I'd just downed a cup of hot coffee when the doorbell rang downstairs. I breathed a sigh of relief. It had only taken him fifteen minutes.

"I'll be down straight away," I said over the intercom as I hurriedly put my coat on.

I kissed Montse and ran downstairs without waiting for the lift: when I went out into the street, another surprise awaited me. It was snowing, apparently had been for some time, and a very fine layer of white powder was forming on cars and pavements. As it was night-time and curtains were drawn, we'd not noticed the snow falling. I tried to tell Montse over the entryphone, because snow is headline news in Barcelona.

"Montse, look out of the window! It's snowing!" I shouted without a response. The system doesn't work very well but we unneighbourly neighbours can't reach an agreement to get it changed.

"Come on, hurry up!" exclaimed Borja impatiently.

My brother was waiting in a taxi whose engine was running and I had to get in quickly. He looked exhausted but seemed to have recovered from his bout of flu. He also seemed pretty excited.

"What a business! On Christmas Day as well!" I said as I settled down next to him. "Did he push her?"

"Shush! Not so loud!" he warned lifting a finger to his lips.

"I'm sorry," I muttered. "But did he?"

"Don't be ridiculous! I mean . . . I don't really think so."

"Perhaps he had a bad turn. He told his wife about the painting, they rowed and . . ." I whispered so the taxi driver couldn't hear.

"It's not this kind of person's style," Borja shook his head. "Men like Lluís Font don't kill their wives when they discover they're having a bit on the side. They ring their lawyers or find solace with their secretary," he pontificated.

"In a nutshell, you haven't got a clue," I concluded.

As it happened, Lluís Font had phoned Borja and merely asked him to go round to his house because something terrible had happened. On the other hand, our taxi driver, who looked intrigued, was more attentive to our whispers than to his driving. My brother signalled to me to pipe down.

"When we get there, let me do the talking."

In fact, I always did, but I was bemused to know how Borja would justify our sudden appearance at the Font household to the police or the judge. I thought of our company that didn't exist and the taxes we didn't pay, I imagined the forensic crew checking out our office and discovering there was only brick and plaster behind the flash mahogany doors . . . and felt a lump in my stomach. I also remembered that the only dead I'd ever seen were peacefully tucked into a coffin in the morgue, surrounded by flowers, their faces polished, and the mere thought I might soon be in the presence of a bloody corpse, possibly disfigured or mutilated to boot made me go weak at the knees. I felt my stomach begin to go queasy and was afraid I'd be sick there and then. I desperately needed a cigarette but it's been years since you could smoke in a taxi.

As we drew nearer the upper reaches of the city, Barcelona was slowly transforming as the flurries of snowflakes got bigger and whiter. There wasn't a soul in the streets, which were eerily silent and phantasmagorical under the Christmas lights. What a cruel paradox – amid the peace of that white Christmas we were heading to the scene of a crime.

In front of Lluís Font's house we saw an ambulance, a fire engine, three police cars and people who looked like journalists. Apparently, the police were expecting us, because they let us straight through when we gave them our names and explained the MP was waiting for us. For obvious reasons, Borja told them he'd left his documentation at home and they were content just to inspect my ID. The journalists warmed towards us when we got out of the taxi, but we were canny and our lips remained sealed.

An Oriental-looking slip of a girl opened the door to us, in a black satin uniform with white pinafore and cap. She was frightened.

"Sir in drawing room, with poleece. Lots of poleece," she said waving her hands wildly. "Ladee dead suddenlee. Sir come now. Wait him here!"

Lluís Font took less than a minute to come and welcome us. He looked concerned but seemed to be in control of the situation.

"Thanks for coming so quickly," he said, looking serious as he held out a hand to Borja. "Something terrible has happened."

Borja hugged him and gave him his deeply felt condolences, as if they were lifelong friends. I merely shook his hand and said how sorry I was.

"The judge hasn't come yet," he informed us. "They can't locate him, apparently. The police have photographed everything, but I'd like you to take a discreet look. They won't try to stop you."

"Naturally," replied Borja, assuming a very professional air, heaven knows on what basis. I just followed behind, praying I wouldn't make a fool of myself and faint if there was blood all around.

We accompanied the MP down a spacious passageway full of paintings by famous artists (including, of course, a couple of Tàpies), until we reached a reception room that was as big as my flat. I was very struck by the fact that everything inside was white: the walls, the furniture, the settees, the carpets, the ashtrays, the porcelain vases, the flowers . . . Even the decorations on the huge Christmas tree, standing in a corner by the fireplace, were silvery. All the lines in that interior design magazine idyll converged on Lídia Font's lifeless body that, dressed in red, was lying theatrically on one of the carpets.

Both her long elegant party dress and her high-heeled shoes were a bright fiery red. The shoes reminded me of the ones she wore in the painting reproduced in the catalogue her husband had showed us a few days ago, although they weren't the same ones. I looked at her, looked at Borja, and scratched my nose as decorously as I could so my brother realized the deceased was wearing one of the two colours he cannot see. It seemed as if Lídia had been placed there to give the room a touch of colour, and I thought how she had class even in death. Her eyes were wide open and her face was contracted in a horrible grimace of pain, but there were no bloodstains and she didn't appear to have any wounds. A thread of saliva and blood dribbled almost imperceptibly from her lips.

"God!" I muttered, feeling my legs giving way.

"Everything seems to indicate that death was instantaneous," the MP explained, as if that made the scene somehow less horrific. I noticed our client's face was tense but that his eyes remained dry.

I wouldn't have been at all shocked if at that moment I'd just woken up half-frozen in bed next to Montse, because she always eases the bedspread her way and leaves my body exposed to the elements. There are experiences you live in the middle of a hangover that blur into a dreamy haze. That huge white room, the white snow falling outside and Lídia Font's corpse wrapped in a spectacular red dress seemed more a figment of a film director's hallucinations than a scene from the real world.

"Hey, what the hell do you think you're playing at?" shouted one of the policemen.

That brought me back to earth. I'd gone into a complete daydream contemplating the scene of the disaster (and embarrassingly, in a way enjoying an experience one might describe as aesthetic) and had ignored my brother's antics.

"Hey, this man's eaten one of those sweets! . . ." said the policeman. "Do you feel OK, sir?"

Borja was by the piano at the other end of the room, and had just wolfed down a sweet from the box open on its top.

"What do you mean?" Borja went pale.

The police observed him for a few seconds, not sure what to do, and finally one of them said: "Well, it's really not the sweets, sergeant . . ."

"It's really not *what*?" Borja asked faintly.

"Fucking hell! What the hell are we going to tell the judge now?" roared the policeman who seemed to be in charge. "You've eaten just our evidence under our bloody noses. Some fucking Christmas! (If you'll forgive my French). All we needed! . . ."

"Calm down, sergeant . . ."

"Calm down, you're bloody joking . . ." The policeman was beginning to sweat, clearly nervous. "We shouldn't have let anyone in here. And you should have been more on the ball, Capdemuny!"

"Casademunt, sergeant. My name is Casademunt," the man being spoken to had a strong Catalan accent.

"Are you sure you feel all right?" asked the MP, looking genuinely concerned.

"I don't know, I think so . . . I'm sorry, it was a reflex action. I have a great weakness for *marrons glacés*." He explained to the police. "And they're not sweets by the way

123

. . ." Borja suddenly understood what had happened and was frightened. "What do you mean by 'evidence'? Do you think there's something wrong with them?"

"These gentlemen believe they may have a case of poisoning on their hands . . ." the MP whispered.

"I need a cognac," said Borja sounding faint as he reached for the bottle of French cognac on the coffee table next to the body.

"Noooo!" we all chorused.

Apparently, just before she'd dropped dead, Lídia Font had poured herself a glass of cognac and opened the box of titbits. The Christmas wrapping paper was still there, and I noted how the box and the paper came from the renowned Foix de Sarrià patisserie. Only two *marrons glacés* were missing. The one swallowed by Borja and the other, presumably, by the woman stretched out on the floor.

"My wife also had a weak spot for *marrons glacés*," the MP explained. "She was fanatical about them in fact. They're the only thing she wouldn't do without, although she was always on a diet. She could eat them by the plateful."

On this occasion, it was obvious that glamorous Mrs Font had only had time to eat one. The judge still hadn't showed up (the turmoil had begun in the Font household after seven, but it was now gone ten o'clock and the police were still trying to locate the relevant judge). In the mean time, the three policemen in the drawing room, now clearly at their wits' end, didn't take their eyes off us.

The MP took a deep breath and started to tell us what had happened.

"It must have been about seven thirty and everybody had left. We were having a family meal, and had invited our closest relatives as we do every year: my parents, my in-laws, my brother Xavier, his wife and three children, Lídia's sister and ourselves. When they left, I shut myself up in my office to make a few calls and Lídia stayed in the drawing room leafing through a magazine." He paused, as if needing to recover his aplomb. "The girl" – he meant the Philippine in her immaculate uniform who'd opened the door to us – "was tidying up in here. Apparently, Lídia started to scream and writhe in pain, and collapsed. The girl came and told me at once but by the time I got here she already seemed to be dead. She was as you see her now. I couldn't feel any pulse. I ran and called an ambulance, thinking she must have had a heart attack," he said, head lowered.

And then added: "In fact, I still think it must have been a heart attack but the ambulance people weren't so sure and told the police as much. These gentlemen," he said referring to the scowling police, "say she may have been poisoned. Because of the blood around her mouth."

In fact, there was a small pool of blood and vomit next to where Lídia Font was lying, but I still couldn't grasp why the fellow was telling *us* all that, nor even what the hell we were doing there. Nor could I understand why the police didn't simply remove us from the scene of the crime, given that we weren't family and didn't live there. I suppose the fact that he was an influential person meant these civil servants turned a blind eye in situations like this. Meanwhile, my brother, who seemed to have recovered from his fright, was giving himself the airs of a professional detective. What a joke.

"Do you know the provenance of the cognac and the *marrons glacés?*" he asked gently.

"I really don't know," the MP shook his head. "I imagine the cognac must have come in a Christmas hamper. We get a good few. And as for the *marrons glacés* . . ." he hesitated before answering, "come to think of it, Lídia did say someone had sent them with a note. I remember because she couldn't decipher the signature and showed it to me."

"Stop!" exclaimed the policeman who moments ago had lambasted Borja. "You say there's a note? Where is it?"

"I don't know, on Lídia's bureau I suppose, if she kept it. I'll tell the girl to go with you to look for it. Frankly," he added, "it was a frightful card."

Minutes later, one of the policemen returned triumphantly with a very sentimental Christmas card, like the ones my aunt and uncle send me every year. The policeman had placed it very professionally inside a small transparent plastic bag.

"Is this it?" he asked.

"I think so. Though I don't recognize the signature . . ." Our client seemed genuine enough.

"What about the envelope?" asked the other policeman, who seemed to be in charge.

"Well, now you mention it," the MP thought aloud, "the card was in a white envelope which just had my wife's name on it. I expect it ended up in the rubbish bin."

The policeman, who was wearing a surgeon's gloves, took the card out of the bag and examined it minutely. My brother and I craned our necks to get a look in. Somebody had written shakily with a blue ballpoint:

I wish you Happy Holiday
With heart-felt gratitude

In effect, the signature was illegible.

"Do you know if the parcel came through the post?" I asked.

"No, I think a messenger brought it," said the MP. "Perhaps the girl might remember. Or perhaps not. We get so many gifts and seasonal greetings . . ."

I thought of all the people who must send the Fonts presents, whether to thank them for some favour or to anticipate one in the future. At Christmas time, bribes are allowed if they come ham-shaped or in a hamper.

"Wasn't your wife shocked when she received a box of sweets from a complete stranger?" I ventured.

"They are *marrons glacés*," pointed out Borja, offended by this confusion.

"The fact is Lídia receives . . . used to receive lots of thank-you notes accompanied by flowers, boxes of sweets and this kind of gift." And he went on: "Everyone knows she adored *marrons glacés*, anyone slightly acquainted with her, that is. In our position, there are a lot of people who ask us for small favours, and if it's within our hands . . ."

The maid interrupted him, rushing into the room, extremely agitated.

"Miss Núlia sicking upstairs!" she said, looking aghast, her whole body shaking. "Sir coming up now! She very bad, very bad!"

"Good God!" exclaimed the MP, clearly worried about his daughter.

"Casadepuny, accompany him!" the sergeant ordered.

The MP and the younger policeman ran out of the room and up the stairs. We stayed in the drawing room, watched over by the other two eagle-eyed policemen, particularly Borja. After a few minutes, the young policeman came back to say it was nothing serious, just an attack of nerves. Soon after the MP returned, slightly calmer.

"She's very upset, but she's all right," he explained when

even calmer. "She's taken a pill and her aunt will come for her in a minute. She's beside herself, naturally . . . It would be best if she spent tonight at her aunt and uncle's house." And whispered, "Poor Núria, that's all she needed . . ."

"His Honour the Judge has just arrived," one of the policemen waiting outside the house informed us rather nervously.

The judge, who was quite young (around thirty, I'd say), came in looking disgusted. His holidays had obviously just been ruined. He seemed competent but out of his depth, and when they told him it looked like a poisoning by some deadly substance and that Borja had eaten a *marron glacé* from the same box the victim had eaten from, he went berserk. He snarled at the police and threw us unceremoniously out of the room. After giving the body the necessary once over he ordered its removal.

Meanwhile, the judicial police searched the room and took fingerprints and samples. They also took with them the box of *marrons glacés* and the bottle and glass of cognac that still retained a few drops of liquor and the traces of red lipstick.

The judge summoned the MP to go and make a statement the following day and advised him to bring his lawyer. He asked us to ensure we were contactable. As soon as the judge disappeared, Lluís Font told us very quietly he wanted a word in private and asked us to wait in his office.

What with one thing and another it was now two a.m. Despite the upheaval and tension I was exhausted. All this time, Borja had been pretending to survey the scene of the crime, as our client had asked, but I really didn't know what to do or think. I was shocked by the man's sangfroid: after all, he had just lost his wife. He seemed so calm and collected. If anything similar happened to Montse (God forbid), I'd be on my knees, I expect, a blubbing heap of nerves. Our client, on the other hand, was so cold and self-possessed it put me on edge. I considered whether he might possibly be involved in some way in his wife's death, but finally concluded that if he were the murderer, he would logically have acted as if he'd been much more affected in order to allay suspicions. When we were alone in his office, I communicated the drift of my deductions to Borja.

"It's a question of upbringing," he told me in the pedagogical tone he adopts when informing me of the subtleties of the world of the wealthy. "The process is an internal one. These people know how to control their emotions, but it doesn't mean they're not upset."

"Well, if he can impose that much self-control, he can't be that upset," I retorted.

"It's a class-marker, Eduard," he sighed at my incredulity. "The upper classes never cry in public. It's considered to be in bad taste."

"Oh!" I said not at all fathoming his insight.

When the police abandoned the house, the MP came and offered us a drink. Remembering the bottle of cognac the forensics had taken off to test, we prudently declined his offer. Our client also abstained, I expect for the same reason.

"I must ask a favour of you," he began quite nervously. "You're the only people I can trust in this matter."

"At your disposition," said Borja deferentially.

"My personal assistant is on holiday in Sri Lanka. He's away till the end of the year . . ." He paused to light a cigarette. "I mean to say I'm only asking you because he is abroad . . ."

"What is your concern?" asked Borja, wanting him to come to the point.

"The painting, of course. The portrait of Lídia that's in my office is what concerns me," he confessed. "Particularly as we don't know what happened this evening. If it's true, as the police believe, that Lídia was poisoned . . . I don't know what the routine is in such cases, but the police will probably issue a search warrant. Obviously I have nothing to hide, but if they were to find the painting, you know, life might begin to get complicated. I'd have some explaining to do, I mean it's not a portrait I commissioned, but one I discovered by chance, the model being my wife . . ."

". . . there's no invoice," Borja quickly homed in.

"In fact, there is. It's made out to a company name. That's not the problem."

"So I don't see what we can do," my brother said. "Unless . . ."

"Tomorrow is a public holiday, and I don't think the judge will be in a great hurry to sign a search warrant." He paused while Borja and I tried to work out what he was plotting. "If you could, tomorrow night for example, discreetly go and replace Lídia's portrait with another picture and keep it for me for a few days . . ."

"Replace the portrait?" asked Borja.

I hadn't understood either.

"I know what I'm asking you to do is rather strange . . ." the MP recognized.

"And why not just take it and leave it at that?" I asked.

"My secretary has seen the package, but not the contents. She knows it's a painting. If the police asked her if she'd noticed anything missing, she might, without meaning to, put her foot in it. I thought," he suggested as innocently as he could, despite the anxiety our faces betrayed, "it would be best to substitute a similar sized package. That

130

way I wouldn't have to do any explaining. If you do me this favour," he drawled, "I shall be eternally grateful."

Neither my brother nor I said anything for a few seconds. Borja huffed and looked at me askance.

"But what if the neighbours catch us?" he objected. "If they see us coming and going with a big package, they're bound to think we're thieves and inform the police . . .You can't hide a package that size under a topcoat!"

"I'll give you a key." He seemed to have thought his plan through. "And there aren't many people living in the building. Most of the flats are offices like mine. The porter isn't there at nights or on public holidays. Nor are there cameras or other security devices. It's an old building, as you've seen. It'll only take ten minutes . . ." he said, pooh-poohing our fears.

I was convinced that what Lluís Font was suggesting was practically a crime. He wasn't asking us to get rid of the murder weapon or provide him with an alibi, but our client did possibly see a connection between his wife's unexpected death and that mysterious portrait. If we contributed to its disappearance, we would be hindering police investigations and could perhaps end up accused of being part of a cover-up.

"The problem," reflected Borja, "is where to find a picture of that size in the next twenty-four hours."

In other words, he'd already accepted the commission. I should have predicted as much.

"I'm sure you'll think of a way." And saying this, he looked at me askance, opened a desk drawer and took out an envelope. "Here's something towards your expenses."

It plainly looked like a bribe, if not worse. I agree some of the things my brother and I do from time to time verge

131

on the illegal, but to date we've never had to confront a woman's dead body. I was hoping Borja would refuse the envelope, wish him goodbye and we'd disconnect from the whole business.

Instead of that, my brother said thanks and solemnly pocketed the envelope without looking at its contents. Not wasting any time, the MP gave him the keys to his office and thanked us once again for this great favour we were doing him.

"I shall never forget this. You will always be able to count on me," he asserted wholeheartedly. And repeated, "I shall be eternally grateful."

Before leaving the house, we called a taxi. Once inside the vehicle, almost in the dark, Borja counted the notes in the envelope.

"Ten grand! Ten thousand euros!" he whispered in my ear, his voice trembling with emotion.

"Pep," I said – when I was annoyed or particularly worried I'd call him by his real name – "we're getting into really deep water. We should watch out . . ."

At that time in the early morning, Barcelona was dark, silent and hung-over. The snow had covered the city in an eerie layer of white that disguised its Mediterranean character. It was cold and there wasn't a soul to be seen, but it had stopped snowing and a few stars were peering between the clouds. The moon had even put in an appearance.

"Everything will turn out fine," he answered, unable to hide his euphoria. "But if there is a problem, I'll take full responsibility, don't you worry. In fact, you don't even need to come tomorrow. I'll manage it by myself . . ."

"As if you didn't know me! . . ." I regretted my well-meaning comment. "Though I don't know where we'll get a picture that size tomorrow. It's a holiday and all the shops are shut."

"I'll think of something. Just leave it to me," he said in a complacent tone.

But the bright idea my brother eventually thought up was only to make our lives even more complicated.

PART TWO

11

As I'd predicted, Borja rang on Boxing Day to excuse himself from lunch. Lola was invited, as usual, for this annual fixture. Initially I felt relieved, thinking that this way we'd have a quieter celebration, but I was mistaken.

"Well, might we know whose side his lordship's on?" Montse recriminated in the kitchen while she cut the turrón. "Why the hell did you have to say something like that to Lola, in the susceptible state she's in?"

"I only . . ." I started on my self-justification but couldn't think what to say next.

"I'll go and see if she's recovered!" she said, taking the tray of turrón and letting fly with her parting shot, "Eduard, you men always put your feet in it! You kept your mouth shut for the whole meal and then regaled her with one of your stupid comments! . . ."

In fact, I'd only told Lola to bear in mind that love and sex are two different things, hardly an obscenity, or a discovery that's going to win me the Nobel Prize, let alone a slight on Lola, as Montse reproached me later. I might perhaps have kept the comment to myself, but we were halfway through the meal, had been debating for a good three hours the kind of work my partner and I were engaged in and I couldn't stand a minute more. What was our connection with Lídia Font's murder (now reported on the television news)? Why hadn't Borja shown up for the meal? Had she been stood up? What did I think of her relationship (that is, did two shags make a relationship . . .)? Were there other women in my partner's life apart from Merche? Etcetera, etcetera. I was sick and tired of my wife and sister-in-law submitting me to a third degree about whether Borja really had an upset tummy or if it was just an excuse because of what happened with Lola, as if they didn't know perfectly well. Apparently, they'd developed the theory that if you fuck once it's only sex, but if the man comes back for more there must be *something else*.

And all this in front of the girls, who were all ears, and Arnau, who was luckily out of his depth. And it had been more of the same since Lola arrived. Although the cannelloni were delicious, my Montse's are always first-rate, the conversation on the topic of Borja put me off eating them. I only managed seven, instead of the usual dozen. What with this and the previous night's hassle, I wasn't in the best of moods. That's probably why I blurted out a home truth: namely that one night of passion doesn't amount to an engagement ring, with the result that Lola left the table and went for a weep in the bathroom.

"I knew you were in the know! . . ." my sister-in-law reproached me as she left the room sobbing her heart out.

Montse was right that Lola was more susceptible than usual, but I was pretty positive her parlous state was also down to the three large vermouths she'd drunk before lunch and the bottle of wine she'd downed by herself to accompany the hors d'oeuvres.

After shedding crocodile tears, my wife tried to distract her sister by letting her in on the gossip from her Centre and lecturing her on the virtues of new massage techniques from the Orient she was learning somewhere or other. Montse had promised her a session of I Ching with her

coffee, and Lola couldn't wait. The twins, who were beginning to find their aunt's scenes tedious, nibbled on
the turrón and announced they were off to their bedroom
to listen to music. Just what I felt like doing: leaving the
witness box and going to lie down for a while. I didn't obey
my instincts, however, aware that if I vanished mid-crisis,
Montse would take it badly.

Boxing Day is the worst day of the holidays, because it
follows on after the excesses of Christmas Eve dinner and
Christmas Day lunch, and I had a thick head and a belly fit
to explode yet again. I sat down on the sofa and pretended
to leaf through a newspaper supplement from way back
while they both chatted and saw off a bottle of one of those
so-called digestive liqueurs the ladies knock back at family
dos. Finally, despite my titanic efforts at staying awake, I
dozed off listening to coins jingling and my wife's voice
reading those ridiculous predictions in the reverential tones
of a guru inspired. I've always wondered how it's possible
my Montse, who read a more or less scientific degree at
university and even got good marks, can believe that the
way three coins fall can reveal a person's future fortunes
and deliver wise advice on how to behave.

"The fact is you don't understand these things," she always
retorts when I raise an objection. "Men are too rational. And
then you end up killing each other in wars and destroying
the planet with your inane sense of macho superiority. The
wisdom of the Orient," she adds from the depths of her
wisdom, "is infinitely more subtle. And much more ancient.
We have so much to learn!"

As a general rule, when Montse launches into this kind
of philosophical disquisition I opt out. Occasionally I've
tried to get her to see that the main spiritual adviser of the

planetary boss is the God of the Bible, not Aristotle, which is hardly what you'd call rational. As far as I know, Margaret Thatcher, Ana Botella and Imelda Marcos are women (women Montse particularly loathes), and I've yet to have the pleasure of meeting a female Dalai Lama. I argue that the enmity between the Chinese and Japanese, who not so very long ago engaged in mutual slaughter, is as ancient as their venerable philosophies, and that *chakras* are like the Holy Spirit: nobody has ever seen them. Finally, as my parting shot, I remind her that the Orient is all well and good if one is lucky enough not to be a woman or belong to the pariah caste, but, when I say that, she accuses me of hankering for an imperial past and turns her back on me in a huff when we get into bed.

I'm convinced Montse knows all this, but, as a standard-bearer for the hippy movement, she has to cling to this string of incense-scented superstition in order to stay sure the world is still a good place to live in. I'm considerably more pessimistic, because I don't think the problem can be reduced to a handful of wise men from the East and a bunch of perverts from the West. It's my firm belief that the problem is that there are right bastards everywhere, in mass-production, in fact, and they're the ones who fuck us all up.

"Eduard, wake up. Lola and I are off to the cinema," said Montse tapping me on the arm.

The girls had arranged to go and play in the house of some girlfriends (or rather, to talk about boys, which is what they do at their age) and Arnau was asleep.

"They're showing Oliver Stone's *Alexander* with subtitles at the Verdi. Perhaps we can have a bit of light entertainment!" she said.

140

I think Montse was also beginning to tire of banging on about Borja.

"They're showing a French flick that's won loads of prizes too . . ." suggested Lola, who liked to give herself intellectual airs.

"No gloomy dramas thank you very much!" Montse shook her head.

"I need an adventure film with a handsome hero. And then we'll go for a drink at the Salambó. You don't need to go out, do you?" she asked in a tone of voice that wouldn't accept I couldn't baby-sit Arnau.

"Well . . . no, of course not."

I imagined – foolishly – they'd be back early. I didn't want to tell Montse (especially in front of Lola) that I'd have to meet up with Borja at some point in order to do a job for our client. I'd risk another avalanche of questions and recriminations. I didn't know then that the film they were going to see would last nigh on three hours and that the famous drink in the Salambó would be prolonged to midnight.

Just after six, with Montse and Lola gone, Arnau woke up. I gave him the snack-supper Montse had left ready and we watched telly for a bit. Borja rang at around nine.

"Is Lola there?" he asked warily.

"No, she's gone to the cinema with Montse."

"I'll pass by your place in a minute," and added, "Eduard, I've had a fantastic idea."

My brother tends to frighten me with his fantastic ideas, but I have to recognize that this time he'd come up with a winner. Twenty minutes later, Borja turned up with a big roll of brown paper, a few empty boxes and some rolls of paper for wrapping presents. It was lurid paper, with thousands of colourful Christmas motifs against a red background.

"Let me explain," he announced, very pleased with himself.

My brother had evidently spent the day ruminating over logistics. We had to ensure the neighbours didn't catch us in the act walking up or down the stairs of the building where the MP had his office. Perhaps there weren't many residents living there, as our client had assured us, but we could have a problem if one of them caught us carrying a very large package on Boxing Day night. It would be difficult to hide the fact it was a painting, however well wrapped it was. The neighbours might well deduce we were burglars and would ring the police.

"Eduard, I have found the solution!" he exclaimed as ponderously as if he'd just hit on the theory of relativity. "It's the Christmas holidays and people go visiting from one house to another, so it won't seem strange if two well-dressed people are seen going in and out of a front entrance . . ."

"Possibly not. The problem is the painting. It's too large to hide," I pointed out.

"Precisely. So we won't hide it. Quite the contrary," he smiled. "We'll cart it out without any inhibitions."

I couldn't tell where he was heading and eyed him sceptically.

"Tell me now. Where would you hide an elephant?" he asked raising his eyebrows.

"I don't get you."

"Well, it's clear enough. What you need is a zoo," he said emphatically. "Look, that's why I've brought these boxes and this gift wrap. And hey presto."

His idea was as follows: first we'd wrap the substitute picture in brown paper and then cover it in gift wrap. Previously we'd stuff the package with empty boxes to give it a weightier look and camouflage its contents. Once in the office, we'd repeat the operation with Lídia Font's portrait, that is, we'd use the boxes to conceal the fact it was a painting and wrap it in the same festive wrapping paper so it looked as if we were carrying the same package.

"At this time of year the least possible suspicious activity is walking around with a Christmas present," he said proudly.

The boy had done good and I was annoyed I'd not thought of it first.

"But we don't have another painting," I objected, noticing Borja wasn't carrying one. "Where will we get one? If we don't have a painting to make the big swap, then you tell me . . ."

"We do. There's a painting that's more or less the same size."

"As soon as Montse gets back, we can go and get it."

"In fact, that won't be necessary. It's right here," Borja declared, as if it were a self-evident truth.

"Right here? Right where exactly?"

From the look on Borja's face I knew he had in mind one of the paintings hanging on the walls of our flat. I wasn't mistaken.

"That landscape you've got down at the back of the passage will do us very nicely."

We had several paintings in the passage, but I realized immediately which one my brother was referring to. There was a frightful oil painting in the darkest corner where Montse and I thought it would be out of sight, a present from my mother-in-law a couple of Christmases ago. It was, in a word, awful. An attempt at a landscape, but in fact a messy swathe of colour in true schoolboy style. But Borja was right. It was roughly the same size.

"You must be joking!" I protested. "It's a present from my mother-in-law! And apart from that, it's horrific . . ." I noticed that detail didn't seem to worry him in the slightest. And I added, "And what do I tell Montse when she sees the empty space on the wall?"

"I don't know . . . We'll think of something. I'm sorry," he justified himself smiling angelically, "none of mine would have done, I can assure you . . ."

No, I thought, especially since they must all belong to Merche. Like everything else in "his" flat.

"Come on . . ." he insisted. "It's only for a couple of days. Then we'll return it to its rightful place." He paused while I reached a decision. "Just think about what Font said: "I shall be eternally grateful to you." *Eternally*, Eduard. That can mean one hell of a lot of dough."

"Montse will kill me!"

I don't know how I let him bamboozle me, but I went and unhooked the painting and, between the two of us, we wrapped it as Borja had suggested. After stuffing the boxes in, it looked a lot fatter, not like a painting. Perhaps we'd manage it, after all. Ten o'clock had crept up on us, and still no sign of Montse. I suspected that after the film she and her sister could spend hours gassing in the Salambó, particularly if fuelled by a drop of alcohol.

"Better still, we'll take Arnau with us," suggested Borja, not batting an eyelid. "If two men with a big Christmas present aren't suspicious, two men, a big Christmas present and a little boy are even less so."

"But he's still asleep! . . ." I said half-heartedly. In fact we had no alternative.

"We'll only be an hour. We'll be back before Montse, you just see."

I wasn't very happy about involving my young son in this rigmarole, but, to innocent eyes, we were only going to leave one parcel and pick up another, and I could see no other option except for Borja to see to it solo. If we took a taxi (because we wouldn't all fit in the Smart), we'd be even quicker. I probably wouldn't even have to tell Montse we'd taken Arnau. At this time of night he slept so soundly he'd most likely think it had all been a dream.

"Come on then!" I said finally.

Borja rang for a taxi as I got Arnau ready, coaxing on his coat, scarf and cap.

"Come on, love. We're going for a ride."

"I'm sleepy, daddy. I want to sleep," said Arnau, rubbing his eyes. "I want mummy . . ."

"We're going to get mummy," I replied persuasively. "You be a good boy."

Luckily the taxi soon arrived. There was hardly any traffic and we were outside Lluís Font's office within ten minutes.

"I want a wee-wee . . ." announced Arnau the minute we got out of the taxi. I expect it was the cold.

"We'll go for a wee-wee right now, just wait." He seemed to have woken up.

We opened the front door and went up in the lift without bumping into a single resident. Everything was going to plan. We got into the office with the key the MP had given us and, while Borja saw to the paintings, I saw to Arnau and his wee-wee.

"It's not coming out," he said, rubbing his eyes again.

I was patient and turned the tap on, as Montse had shown me. The lavatory door was open and I could hear the noise Borja was making with the packages.

145

"Now I've got to wash my hands," said Arnau after he'd finished.

"Leave it for now, we've got work to do and Borja needs some help. You wash them at home," I said taking him out of the bathroom.

Just after we shut the door behind us, my son and I had the fright of our lives. We heard a loud crash, the floor shook and we were plunged into darkness. We also heard a woman shout, right next to us, and I protected Arnau instinctively with my body as we both threw ourselves to the floor. I didn't know whether it was an earthquake or an explosion. A few seconds later, I checked there was no smell of smoke or burning, and that calmed my nerves slightly. We were in complete darkness and could see nothing at all.

"Help!" I heard a woman shout, her voice choking.

"Hey, what the hell's happening?"

Borja groped his way towards us, his cigarette lighter guiding his way. Arnau had started to cry.

"Ouw . . . ouw! Help!" The shouts were coming from the bathroom.

We opened the door as best we could. There was a naked woman in the bathroom covered in dust and rubble. The ceiling was one big hole and someone looking very scared was peering down. The light still worked in the flat upstairs.

"Ow, heavens! . . . Sílvia, *amor*, are you all right?" we heard a young man ask in a Cuban accent.

"Ouw! . . . Ha, ha, ha . . . Ouw! Ouw! . . ."

The woman said something else we didn't understand. Apart from being injured, she seemed high as a kite.

It wasn't a bomb, a gas explosion, or an earthquake, which was what I'd thought at first. It was much simpler.

146

The bathroom in the flat above had collapsed while that woman was having a shower and the fuses (or whatever) had blown. Maybe God wasn't playing dice after all tonight, I thought, because the disaster occurred only a few seconds after Arnau and I had left the bathroom. We'd been lucky, because a few seconds later and ceiling, bath and woman would have fallen on our heads, although it was already quite some coincidence that that ceiling had collapsed at the very moment Borja and I were carrying out a rather shady commission.

"You should call an ambulance!" I shouted at the Cuban up above. "I think she's hurt herself. Hey? Are you up there?"

No one answered. Seconds later we heard a door shut suddenly and footsteps running downstairs. The Cuban hadn't had second thoughts about scarpering.

The woman seemed to have fainted and Borja decided we should take her out of there before trying to switch the light on. The bath was full of water and rubble and we were afraid there'd be a short circuit and the woman would be fried alive.

We left the stranger in the lobby and managed to get the lights back on. She'd recovered consciousness but was raving. In her wet and naked state, we tried to wrap her up as best we could in our topcoats. To judge by her whimpering she'd only broken a leg. The bell rang and the neighbours were beginning to gather, visibly angry. Some wore dressing gowns and slippers, and looked threatening. Borja announced he was going to ring for an ambulance and disappeared.

"So who might you lot be? You don't live here . . ." a woman in her sixties shouted accusingly, pulling her turquoise, size-24 housecoat tight. "I must inform you," she introduced herself ceremoniously, "that I am the chair of the residents committee."

I explained that we worked for the MP and had come to the office on his behalf to collect some papers our boss urgently needed. The majority of residents looked as if they didn't believe a word.

"What about this poor little child? Can't you see he's very frightened?"

Arnau was no longer crying, but he was shit-scared.

"It's my son," I explained. "He insisted on coming for the ride."

"I want my mummy! I want my mummy! . . ." sobbed Arnau.

"We'd better call the police," said the woman in the turquoise housecoat wrinkling her nose. "Something odd's going on here."

The rest of the neighbours seemed to agree and their chair left the office, presumably to look for a telephone. That word "police" was like a knife thrust into my stomach and it set off a cruel comic strip of events in my imagination. I saw Borja and myself leaving the building handcuffed and accused of some dreadful crime. I imagined myself in the Modelo raped by inmates, ill-treated by the guards and abandoned by Montse and I had a dizzy turn. It was my second queasy spell in two days. I was beginning to behave like a pregnant woman.

"Are you really sure that's . . . necessary?" I managed to ask. "An ambulance . . . It seems there's been an accident. The ceiling's collapsed . . ." I tried to explain.

"No, not the police! . . ." bawled the injured woman.

"You bet we're going to call the police!" shouted another

neighbour, a man in his fifties in dressing gown and pyjamas on the arm of a woman whose nightshirt was peeking out from under her overcoat and who was nodding.

"I've just rung them. They're on their way," Borja stated cool as a cucumber. He'd just emerged from the MP's office and looked totally unfazed. "I thought it must be the right thing to do. Of course, I rang for an ambulance as well."

That disconcerted the neighbours and meant the woman in the turquoise housecoat came back with her tail between her legs, but it was obvious none of those present had the slightest intention of leaving until the police arrived. I thought my brother had gone mad, because we'd have lots of explaining to do, for sure.

Nevertheless, his news seemed to soothe the neighbours. The injured woman, for her part, kept shouting incomprehensibly, laughing and groaning simultaneously. Arnau cried and I wished I was far away. My brother, on the other hand, didn't seem at all worried. Quite naturally, using all his charm and politeness, he'd succeeded in asserting control over the situation.

"This lady doesn't live in this building!" explained one woman in a pink tracksuit whose face bore greasy traces of moisturising cream. "In fact, the flat upstairs is empty. No one lives there."

"That's a lie!" countered the injured woman, who swung from the delirious to the lucid every few seconds. "This flat belongs to a friend . . . Ouch, my leg! It really hurts!"

"And I'm telling you that nobody lives there," repeated the track-suited woman. "Both this flat and the one opposite are empty. So you might like to tell us what you were doing there . . ."

The injured woman tried to pull herself up but fell back on the floor writhing in pain. Borja ran over to help, but she signalled she wanted nobody touching her.

"Who the hell do you think you are anyway? I've no reason to give you any explanations! . . ." She shrieked angrily.

"No, you can give them to the police," said the woman in the turquoise housecoat who clearly suspected she was a streetwalker who'd taken advantage of the empty flat. "You two as well," she fulminated in our direction.

I swallowed, but Borja looked at me as if to say keep calm. After several interminable minutes, the ambulance men arrived as did a couple of city police cars. Borja introduced himself and summed up what had happened. He said we were working for Lluís Font MP and had come to the office on his behalf to collect some urgent documentation and that they could phone to check if they so wished. He also showed them the keys the MP had lent us and the card with his telephone numbers.

"Lluís Font? You mean the politician?" one of the policemen asked, sounding surprised.

"The very same," nodded Borja.

"Wasn't his wife murdered yesterday?" asked his colleague, a much younger man who looked more like a university teacher than a policeman.

"Yes, very unfortunate . . ." my brother replied. "But what's happened here has nothing to do with that. There's been an accident. Presumably water leaked, built up and the ceiling finally gave way . . ." He paused. "And now, if you'll forgive us, we must be on our way . . ."

"Not so quick, policeman," trumpeted the woman in the turquoise housecoat like a general from the bad old days, not knowing which policeman to address, "I am the chair of the residents committee and I can assure you nobody lives upstairs. This flat's been empty for years." And she added, "We don't know who this lady is. Or these gentlemen for that matter!"

"So they'll have to wait a moment until we've cleared all this up . . ." sighed the policeman who was apparently in charge.

While we argued, the ambulance men tried to attend to the injured woman, which wasn't at all easy because she was still under the effects of something rather more potent than her crash. They wrapped blankets around her, took her blood pressure and announced they were ready to take her to hospital. The woman did nothing but complain and snarl incoherently.

"So what have you got to say for yourself?" asked one of the policemen bluntly.

"I shall only speak when I am in the presence of my lawyer," the injured woman muttered contemptuously.

"Calm down, madam, nobody's accusing you of anything. What's your name? Where's your ID? Upstairs?"

"In my handbag."

"Is there anyone else upstairs?"

"Hmm . . . well . . ." the woman hesitated. "No, nobody. Nobody at all." And repeated, "I'd like to speak to my lawyer. I'm within my rights."

"Very well," said the policeman. "You can ring him from the hospital, if you consider it necessary. But at least tell us your name. We'll find out in the end, because we have to include it in our report."

The woman pulled a face and swore. She was shivering with cold and her face looked shaken. The police had failed to clear the neighbours out, in fact their presence

151

had attracted several more and they'd formed a whispering circle around us. Some were overtly nosy, and I spotted the woman in the pink tracksuit shift an expensive cut-glass ashtray into her pocket. One of the policemen, now beginning to lose patience, asked the woman what her name was yet again.

"I am Sílvia. Sílvia Vilalta," she said finally. "I am Lluís Font's sister-in-law. You can check that." And added, with an exhausted sigh, "*He* is my lawyer."

12

That unexpected revelation knocked us all sideways. Borja
and I looked at each other nonplussed while the ambulance
men carried a woman downstairs who was either high or
insulted and claimed she was our client's sister-in-law. From
what you could deduce from her surname, she was the
stepsister of the woman who'd allegedly been murdered the
day before. While we recovered from our shocked surprise,
one of the policemen, harassed by the neighbours who
assumed we were thieves, tried unsuccessfully to phone the
MP. His lines were regrettably all engaged and I could see
myself spending the night in the police station, or worse
still, in a prison cell.

"Would it be a good idea if we drove over to Mr Font's
house in the patrol car?" one of the policemen asked
graciously. "If he corroborates what you've said, that will be
the end of the matter. If we have to go to the station, you
could be there for hours. And you've got a small child with
you . . ."

The fact we were well dressed and cradling Arnau played
in our favour. I noted that, unlike the neighbours, the police
seemed to believe the story Borja had spun. Nonetheless,
the woman in the purple housecoat was relentless and
demanded we should be taken to the police station. The
police ignored her.

"I would really appreciate that," said Borja. "I suppose
that after last night's misfortune, the MP's phone hasn't

stopped ringing. Condolences and the like. Not to mention journalists . . ."

"Yes, they must be happy. The crime pages have got copy for several weeks . . . And we've got a real headache!" That extremely polite policeman with a slight squint didn't seem to be a big fan of the press.

"Perhaps we should have left the kid at home," I conceded. "He's knackered . . ."

I'd been ringing Montse so she didn't panic when she got home and found the house empty, but her phone didn't respond. She and her sister must have been conversing animatedly in the company of a bottle of wine, and I expected she'd forgotten to switch her mobile on when they left the cinema. I knew that if Montse came home very late and didn't find us in, she'd be alarmed, would assume something had happened to Arnau and would start ringing round hospitals and making one hell of a fuss. I made one last attempt, and this time Montse answered. She'd just arrived and seemed on the merry side.

"Don't worry. We went for a drive with Borja and Arnau and it's suddenly very late (. . .) No, nothing's up. (. . .) Really, I'm telling you (. . .) Arnau's fine. We're on our way."

I looked at my watch and saw it was a quarter past eleven. I put Arnau's coat on, he wasn't crying anymore but rubbing his eyes, and went to the lift with the policemen.

"Heavens! We almost forgot the papers we'd come for in the first place! And the present for the twins!" Borja exclaimed with all the sang-froid in the world as we were about to enter the lift.

"What present? I want a present too . . ." said Arnau yawning.

154

Borja turned round and went back to the flat. He picked up one of the folders that were scattered around the office and the Xmas wrapped present.

"Here we are!" he said waving the report in the eyes of the police while he carried the voluminous package with the painting. I saw out of the corner of my eye that it was a report on the impact of liquid manure on farming in the Garrotxa.

"OK, we can go now."

We got into the patrol car, with Arnau half asleep in my arms, and I had no option but to give them my address. I didn't even want to think about the neighbours crowing about our triumphal arrival in a gleaming patrol car. The police were thoughtful to the point of not using their flashing lights or sirens, but even so, when the car halted outside the main door, I noticed the curtains in flat 2 on the fourth floor half-opened. That flat belonged to the chair of our residents committee, a neurotic spinster who liked to poke her nose into everything and I was reminded of her colleague in the turquoise housecoat. These gossipmongers would have a field day the next morning.

One of the police said he had to accompany me upstairs and that Borja should stay in the car. Arnau had fallen asleep and I was carrying him in my arms. Once more, my brother chanced his luck.

"Hey, we don't need to take the twins' present all over the place. As you're going upstairs, why don't you take it with you," he said.

"You're right. Don't worry, you see to the boy and I'll look after the package," said one of the police very considerately.

I tried to swallow but my mouth was dry. I knew the worst was yet to come. When Montse saw me escorted in by that stout policeman and Arnau asleep in my arms, she'd be alarmed and rightly so. The moment I opened the door, I assured her there was no reason to be worried, that the boy had fallen asleep but was fine. I then explained that Borja and I had to go to take some papers to the MP's house. There'd been a misunderstanding and that's why the police were accompanying us. Montse didn't say a word but was evidently annoyed.

"Nothing to worry about, madam. We're just making a routine check," the policeman corroborated, throwing me a lifeline.

"And what's this? Can you possibly tell me what this is?" whispered Montse when the policeman put the Christmas wrapped present on the floor.

"It's a present from Borja for the girls. We brought it up now so we're not carrying it about all over the shop . . . Just put Arnau to bed and I'll be back in a jiffy. Within the hour, you'll see."

I preferred not to think of the row and third degree I'd be in for when I did get back. The policeman and I went down the stairs trying not to make any noise, but before we got to the lobby the residents' committee chair had caught up with us. She was wearing a housecoat and was out of breath.

"Is anything wrong?" barked the Rottweiler (the nickname the residents have given her). It was clear she desperately wanted the answer to be "yes".

"Not at all, madam. Nothing at all," rasped the policeman. "Good night."

On the drive to the MP's house, Borja decided to play Mr Nice and joke with the police but I stayed silent. I was thinking it was a big coincidence our client's sister-in-law should be entertaining a young Cuban in a flat precisely situated over the flat belonging to her brother-in-law, and only a day after her sister (stepsister, really, as Mariona told us) had died in mysterious circumstances. I was also worried because of Borja not being Borja but Pep, because of our company that didn't exist and because of that portrait of Lídia Font that a policeman had helped me carry up to my place.

"We're here!" announced Borja when the car pulled up next to the MP's house.

The same oriental girl opened the door, now wearing a less showy light grey uniform. She gave a start when she saw it was the police knocking yet again on the door of the honourable mansion.

"Sir now coming. Is phone," she said, her voice shaking.

She let us into the lobby and disappeared down the passage. The MP came a minute after, his mobile still stuck to his ear. He was saying goodbye to his interlocutor and thanking him for his condolences. After hanging up, he invited us into a small, very welcoming, much more colourful room than the huge reception room where his wife had dropped dead the day before. It was furnished in colonial style and adorned with cheerful flowery cushions and curtains. There was a parrot in a cage, a cat snoozing on one of the cushions and big pots of tropical plants. Lluís Font invited us to sit down and asked if we wanted a drink, but we all turned down his invitation.

After apologizing for the late hour and giving him condolences for the loss of his wife, one of the policemen asked the MP if he knew us and if it was a fact we worked for him. Lluís Font looked surprised and said we did, that we were his political advisers, and demanded to know what all

157

those questions were in aid of at that time of night. Despite his calm and collected mien, the MP must have caught the drift of what had happened: we'd been caught in his office carrying a huge package and someone had given an alarm call.

"It's only a routine enquiry," explained the policeman. "These gentlemen were in your office, but the neighbours said they didn't know them. We tried to speak to you by phone, but you were engaged . . ." he justified their actions. "Of course, these gentlemen don't look like thieves," he smiled to relieve the tension, "and that's why we have brought them here."

"I personally gave them the keys yesterday and asked them to go and fetch . . . something I needed urgently," our client replied rather nervously.

"Given everything that has happened, I couldn't possibly go to the office myself. You've seen how the phone hasn't stopped ringing!"

"Here's that paperwork," said Borja, handing him the strange file. And added soothingly, "All in order."

I prayed neither of the policemen would wonder how a report on liquid manure could be so important the day after Lluís Font had lost his wife and in the middle of the Christmas holidays. But it was obvious that they had another question on their mind. Once they'd clarified the fact we weren't thieves, the young, squinting policeman hurriedly explained that the confusion had arisen because the ceiling to his bathroom had collapsed while a woman, who claimed she was his sister-in-law, was taking a shower in the flat upstairs. The victim, he went on, was injured, the office was full of rubble and the firemen had had to be called. There was a frightful commotion, on the stairs, he added.

The MP looked astonished. I noted how he was gritting his teeth because his facial muscles had tensed. "The neighbours are adamant that nobody lives in the flat above and are worried. Naturally if the lady who suffered the accident is your sister-in-law, there must be an explanation . . ." the policeman said prudently.

"Was she hurt? Where is she now?" asked the MP with genuine anxiety.

"In other words, the lady is your sister-in-law," deduced the other policeman, who hadn't opened his mouth up to that point.

He was older and stouter than his colleague and sported one of those bald heads that's trying to hide behind a comb-over.

"I suppose so, it must be her," Luís Font paused before continuing. "My sister-in-law has keys to the flat. But where is she now?" he insisted. "Is she all right?"

"I expect they've taken her to the Clinic. She's apparently broken a leg, but it's nothing serious. The shock more than anything else!" he said, trying to downplay the incident.

Despite his affable tone, I began to suspect that this old hand was starting to smell something fishy.

"You know, really . . ." continued the squinting policeman. "Isn't all this rather odd?"

Lluís Font took a cigarette and offered us one. I think he was playing for time. The policeman turned down his offer, although I could see they smoked from their nicotine stained fingers.

"In fact, it couldn't be simpler." The MP reassumed an air of VIP authority. "This property belongs to a company by the name of Diagonal Consulting. I am the main shareholder. The person in charge is Pablo Mazos, and he's also my personal assistant. The fact is we don't use the upstairs flat, but we've been intending for some time to turn the two flats, the one upstairs and my office into a duplex in order to gain more space. My sister-in-law has a key," he continued while he smoked his cigarette slowly as the rich like to do. "Although the upstairs flat needs some attention, Sílvia occasionally shuts herself in there when she feels like being alone and not bothered. She says," he attempted a smile, "that she's writing a novel or something of the sort."

"Right. I suppose you can prove this," the squint-eyed policeman said rather aggressively. "I don't like to do this, particularly in the circumstances, but it's our job . . ."

"I've got the documentation in my office. Do you want us to go this very minute?" the MP asked in a tone clearly designed to elicit a no for an answer. "It is on the late side . . ."

"Of course not, Your Honour!" exclaimed the balding policeman. "We can drop by in the morning, at a time that suits you, you can show us the paperwork and case closed." And getting up he spoke to his colleague: "Come on, time to hit the road, it's late. Very sorry to have bothered you."

"If it would help, we can take you home in the patrol car," the younger policeman suggested with a smile.

He was trying to win brownie points.

"I know it's rather late," said Lluís Font addressing us, "but since you are here, there are a couple of things I'd like to discuss. It's to do with this . . ." he glanced at the file on the impact of liquid manure.

Borja and I looked at each other askance. I looked impatiently at my watch.

"Perhaps just I could stay behind . . ." Borja suggested. "My partner was expected home some time ago, weren't you, Eduard?"

My brother must have been imagining how worried Montse was and so he gave me a helping hand. The truth was that after all that had happened, regardless of when I turned up, I'd be in for a hell of a blasting.

"Of course, of course! You go," agreed the MP. "The two of you don't need to stay. And my sincere thanks to you," he turned to the policemen. "It's so gratifying to see how well our security forces work!" Now it was the politician speaking. "Naturally if we were in government," he smiled, "the home affairs budget would get a real boost . . ."

"Great, you'll get our vote, and then fingers crossed for a rise . . ." said the squinting policeman unenthusiastically. "Because we're always last on the list, right?"

"Come on, Ruiz," said the other policeman rather nervously. "These gentlemen have been very patient with us. Sorry to have bothered you," he apologized a second time. "But you know what neighbours are like sometimes . . ."

"Not at all. You have a job to do. It was most kind of you to bring these gentlemen to my house."

"The least we could do. Good night. And we are very sorry about your wife. If we can help in any way . . ."

"Thank you very much," the MP repeated, "have a good night."

I left Borja alone with our client and went off with the policemen. The patrol drove me home while I wondered what tale I could spin Montse, who was certain to be waiting up for me. I was feeling tired but slightly calmer now the night seemed to have ended satisfactorily. From the main door, I saw the curtains of Flat 2 on the fourth floor twitch again (and the ones in our dining room too), and went up prepared for the worst. To my surprise, the moment I opened the door Montse threw herself around my neck,

161

kissed me and asked with tears in her eyes if I was all right. She'd thought I was in jail.

"What nonsense! Of course they didn't arrest me!"

I told her about the paperwork we'd fetched and the business of the woman falling through the ceiling.

"And this?" Montse had unwrapped the package. "It's not a present for the girls, is it? The painting my mother gave us has gone missing by the way."

I had to think on my feet and say there was a problem with the invoice for the painting, which was very valuable, and we'd had to swap it for her mother's oil painting until it was sorted. It was very likely, given the circumstances, that the police would search the MP's house and he'd asked us to keep hold of the painting for a few days. As he was a well-known politician, there was a risk his enemies would accuse him of buying it and the newspapers might stick the knife in.

"So he's trafficking in stolen art works! . . ." summed up Montse, scandalized.

"It's just a favour we're doing him, dear. We're also giving him advice on his investments . . . His wife's death is pure coincidence."

"I want this picture out of the house in the morning," she said definitively. "Let Borja look after it, or whoever, I don't want it here. It will cause us problems."

I assured her I would remove it early on and persuaded her to come to bed without more ado. Arnau was asleep in his bed, the twins were at their friends' and I was exhausted. Once we were in bed, my wife and I still took a while to get to sleep. When I felt the touch of her skin I realized I wasn't as tired as I thought I was. Despite all the shocks and surprises, the night was still young.

162

13

Next morning, before Montse woke up, I wrapped the picture up again. My wife had apparently not noticed it was a portrait of the murdered woman, and so much the better. I went down to buy chocolate croissants to mollify her and got the coffee ready. After last night's hullabaloo Arnau was sleeping like a log, and while Montse was in the shower I phoned Borja. He was still asleep in bed.

"Hey, there's no way I can keep the picture here. I'm sorry, but Montse won't hear of it."

"All right," he said drowsily. "Bring it to my place."

Before hanging up, he told me he'd got to bed in the early hours because he'd had a very long and insightful conversation with the MP. I was intrigued and told him I'd be there within the hour.

Montse didn't have to be at the Centre till the middle of the morning so the girls would be back in time to look after Arnau. As I was still trying to get back into her good books, I told her I'd be back earlier and would get lunch ready for everybody. She'd not be home till three o'clock, would have a quick bite and then rush back to work. As it was party time, women wanted to be beautiful and Montse was run off her feet.

When I got to his flat, my brother was already showered, dressed and shaved, though his face looked sleepy. We put the picture under his bed and hoped Merche wouldn't start sniffing around – not that she was likely to. And if she did find it, it was so well packaged Borja could tell her it had to do with one of his lines of business.

"I think this guy has put us right in it," Borja started off.

"Why do you say that."

"The whole matter is much more complicated than I thought."

"Fine, we've still time. Look, we just take the damned picture, return it to him and tell him our job's over," I suggested. "His wife is dead, isn't she? She can't have any lovers now."

"It's not so simple. Want a coffee?"

While he prepared coffee in the kitchen, he began to tell me in detail about his conversation with our client. First things first, the autopsy confirmed she'd been poisoned, although it would be a few days before the forensics identified the kind of substance that had caused death. But that wasn't all.

"It turns out this Sílvia and the MP have been lovers for almost a year," he let drop.

"Fucking hell!"

"He went stiff as a board when I told him there was a naked Cuban in the upstairs flat as well, twenty years younger than his sister-in-law, who disappeared in a flash when the ceiling collapsed," he went on as he gulped down his coffee.

"Well, well . . . And the guy was upset in case his wife was carrying on with a painter!" I said scandalized. "And all the time his lover was having it off with someone else!"

"Just so. And we were happily investigating his wife while he was carrying on with his sister-in-law. Of course I already suspected something . . ." he said, playing the wise guy.

Apparently, when they were by themselves, Borja decided to make a few stabs in the dark and the MP had finally confessed the usual old story: his marriage had been on the rocks for years and he'd fallen in love with another woman; unfortunately the woman in question was his sister-in-law. Given his position, divorce was unthinkable, apart from not being a very practical solution. As Mariona had told us, Sílvia was Lídia's step-sister, daughter of her father's first marriage to a woman who broke her neck skiing in Cortina, and, unlike Lídia, she was a good listener, an affectionate, understanding woman he could relax with (with the occasional bit of rumpy pumpy, no doubt, I thought to myself). On the other hand, Sílvia Vilalta was quite an attractive woman, although not to be compared to her sister. She was divorced and childless. In Borja's view, Lluís Font spoke about her as if he sincerely loved her and found it difficult to accept she was having it off with a mellifluous gigolo.

As for the flat the neighbours thought was empty, as the MP had told the police the previous night, he was its owner. He'd found it an unobtrusive way of being able to meet his lover without his movements giving rise to suspicion. Behind his wife's back and through that company called Diagonal Consulting, he'd bought the flat so everything stayed in the family. The only precaution the MP and his lover had to take was to ensure the neighbours didn't catch them going up or down the flight of stairs that separated his office from the bachelor pad, but luckily it was an attic and opposite was one of those phantom companies that act as a tax address. The ruse had worked reasonably well up to then.

"Christ, what a mess!" I said, rather confused. "Naturally if these two are lovers, they had a good reason to get rid of the deceased. Either together or separately."

"I expect that's what the police will think if they ever find out. He swears it wasn't the case and I believe him."

"At this point I really don't know what to think!" I responded, shrugging my shoulders. "Perhaps he thought if he killed her in this recondite way, using sweets or poisoned cognac sent by a stranger, he wouldn't be caught . . ."

"It hardly makes sense," he shook his head, "why should he implicate us with the picture business? And what if his daughter had eaten the *marrons glacés*? Or if the maid or someone else had poured a shot of cognac?"

"In any case, we still don't know what killed her. You ate one of those things and you're all right . . . So it must be the cognac."

"I suppose so. But I think if our MP had wanted to see off his wife he'd have found a simpler way than putting poison into a bottle of Courvoisier. An accident in the house, for example," Borja speculated.

"Yes, he'd have avoided the publicity," I conceded.

"The newspapers have talked about nothing else for a couple of days, and I don't think a murder in murky circs will help his political ambitions. Conversely, the poison implies premeditation, that the person who put her away thought carefully before acting." He paused and sighed, joined his hands together and half-closed his eyes. "Eduard, this is no crime of passion."

"Elementary, my dear Sherlock," I laughed, because it was the first time I'd seen him play that role. "And do you have any idea what might have happened?"

"This Sílvia woman came to their Christmas lunch. She was probably connected to the poisoning," he suggested. "She was probably unhappy with her role as second lady and thought the most expeditious way forward was to make her brother-in-law a widower."

But that wasn't all. Borja extracted from the drawer of his night-table an envelope full of 100 and 500 notes. He reckoned 12,000 euros all told.

"The MP wants us to continue with our investigation. Discreetly, of course. He says he's got a contact in the police who'll tell us how *their* investigation is faring and will get us copies of their reports. Apparently it's the nephew of a friend."

"So he wants us to spy on what the police find out!" I said, shocked. "So he can cover his own back, I expect!"

"I suppose so. Well," my brother turned serious, "if he's guilty, we'll also find out."

"And will we also cover it up?" I wondered, though not daring to voice the question out aloud. "At what price? How stuffed does an envelope have to be in such cases?"

"Pep, it's one thing to be a prying eye for the rich and quite another to cover up a murder. Besides, I should remind you we're not detectives."

"He knows. Listen, I give you my word that if we discover he murdered his wife we'll go straight to the police. But I think he's innocent. People who can afford lawyers don't usually opt for violence."

"Only if divorce is too expensive," I retorted, "and I'm not just referring to money."

12,000 euros were tempting enough, not to mention the 20,000 he'd already shelled out in less than three weeks. On the other hand, what Lluís Font asked of us bordered on the illegal, although so far, when all's said and done, we'd done nothing to keep me awake at nights. Even so, keeping hold of his wife's portrait in oils to avoid her adultery hitting the headlines, or having furtive conversations with a policeman so he could tell us how their investigation was going, wasn't the same as turning a blind eye to cold-blooded murder.

I was convinced Borja and I would never cross that frontier however much cash the MP might offer us. Besides, I had my brother's word, and he didn't usually go back on his promises. I agreed to carry on with the case, although I didn't have the slightest idea where we should start.

"We'll go to Paris and see Pau Ferrer," Borja decided. "If he and Lídia were lovers, he may be implicated or perhaps can give us the name of somebody who had it in for her. Perhaps she suspected someone wanted her out of circulation, her husband even."

"Yes, that makes sense," I agreed.

Given the circumstances, we decided we would bluntly ask the painter how he got to know Lídia Font and what kind of relationship he'd had with her. We were quite sure a conversation with the painter of the picture that had caused such a stir would clear up many of our doubts.

I'd promised Montse I would get lunch ready, so I told Borja I'd see him in the afternoon. We'd have to pass by a travel agency to order the plane tickets and book a hotel. I'm not over fond of flying, but knew that Borja wouldn't agree to take the train.

When I told Montse my business partner and I were off to Paris she got all furious again. She harped on about the murder, the picture and the police, and it began to look as if I had a full-scale matrimonial crisis on my hands.

"You know," I said, trying to change the subject, "I think Borja really likes your sister."

It was as if I'd uttered words of magic. The long face and reproaches went and suddenly the conversation centred on the relationship between my twin brother and much adored sister-in-law. Women always go for the romantic, some at least, and Montse took the bait immediately. Of course my timely comment would generate futile expectations for Lola and a future problem for Borja, but I thought it better they focussed for a couple of days on the Borja *affaire* rather than on the business of the painting.

"Well, I had thought Borja was rather taken by Lola . . ." said Montse excitedly. "Do you think he'll bring her a present from Paris? And what about you? Will you bring me something?" she asked sweetly.

The truth was I'd not given it a thought, but obviously we'd find time to buy a few presents in Paris, although it isn't as simple as it sounds. It used to be easy when you travelled abroad to find a little present that would go down well. Now, you buy something with high hopes it will please, cart it around in your suitcase only to find it's on sale at half the price next door to where you live. Luckily, I was going with Borja, who loved shopping.

The tickets bought today to travel tomorrow cost us the earth. However, thanks to our MP's generosity money was no longer a problem, and we booked two rooms in a small hotel near the Opéra. Paris is enormous, and it's better to go for somewhere central than to bankrupt yourself on taxis. Because the plane would be departing at the crack of dawn, Borja and I left for our respective homes. We still had to pack our bags and I wanted to get to bed early because I'd had a backlog of sleep owing ever since Christmas Day. That night my brother had arranged to have dinner with Merche, whom he'd not seen for days, and I advised him to disconnect his mobile.

"Lola will probably give you a call . . ." I said casually.

I didn't dare tell him about the comment I'd made to Montse. It was stupid, but I knew Borja would lose his temper with me, and then eventually take it on board. I was getting desperate for a zoo where I could hide this elephant that was getting bigger by the second.

14

"*Mésépamafótsivúnevusavépabian'xpliqué, mesié!*" rattled the taxi driver at Borja's third remark about the route we were taking.

We'd taken the taxi at the Gare du Nord and were now embarked on a rough-and-ready tour of the most historic sights in Paris. When the driver saw our luggage and heard that our destination was a hotel, he'd deduced quickly and correctly we were foreigners and we ended up paying fifty euros for a journey that should have cost twelve. Despite my brother's excellent French, the guy took us on the classic sight-seeing route, and not content with that, he got very angry when Borja pointed out most politely it was the third time we'd passed that same *église*. Of course, the wiles of Parisian taxi drivers are something you have to anticipate when travelling to the city, as my brother explained. No need to kick up a fuss or tear one's hair out.

I'd always told Montse I'd never been to Paris. It's one of those stupid lies one makes up on the spur of the moment and then have to sustain for a lifetime so as not to look silly or like a liar. What happened was that one afternoon soon after we'd started going out, after making love in the tiny flat I used to rent in Sants, Montse asked me if I'd been to Paris. She'd just confessed that she'd never set foot in the city and really looked forward to the day we would discover it together. Faced by such blossoming tenderness, I didn't have the guts to tell her the truth.

"No, no, I've never been," I said quietly as I caressed her hair. "I was leaving it till I met you."

That little white lie was meant more as a romantic aside, but the consequences have haunted me ever since. In fact, I was twenty when I first went to Paris with a girlfriend by the name of Olga who lasted six months. With hindsight I can see she was quite crazy and I thank God things never turned serious, but all the same I was mad about her at the time.

We went to Paris together over a long All Saints Day weekend, in one of those awful trains that left the estación de Francia and took three decades to arrive, at the time our passion had reached its culminating peak. Days I shall never forget, that's for sure. It was autumn, and the golden leaves on the trees in Paris rustled and fell on the pavements to form a carpet that crackled under our feet. Postcard skies, of unimaginable colours, framed some of old Europe's most emblematic buildings while Olga and I crossed, one by one, the bridges of the river that has surely witnessed the most lovers' suicides throughout history. I also remember the small, cheap, unheated hotel where we stayed just over four days, and a passion driven by youthful hormones that steamed up the windows and prevented the bright moon beams shining in.

I felt guilty about staying in Paris with a girl who wasn't Montse. The intensity of my memories made me feel uneasy, as if I'd been unfaithful to my wife, even though it was a fling from years before I met her. The truth is that both Paris and Olga had captivated me in my early twenties. It had been only my second excursion abroad (I'd been to Italy with some friends before that, but it wasn't the same), and my brief stay in that paradise of freedom, hedonism and *philosophie* brought me back to Barcelona thinking I lived in a small, boring provincial capital. Franco hadn't been dead long, the first democratic elections had been held, and in my eyes and those of all my generation Paris possessed the magic the Generalíssimo had snatched from us.

Our plane had left and arrived on time, and Borja and I were in our hotel by mid-morning. We unpacked, changed our clothes and prepared to visit the gallery where Pau Ferrer had exhibited the portrait purchased by our client just over a month ago. Borja forced me to put on my Armani suit and the tie Mariona Castany had given me, and he lent me one of his overcoats – black, in fact – to round off the image. I had to pass myself off as a Spanish art collector who spoke no French, and my brother had given me very precise instructions about how I should perform.

"While I talk to the person in charge and try to get the painter's address," Borja told me, "You look at everything as if you're interested in buying. When you find the most expensive painting in the exhibition, come over to me and say you'll be back in the morning with your wife. Don't smile, look as if you're suffering from a stomach ulcer and look at your watch now and then. Leave the rest to me," he added with a smile.

The gallery was near the Jardins de Luxembourg, so we caught a taxi. This time, with no luggage and Borja's impeccable French, the taxi driver spared us the roundabout route and we were there in a few minutes. It was a modern outfit in an old building, and stuffed with quite abstract pictures at a price to cure your hiccups. First, a young West Indian woman attended to us, and then the man who must have been the gallery owner, a middle-aged Frenchman, snooty, precious, heavily scented and as charming as pie. I performed to prior instructions, and while acting the indecisive buyer I tried to decipher what the shop manager was explaining to my brother in French.

"Well, then?" I eagerly asked Borja as we left. "What did he tell you? Have you got the address?"

"We're out of luck again." He shook his head. "Pau Ferrer had a stroke a week ago and is in a coma in hospital."

"Fuck! What a coincidence! Wonder if he's been poisoned as well . . ."

"I doubt it. Apparently, he's a glutton for punishment," he explained. "He wouldn't give me the name or address of the hospital, but I did get his dealer's number. It's a woman."

"Well, every little helps. Perhaps she can."

"Don't get too hopeful. She's out of Paris, abroad, and won't be back before the end of the year."

A pointless trip, I thought, because we couldn't stay that long in Paris. We'd have to go back empty-handed and perhaps return later on.

"We've still got one card to play," my brother said mysteriously. "Let's go for a bite to eat."

Borja seemed withdrawn and I could tell he was in no mood to talk. I know him and realized he was plotting something. We went into a café and ordered a couple of *croque-monsieurs* and two beers. While we downed our frugal repast, Borja revealed the ace up his sleeve.

"I know someone in Paris," he said finally. "I'd have preferred not to have recourse to her, but as we've come this far . . . Obviously, she's probably on holiday. It's not a good time . . ."

"It's worth a try. We've nothing to lose," I encouraged him.

"I need a cognac first."

Without going into great detail, he explained that the

174

woman he was thinking of contacting was, as I worked out, the woman who'd broken his heart in a previous life. It was a typical, clichéd story, one to inspire the screenplay for a profound film or a tear-jerking melodrama. Since our reuniting, Borja had told me very little about his life, except for a few disparate, entertaining anecdotes I could never quite believe. I'd got wind of the fact that it hadn't been a path strewn with roses, since, as Montse says, when somebody refuses to talk about their past it's because they have something to hide or a painful wound that has yet to heal.

She was a penniless art student dreaming of becoming an artist. Borja was working as a waiter in a café and both survived on the wage and tips he earned. They lived in one of those tiny attics that have made Paris so famous, without heating or bathroom, and for a couple of years Borja acted as her patron, for want of a better word, while she painted and strove to become that great artist. Apparently, at the same time my brother also wanted to be a writer (you see, we are twins!), but what with his work in the café and the devotion he showed her, he never managed to write a single worthwhile word.

The upshot was that the girl, who was very pretty according to Borja, met a gallery owner thirty years older than herself and thirty million times richer than he was. She married the gallery owner and dropped Borja, who for another couple of years at least paraded his depression and drunken habits around the bars of Paris without writing a line. My broken-hearted brother finally left, and the girl, who was called Camille, stopped painting to devote herself body and soul to her rich spouse's prosperous business. According to Borja, the married couple owned one of Paris's most famous contemporary art galleries.

"It must be fifteen years since I last saw her," he said after he'd ordered his second cognac. "Even so, it's still a kick in the teeth."

"You still feel . . ." I hinted gently.

"I feel I acted like an idiot for five years of my life," he said angrily. "But as things stand, going to see her is all that comes to mind."

I asked him if he preferred to go alone, but he said he'd prefer if we both went. It wasn't too far away and we walked, although it was drizzling and quite cold. Protected by our umbrellas, we reached this particular Parisian temple of art just as tiny snowflakes began to fall.

"Pep, good heavens, I wouldn't have recognized you!" said my brother's ex looking surprised. "I mean . . ."

"You're as beautiful as ever," said Borja giving her three big kisses with a broad smile I knew wasn't genuine.

I'd not had the pleasure of meeting Camille when she was my brother's girlfriend, but knowing his tastes I reckoned she'd not worn very well. She was a very short, incredibly thin woman, skin and bones to be precise. She wore her hair short, dyed various colours and thousands of tiny wrinkles furrowed her face, which was caked in make-up as if she were going to a party. Her patterned dress was hideous. She wore big earrings and rings on every finger. I suddenly realized her over-the-top appearance reminded me of Lola, and things then clicked.

"I suppose you feel peculiar seeing me after so much time . . ." Borja began rather nervously.

"Let's say I wasn't expecting you," she replied curiously, with a big smile.

"You look great. Really," lied Borja.

"I'm older. *Caramba*, Pep, what are you doing here in

176

Paris?" she asked looking him up and down, "Have you been here long?"

"We've just arrived, you might say. Perhaps you can do a favour for my friend. It's the Christmas holidays and so many people have gone away, I could only think of coming to you for help . . ."

Camille smiled at me and Borja did the introductions, "Camille, meet Eduard . . . Eduard Másdeu."

As that woman knew him as Pep Martínez, he'd decided to change my name. He added: "He's a collector."

"*Enchantée*," she said offering me a hand.

"Pleased to meet you," I responded.

"The thing is," Borja cut to the quick, "my friend would like to contact a painter who's famous here in Paris: Pau Ferrer, but we were told he's in a coma in hospital."

"That's right, poor chap! And by all accounts he's done for this time." She shook her head. "It's the second attack he's had . . . Apparently," she said confidentially, "his nose is wrecked on the inside . . ."

"Our problem is that his dealer is away from Paris and won't be back till after the holidays," explained Borja.

"And?"

"He painted a picture my friend bought not long ago, the portrait of a woman. He requires some information about the model used and we were hoping to talk to him. But since he's ill and his dealer isn't here . . . I thought perhaps you might know him, the model or might know someone who knows her." Borja showed her the photograph that was printed in the catalogue.

"Is this the painting he bought?" she asked. "I know it well. He's made a good investment."

But suddenly she burst out laughing and said: "But

177

don't you know? Don't you know how Pau paints these portraits?"

Borja and I looked at each other dismayed.

"Pau takes photos of people behind their backs and then uses the photos as the basis for his portraits. He says that what excites him is painting people, but also that people who commission painters to paint their portrait in oils are vain in the extreme and don't deserve the efforts an artist has to make. What's more, Pau thinks studio models are too stagey. Apparently," she added playfully, "on one occasion *le roi* himself wanted to commission a portrait and he said no."

"The guy's got balls," I said.

"But here in Paris, everyone knows . . . the way Pau Ferrer works."

"But, obviously we don't in Barcelona," Borja retorted.

"I bet this woman is a complete stranger to Pau. He must have taken her photo when she wasn't looking. I'm sorry," said Camille. "I can't help you."

It had its funny side. With all the women there are in the world Pau Ferrer had to choose to paint a woman he didn't know, whose husband was an art-collector and a politician in Barcelona who feared for his reputation.

"You say he takes photos . . ." Borja had had a brainwave. "Do you think we could talk to his wife or a friend of his? Perhaps we could get hold of one . . . You know, this is more important than you think."

I imagine Borja wanted material proof to take to the MP. Camille looked intrigued.

"I don't know what you're up to . . . but one of Pau Ferrer's friends is a good friend of mine. I think they split up about a year ago, but they're still friends. I don't know whether she might be able to help you," and she jotted a name and telephone number on very elegant notepaper. "She's Cécile Blanchart. Tell her I told you to phone her."

"You don't know how grateful I am," said Borja.

Camille beamed at Borja. She started playing with one of her necklaces with one hand while with the other she stroked the hair around the nape of her neck.

"I hope, after all these years, you won't leave just like that, Pep? You must have lots to tell me . . . You've changed so much! You're a real gentleman now!"

"My business is going well. I can't complain," my brother replied contentedly. "How is Fabien?"

From my brother's smile that tailed off in a grimace, I deduced that this Fabien must be Camille's husband.

"Oh! He hardly ever comes to the gallery these days. He's in a delicate state." And added in a seductive, honeyed tone, "You have forgiven me, haven't you, Pep?"

"There was really nothing to forgive. We were youngsters . . ." Borja replied condescendingly.

"Why don't we have dinner tonight? Like two old friends."

"Such a pity! I've got a prior engagement."

"What about tomorrow?"

"Fine," agreed Borja. "Let's have dinner tomorrow. At eight in the usual place. All right?"

"Heavens! It's years since I've been there . . . It might have closed down . . ."

"It's not changed a bit," said Borja. "I'll book a table. At eight o'clock sharp."

One of the things I've learned as I've followed my brother throughout the world is never to contradict him in public because I always put my foot in it. However, as soon as we left the gallery I reminded him that our return flight took off at the same time as his dinner-date.

"Quite," he smiled sulkily, signalling our conversation was at an end.

We took a taxi back to our hotel. It had got dark and, although it wasn't raining, an icy wind was blowing. Moreover, we had to talk to Camille's friend and try to fix a meeting with her as soon as possible. It wasn't the end of the world if we didn't get a photograph, because Camille's explanation seemed persuasive enough and we could certainly document it elsewhere. The art catalogue Lluís Font had given us didn't supply us with that information – there's all manner of things in that kind of publication except for info that is useful. Most catalogues seem to be written at the height of an attack of delirium tremens, but I suppose art critics have a right to earn their daily crust.

While Borja rang Pau Ferrer's friend and agreed a time to meet the following day, I spoke to Montse, who seemed more than busy. That night Borja and I decided we deserved a slap-up meal and he took me to one of those restaurants tourists never see the inside of. We ate and drank like lords, none of your *nouvelle* rubbish, traditional French cuisine, and we managed to let our hair down for a while. Two bottles of Bordeaux bit the dust, and dishes with such complicated names that I can't remember them, just that we started on *foie* cooked four different ways and Borja ate fish and I ate some kind of meat done in a really delicious purple sauce.

"So, dear partner, case closed!" I said as I decided whether to dunk my bread in that sauce. "Poor Pau Ferrer clearly wasn't involved in the mysterious murder of Lídia Font. He didn't even know her."

"So it would seem."

"In other words, as far as we're concerned, we've done our bit," I insisted.

"Aren't you curious to know what really happened?"
Borja was starting to worry me.

"You mean about finding out who gave her a push?"

"Well, you can't deny it, this case is far too similar to the novels we read when we were kids. And we did promise the MP we'd talk to that policeman."

"You mean the case isn't over!" I acquiesced forlornly.

After polishing off the desserts – wonderful home-made cakes, mine a bitter chocolate and Borja's an apple tart – we lit up and ordered a couple of cognacs. We were surely the last generation of privileged sybarites to enjoy that kind of dinner, because smoking would be soon be banned in restaurants and no doubt alcohol would follow suit. And then maybe they'd decide to prohibit sugar and fats, if our local feminists hadn't already sentenced us all to being alcohol-free, Catholic and vegetarian.

"And tomorrow you're going to stand Camille up, I presume . . ." I jibed.

"Well, she did give it to me on a plate. It's the least I owe her."

"She'll probably not show up."

"Possibly not. But if she does, and I think she will, she'll dine alone," and in that confidential tone he only uses when the alcohol's flowing, he added, "I spent many an hour waiting for her in that place. It was our favourite restaurant. When we had any money, that is, which wasn't very often."

"Is that why you turned into Borja?" I plucked up the courage to ask.

It was the first time I'd openly touched on the reason for his change of identity.

"It's late. We should get back to the hotel."

And with a half smile he curtailed our conversation.

We walked back to the hotel, despite the intense cold and the threatening clouds looming overhead. I was tired, but my intake of alcohol and coffee meant I didn't fall asleep immediately. That night I dreamed of Olga, and also of Camille, and the following morning I woke up dead tired and furry-mouthed. Borja, on the other hand, beat me down to breakfast and was as fresh as a daisy.

As agreed, we turned up at Cécile Blanchard's house at eleven sharp. She was about the same age as Pau Ferrer and seemed very affected by his illness. She was an intriguing woman with a house stuffed with books, paintings and cats. Her long curly hair was dyed saffron and she wore a bunch of necklaces over a blue tunic of sorts. Her blue eyes sparkled, and she spoke in a warm, gravelly voice while puffing on a pipe. She offered us a cup of tea.

Cécile confirmed everything Camille had said about Pau Ferrer's method of working. We tried to make her understand it was very important for us to get one of the photos his friend had taken of Lídia Font. We explained what the problem was, without divulging any names: the model had died and her husband, who'd discovered the painting by chance, suspected the two must have been having an affair. That amused her no end and she burst out laughing.

"I remember when Pau painted that portrait . . ." she drawled in a French that was easily understood. "At the time, over two years ago, we saw a lot of each other . . ."

Apparently, there were several photos of Mrs Font around, and Cécile promised to have a good look for them in her ex's study. Although they were no longer lovers, as she explained quite unashamedly, she still had keys to his studio. She also remembered that the woman in the photo was asleep.

"But Pau decided to paint her as if she were awake, he did that kind of thing sometimes," she said as she accompanied us to the door. I could see she was making an effort to hold her tears in check.

We thanked her and said our farewells, wishing her friend the very best. Before returning to the hotel, we went present shopping, and then, as the weather was good, decided to go for a stroll and enjoy the city for a few hours.

So far my reunion with the Paris of my youth had been a deeply disappointing experience. At no time had I managed to relive any of the emotions that had swept me off my feet the first time I'd visited. I felt unmoved by the sight of the Seine, the Notre Dame and even the Jardins de Luxembourg, which twenty years earlier had been the scenario of my youthful passionate love for Olga. On the trip with my brother, none of those emblematic places had succeeded in arousing the same sensations. I was terrified by the thought that, if I did come back one day with Montse, I'd have to feign emotions I was no longer able to experience in order to make my wife happy, and that prospect made me feel empty and despondent. I said nothing of this to Borja, but Paris was no longer my Paris. I could only see a huge metropolis full of frantic cars and people, imposing enough but stripped of the unrepeatable magic that had enchanted me twenty-five years ago when he was in his twenties. Borja and I strolled silently, laden with bags of presents, when my brother stumbled and saw one of his shoelaces had come undone.

"Christ! Let's sit down for a moment," he suggested.

We were near the river and walked over to one of the seats next to the bank, between the old *bouquiniste* stalls. While Borja did up his shoe, I put my bags on the floor and enjoyed a few moments' rest. We'd been walking for almost two hours and my feet were beginning to hurt.

Suddenly the wind started to blow in gusts and the heavens opened and turned black. Drops of rain fell on our heads from the clouds gathered above and were the size of walnuts when they splattered on the ground. The unexpected storm changed the smell of the city that was now filled with the perfume from the trees and the rainwater and the river. I closed my eyes for a few seconds and, as if the guy up there had been listening to my thoughts, Paris was transformed once again, magically, into the mythical place it used to be for me. Sitting there, while Borja tied his shoelaces and cursed the downpour, I was stirred by the disturbing emotions from my early twenties. For a few moments, it was as if no time had elapsed between that first trip and now. Finally Paris was Paris again.

"You look spellbound!" I heard Borja shout as he tried to make himself heard above the gale. "Come on, hurry up. This is one hell of a downpour!"

I could have stayed there transfixed under the rain, savouring that part of me that had been fading away over the years and that I'd suddenly recovered. I knew it was an ephemeral feeling sentenced to disappear, and that however long I sat on that bench on the banks of the Seine I could only hold on to it as long as the spirited, surprise shower lasted. I got up disconsolately and walked after Borja, who was running towards a taxi rank as if the devil were at his heels. As I got into the car, soaked, in emotional turmoil but happy, I bid farewell to the Paris of my twenties and the memory of the girl who finally ensured those days of my youth were what they ought to have been.

15

"We're late . . ." said Borja as we tried to park the Smart in the blue zone, which was no easy feat at that time of day.

We'd agreed to see our client in his office on the Diagonal. Our appointment was at twelve and Borja was right. We were late. All the parking lots in the vicinity had posted the red "FULL" signs and we'd been driving around for twenty minutes. As on any 30 December, the city centre was a chaotic, seething mass. It was Friday and everybody seemed to have rushed out to do their last-minute shopping. The weather had inspired people because the sun shone brightly and few people were wearing coats. Women of all ages were desperately combing this shoppers' paradise for that party dress to show off on New Year's Eve.

"Thank God the plane arrived on time!" I said in a foul temper. "I don't understand why we couldn't see him this afternoon . . . Montse was pretty angry when I told her I wasn't going home. You know she's not used to being by herself. And she's been coping with the children for the past three days . . ."

"Don't worry. Lola will have kept her company."

"Sure, that's part of the problem."

One of the things nagging me was the fact Montse and Lola had enjoyed three days to devote to the single topic of Borja. I bet they'd plotted something and would try to involve me on my return. I was also worried about the possible fallout from the comments I'd made to Montse

before going to Paris, my rash statement to the effect that
Borja really fancied Lola. I just prayed that, after a brief
tête-à-tête and a few glasses of wine, Montse hadn't told her
about the little matter of the painting. I expect my sister-
in-law hadn't noticed that her mother's landscape had
vanished from the passage in our flat.

"You know the MP was in a hurry to talk to us," said Borja
justifying himself. "He wants to see us in person."

"Fine, but we've only just arrived from Paris . . ."

They cancelled the flight we should have flown on at eight
o'clock the evening before, the exact time Borja had agreed
to meet his old flame for dinner fully intending to stand her
up in honour of the good old days. We never discovered
why. We were kept waiting hours inside the plane without
anyone bothering to offer the slightest bloody excuse as
to why we weren't taking off, until finally the loudspeakers
announced that we couldn't fly till the following morning
because of technical problems. It was a really mean trick
but fear of terrorist attacks meant no one protested. We
had to leave the plane and were ushered to a hotel next to
the airport. What with the noise from planes, the late hour
and the stress caused by the knowledge we'd have to get up
at six in order not to miss our new flight, I barely got a wink.
The following morning I was a wreck.

The previous evening, before leaving for the airport, we'd
rung the MP to tell him of the positive results from our
investigations. However, as soon as he heard Borja's voice,
our client told him curtly "nothing by phone", and that he
expected to see us in his office as early as possible in the
morning. According to Borja, Lluís Font's voice sounded
very distressed. My brother tried to explain it had all been
a misunderstanding and that he could stop worrying about

the portrait, but the MP rudely cut him short in a tone we'd not heard before and we imagined it must be because he suspected his telephone was being tapped. In a harsh, imperious voice he told us to be in his office at nine a.m. sharp.

When they cancelled our flight, we had to ring him again to defer our appointment, but he insisted we go straight to his office from the airport. We had barely time to pass by Borja's place to drop off our cases and presents. Without even changing our clothes, we jumped into the Smart and headed for the Diagonal.

"Pep, I reckon the thing's taken a turn for the worse. The murder's hitting the headlines again."

"But there are no new revelations. And since the judge has decreed that the hearing should be in secret . . ."

"Then they've probably found some thing out that the newspapers haven't published yet. The MP must have his contacts among the judiciary, and it's very likely there are new developments," I suggested while we were still trying to park.

We finally found a space to park the Smart but with one thing and another we reached our appointment half an hour late. His secretary wasn't there and Lluís Font opened the door himself. We were shocked to see that the man who now welcomed us wasn't the same self-confident politician who'd contracted us a few weeks ago to keep an eye on his wife, nor was he the calm and collected bereaved husband we'd watched replying with such aplomb to the questions of the police while his wife's body lay theatrically on the carpet in his drawing room.

To begin with, his suit hung off him as if he'd shrunk, and he looked much the worse for wear. He was no longer the all-powerful MP, but a man running scared. He listened gravely to our explanations, but his attitude didn't change despite our good tidings. His face still looked as distressed as when he'd opened the door to us.

Rather than bringing him some relief, Borja's explanations deepened his disquiet. I saw that his eyes had the same vacant look as Montse's when she takes a valium, although in the MP's case there was something else that the valium – or whatever he'd taken – couldn't conceal. The look on the face of the man opposite us, as Borja had already suspected when speaking to him on the phone, belonged to a man running scared.

My brother gave him a blow by blow account of our activities in Paris (obviously omitting any mention of his old flame) and told him of the happy conclusion to our enquiries. As detectives, we weren't performing so badly.

"In short, the painter took a photograph of Lídia when she wasn't looking," our client said, visibly displeased.

"Apparently it happened in a train, some two years ago," explained Borja. "She must have fallen asleep and the painter took the opportunity to photograph her. Then he painted the portrait. Cécile Blanchart, the painter's friend, promised us she will try to get one of the photos he took, but I believe her all the same. Art connoisseurs in Paris know how Pau Ferrer works."

"It's an explanation that's too simple and surprising not to be true," I added. "It was also our bad luck the painter had had a stroke only a few days ago . . ."

"I expect if he doesn't survive, his paintings will leap in value," observed Borja, who thought of everything.

The MP shrugged his shoulders as if to say that at that precise moment he wasn't impressed in the least by that spin off. He seemed despondent. Leaning back on his chair he muttered sourly: "In other words, Pau Ferrer wasn't involved in Lídia's death. You don't think he's a suspect . . . In fact, the photograph explains everything," he conceded gloomily. "Lídia never travelled by train, and that's why I remember how once when she went to Paris (for reasons of work, she claimed), she came back in the Talgo. There was a strike of . . . air-traffic controllers, I don't remember exactly. She did that because we'd been invited to a gala banquet with the King, Queen and Prince in Pedralbes, and the President of the Generalitat, the Mayor and a few other MPs . . . Lídia didn't want to miss the reception, naturally. She had spent a fortune on her dress," he sighed sounding annoyed, "and besides she loved that kind of thing. So she decided to come back by high-speed train."

"You obviously remember it well . . ." said Borja.

"Lídia was in a temper for days. She spent the whole dinner complaining about the bags under her eyes and the fact she was exhausted. She even got the king into a stew over her journey. And obviously as he's so good-natured . . ."

"Not half!" Borja chimed in to endorse his flattery.

"So it all fits perfectly," I spoke up in an attempt to ensure the conversation didn't turn into a eulogy of the virtues of the monarchy. As a good republican, I'd started to twitch.

"Not entirely," Lluís Font shook his head and looked down. "The ambulance workers were right. Someone did poison Lídia."

He lit another cigarette and stiffened slightly in his chair. He was tense and felt uncomfortable, but his attitude didn't seem a result of his loss.

"I wasn't at all convinced, but it was confirmed by the tests," he said slowly. "It was the *marrons glacés*. Some of them were poisoned. You," he said addressing Borja, "were very lucky."

"I don't know what came over me in those circumstances. It must have been nerves . . ."

I saw Borja go slightly red, a colour he can't see. Eating the sweets or whatever they were while Mrs Font's body was lying dead had been one hell of a blunder. We still lived in hope that his greediness wouldn't lead to problems with the police or the judge.

"There is something else," said the MP, " that I'd better tell you." He took a long drag on his cigarette. "I didn't want to tell you on the phone because it's not a secure channel at the moment. I wanted to say," he said grimly, staring hard at us, "if you are thinking of taking this story to the press, I can assure you . . ."

Borja shot out of his chair, as if catapulted by a spring. He seemed very offended.

"Let's bury this here and now. I don't know what kind of people you think we are!" he exclaimed pretending to be highly indignant.

I followed suit and also got up, though somewhat less angrily. When the MP saw our reactions he immediately corrected himself and adopted a diplomatic tone of voice. He was in no position to threaten anyone.

"I didn't want to cause offence. I do apologize, Mr Masdéu. And to you, sir . . . I'm very sorry I doubted you, but you must understand that I'm at my wits' end. Journalists are after me all the time, and yesterday they broadcast a report on Lídia's death on one of those programmes they show on breakfast television that so many people watch. They even showed interviews with Yanbin, our housemaid . . ."

"It's disgusting!" exclaimed Borja sitting down again. "Of course, not everybody is like that . . ."

"No, of course not . . ." the MP agreed.

I wasn't at all clear that the idea hadn't passed through Borja's head. These programmes that feed on gossip and scandal have been the fashion for years. The chat and rumours that used to go no further than the bar, market or office have now become our main source of entertainment. People no longer read novels, crochet or go to political meetings to protest or put their demands. Nowadays, they like to spend weekends buying special offers in shopping centres, watching football all the time and then going to bed in the early hours after seeing a few sex and adultery dramas on telly. Even though the pariahs now get their moment of glory on reality shows, it's the scandals of the rich and the powerful that spark infinitely more interest, and all the more so if they come with a juicy crime attached.

"You mentioned there was something else . . ." I spoke up in order to break the uncomfortable silence that had descended after the MP had confessed his worries over our integrity. I was curious to know what was suddenly upsetting him.

The doorbell rang before the MP could answer. Our client gave a start and Borja and I realized his heart was beating at full pelt. He went pale, half-closed his eyes and, downcast, got up out of his chair muttering that he wasn't expecting anybody. He repeated this to himself three times as if that improvised litany would help quell his fears.

It was the judicial police. Two men and one woman in plainclothes: young, polite and pleasant. None looked like police or had the rough, bullying ways of the pigs of yesteryear. When they identified themselves, the MP was quite taken aback. They were carrying a search warrant from the judge.

"It's the procedure in such cases," said one of the policemen. He seemed very nice and his accent betrayed that he was from Lleida.

"We'll try not to take up too much of your time. We'll only be a minute, you'll see," said the woman with a would-be soothing smile as she glanced quickly round.

The other policeman, a rather scrawny young man wearing spectacles that looked too thick for a man of the law, hovered silently in one corner. He didn't even deign to look at us. Lluís Font introduced us yet again as his advisors and resigned himself to the fact they were about to turn his office upside down. He had no choice. When he realized it was a search, he looked relieved, as if it could have been much worse.

The police took their coats off, put on white, thin gloves, like the ones hairdressers and surgeons use, and started to search the room quite gingerly. The three of us remained silent though we couldn't avoid glancing furtively at the package behind the door.

They looked in every drawer and checked every scrap of paper. The police who had done the introductions spotted the huge package wrapped in brown paper. It was exactly where Borja had left it on the night the MP's sister-in-law had crashed down so dramatically from the flat upstairs. Although he didn't have to, the policeman asked for permission before he unwrapped it very, very carefully.

"So what is this?" he asked when he came face to face with the hideous sight of one of my mother-in-law's most dubious expressions of her artistic genius.

Lluís Font swallowed. His mind had gone blank. After seeing what was hanging on the walls of his house, I imagined he couldn't think of an excuse to justify possession of that monstrosity. In the full light of day, it was even worse than I remembered. As usual, Borja was the only one who kept his sang-froid and rescued the situation.

"Well, if it isn't the painting that supporter of yours gave you at the end of a meeting!" he exclaimed totally matter-of-fact, looking at the MP. "How thoughtful of you to want to hang it here. Of course you might want to change the frame. It doesn't go with your furniture . . ."

"Yes . . . No, quite . . ."

"It's signed by one 'J. Mir' . . ." the policeman remarked. "It's vaguely familiar. Don't you think?" he asked the policewoman.

She came over to take a closer look. Perhaps it was me, but I could swear that when she walked past Borja she almost lurched into him, regaling him with a smile that wasn't merely polite. Apart from being flirtatious, she was quite young.

"You certainly get a nice line in presents!" she exclaimed after scrutinizing the painting. "Joaquim Mir is one of the most important contemporary Catalan modernists. If it's genuine, this painting's worth a small fortune."

The three of us were struck dumb. She might be a policewoman, but that girl was out of her mind.

"What do you mean? It's an awful painting!" I interjected.

I couldn't tell them that "J. Mir" was the signature of my mother-in-law, Joana Mir, who, as far as I knew, wasn't related to the famous painter. You could bet Montse would one day split her sides when I told her about this mix-up, I thought. Her views on the painting that used to hang in our passage were as scathing as mine.

"If it is a Mir, one certainly cannot say it's awful," the woman opined. "Besides, in matters of taste everything is relative," she added solemnly.

Nobody felt like arguing with her. The six of us focussed back on the painting. It was a kind of landscape with mountains, trees and village houses. A few clouds floated quite gracelessly over a postcard blue sky. The foreground was dominated by shapes pretending to be shrubs with flowers of different colours and sizes, all species that were unrecognizable.

While the policewoman took the painting to the window and examined it expertly, her colleague explained that the young woman had a degree in art history. As I already knew my mother-in-law's painting backwards, I concentrated on the woman. Although she was dressed unobtrusively, her clothes were one size too small for her, thus emphasising her generous curves that must have caused more than one colleague on night duty to look up. The policeman with the Lleida accent said he was an anthropologist while his colleague, who was still scrutinizing the files piled on the table, was, he explained, a mathematician. He'd not said a word since he walked in.

"If you don't have any paperwork to certify that this painting is legally yours, we shall have to take it with us," said the woman after seeming momentarily flummoxed. "You can't keep a Mir in a corner like that!" And added: "Besides, there were some problems with Joaquim Mir paintings not long ago."

"That's true," her colleague corroborated.

"All I needed!" The MP looked at us half in despair, half in anger. "Listen," he addressed the policewoman, "I had no idea . . ."

I'd had enough and jumped up: "But this painting is the work of! —"

Borja cut me dead, "Yes, Eduard, we know all that! The woman who gave Mr Font the painting probably didn't know what it was," he said, raising his eyebrows and opening his eyes wide.

"But! . . ."

"You know that fine art, like elephants, has never been your forte," he rasped as if to say I should shut my trap once and for all. "I think it would be best if the police took the painting with them and investigate whatever they have to investigate," he said, seeking our client's approval. "I'm positive this business will soon be cleared up."

"Can you give us the name of the lady who gave you this present?" asked the young policewoman, taking out her notebook and pencil.

"The fact is . . . I don't really know," the MP confessed. "A lot of people come to meetings and say hello to me. People I don't know . . . I get given the odd gift . . ." he improvised.

"I see . . . in that case we'll have to take the painting. We need to check one or two things . . ."

"As you wish. But you are quite mistaken . . ." Lluís Font didn't seem very sure of himself.

The police strode off carrying the painting but took none of his papers. If Lluís Font had another elephant in that office, the police hadn't found it. Borja's certainly very clever, but he's particularly adept when it comes to the business of hiding pachyderms.

When we were alone once more with our client, who was reaching the end of his tether, I explained as best I could that the painting in question was the work of my mother-in-law who just happened to be called Joana Mir. I guessed the MP was thinking we'd used his office to keep a fake or stolen painting out of sight. I don't know if he found my explanation at all convincing.

"I didn't really believe it was a Mir," he finally admitted. "But that girl thinks it is . . ." he said looking anxious.

"Don't worry," said Borja. "An expert won't certify that it's a Mir because it isn't." And he added in a shocked tone of voice: "I don't know what universities are coming to! . . . Fancy not being able to distinguish a Mir from an amateur's work! . . ."

"Yes, I don't know what young people today learn at university . . ." I said. Lluís Font looked at us without blinking. "And these young graduates end up joining the police! . . ."

Borja used the opportunity to side with the MP.

"This country's going down the drain. All this autonomy and sodding—"

But Lluís Font wasn't in the mood for political chit-chat. It was clear his mind was on other worries and the last thing he wanted was to tangle with Borja in an argument about blueprints for nation-states.

"What about that other matter you wanted to tell us about?" I asked changing the subject.

"I don't know about you, but I need a whisky."

Before we could respond, Mr Lluís Font got up and, with a glance, invited us to follow in his wake.

16

He steered us to a small, elegant and expensive bar. We sat over in a corner and my brother and the MP both ordered scotch. At that time of day, exhausted as I was by our journey, I opted for whatever they had on tap. However, they only served bottled and imported beer and the waiter scowled at me.

"The police found something in my house," Lluís Font announced after downing a big gulp of whisky.

Borja and I were all ears.

He went on: "It is," he paused, " a rather delicate matter."

I wondered if there was anything that wasn't delicate in all this.

"To do with your wife's murder?" asked Borja.

"Perhaps."

I glanced warily around to check no one near us was taking an interest in our table. The beautiful people sat near us were too preoccupied with themselves and their respective conversations. Everybody was whispering. Some were talking quietly on their mobiles while others leered over the woman sat next to them. Four aggressive executives were arguing over business matters while, on the adjacent table, some women dripping in jewels openly criticized their respective husbands. The waiters had trained their ears not to hear, or at least to simulate that they didn't. The place reeked of good wine, American cigarettes and expensive eau de colognes.

Lluís Font decided to tell us what hadn't yet appeared in the press.

"The police," he began, "discovered that Lídia had kept files on various people in the house, containing, let's say, compromising information . . ." He paused and lit a cigarette. "I knew nothing about this, I promise you. If I had, I'd have got there before the police did."

Borja didn't flinch at this new revelation. "You mean that there were people who had very good reason to eliminate your wife."

"Exactly. That's what the police think," he replied despondently.

"What have they done with the files?" Borja continued.

"They took them away for further examination."

He explained how his wife kept the reports in one of her desk drawers. The police had broke into them and scrutinized the contents. Apart from cash and papers related to her work, they found some files that were highly suspicious.

"I deduce," said Borja, adopting his newly cultivated detective tone of voice, "that basically they contained dirty linen . . ."

"You could put it that way." The MP sighed. "Luckily there were only three files. But there were no names, only initials and they were quite short. I identified the initials that appeared on two of the files, but I don't recognize those on the third. And I've been turning it over in my mind for days," he admitted.

"Whose initials have you identified?" I asked. "They might give us a lead."

"One set belong to Nieves Dalmau, the woman you probably saw in the Sandor. She's Enrique Dalmau's wife," he clarified, in case we didn't know. "We are the two candidates for the post of party secretary-general. He is more rightwing and is much more popular than me with some sectors of the party, especially outside Catalonia. But of course that's not where the votes will be cast . . ."

"And the other files?"

"One carries the initials "S.M.". It contains a very short report which just says they hadn't found anything. There wasn't even an address or telephone number. Nothing to help identify the individual concerned, as with the others. I can't think who it might be."

"It's probably the man we saw in the Zurich," I suggested, prompted by the association of ideas. "It really looked as if your wife, may she rest in peace, had thrown a bucket of icy water over that poor guy," I said, warily remembering that exchange.

"Yes, but the report said he was clean. It seems very unlikely that he was the murderer," the MP retorted.

"You're quite right," I had to admit. "What about the third file? You say you recognized those initials."

Lluís Font said nothing and looked down at the floor. I also noticed he was gritting his teeth.

"It was about you, I suppose?" murmured Borja.

"Yes," he nodded laconically.

Borja looked at me and sat up in his chair looking pleased with himself. He'd hit bull's eye. Lluís Font finished his whisky and spoke even more softly.

"The truth is that Lídia knew her sister and I . . ." He didn't finish his sentence.

"Good heavens!" I exclaimed, taking pains not to blurt out a "fuck" or a "shit" in such a refined watering hole.

"This makes life even more complicated," was Borja's comment. "I suppose the police have now added you to their list of suspects."

"You suppose rightly. They seem to think the odds are now stacked against me," he sighed.

The three of us sat in silence and Borja ordered another round while we tried to fit that fresh information in the puzzle the case was turning into. The waiter made a mistake, and also brought me a whisky rather than another beer. I must have looked as if I needed one.

"I take it that we can discount "S.M.", whether it's man or woman, since your wife had no way to blackmail him."

"Now just listen up, I didn't kill my wife!" he whispered, clearly rattled. "I didn't even know she suspected that Sílvia and I . . . I give you my word."

I didn't know whether to believe him.

"The fact is, poisoning is a very female method," noted Borja. "The police must know that."

As my brother doesn't read the newspapers, he didn't know that poisoning people is back in fashion with the Russians.

"The thing is, I know Nieves Dalmau!" the MP confessed. "I find it hard to believe that her intellect is up to it. One has to plan a thing like that and have at least one accomplice. Remember how a man delivered the parcel and he didn't belong to any messenger service; Yanbin is sure about that. And naturally it wasn't Enrique because he'd have found disguising himself as a motorcyclist a little difficult. He weighs almost a hundred kilos!"

"I expect she contracted somebody to do that. A professional," I suggested.

Borja shook his head.

"We know," my brother replied, showing the fruits of our week spent trailing the victim, "that Mrs Font didn't have a bodyguard. A professional would have shot her in the middle of the street or put a bomb in her car. He wouldn't have risked delivering personally a box of *marrons glacés* from one of Barcelona's most famous patisseries with a poisoned chestnut and a few handwritten words on the kitschiest of Christmas cards."

"No, you're right . . ." I had to concede.

Borja was becoming a dab hand at making deductions.

Lluís Font was right: this was a delicate matter and got more complicated by the day. What had begun as innocent suspicion about a possible cuckolding was turning into a crime that was tricky for the police and juicy for the press, not to mention the fact that it could destroy our client's political career. The way things were going, all we needed was Alfred Hitchcock mixing a cocktail behind the bar.

"I'm very worried," he confessed in a cold sweat. "If the police persist in thinking that I was involved in . . . I need your help."

"What do you want us to do?" asked Borja solicitously.

"I want you to go and talk to my contact. He will tell you how the investigations are going and what the police have been able to find out. He promised me he would. He owes me a favour."

He took a scrap of paper from his pocket and jotted down a name and telephone number. Borja put it in his pocket.

"We'll ring today and arrange to see him."

"One last thing: we'll bury Lídia on Monday. The judge has at last given us permission to hold the funeral. I would like you to be there and keep an eye out for any strange behaviour. The murderer may come to the ceremony."

"You can rely on us," said Borja. "Where will it be held?"

"In the church in Sarrià, at five."

And he added apparently sincerely: "I swear I had nothing to do with Lídia's death. I agree we weren't the happiest of couples, but we had lives and interests in common . . ."

"The police may be thinking that a divorce wouldn't have

done your political career much good . . ." said my brother, playing devil's advocate.

"If Lídia was upset because she knew I . . . I mean we'd have found another way to sort that. We," he was referring of course to people of his social class, "do not divorce just like that. The family is holy."

"You bloody hypocrite!" I thought to myself. I'm not one to moralize, but at least I don't put on a performance every Sunday at mass and wave little flags in the cathedral when the Pope pays a visit.

"All the same, I don't understand why in the circumstances you decided to contract us to investigate whether your wife was branching out . . ." I responded provocatively.

"I thought that if Lídia did find out some day that her sister and I were . . . that is . . . I mean"

"That you thought it would be useful to have an ace up your sleeve?" said Borja trying not to sound too cruel.

"Well, put that way it seems very unpleasant . . . Sometimes when one has a certain standing, things are not so simple . . ." he replied, looking for sympathy from my brother.

One of my legs had gone to sleep from so much sitting and I could hardly feel my bum. It was past three o'clock and my belly had been demanding fodder for some time: I didn't even want to think about the storm waiting for me when I got home a day later than I'd promised Montse. Luckily, our client decided to end the meeting there and then and asked for the bill. By this time, there was hardly a soul left in the bar.

Once out in the street, our client insisted we should speak as soon as possible to his contact and keep him up-to-date with how the investigation was going. Whether or not he'd killed his wife, it was obvious the MP wasn't willing to bet on a roll of the dice.

17

As the following day was Saturday and we were still worn out, Borja and I decided to give ourselves a day's holiday. Besides it was New Year's Eve, and Montse had been broadcasting for days that we'd have a special dinner party at home. She'd invited her mother who always fell asleep before the clock chimed twelve, her sister and two married couples of our age, her friends rather than mine. After a short restorative siesta, I spent the rest of the afternoon doing penance helping her in the house. Luckily, the present I brought her from Paris – a very pretty, lilac silk shawl, that Borja helped me choose – and the promise that we'd both soon spend a long, romantic weekend there helped defuse her anger.

"I think you've miscounted," I told Montse as I was laying the table. "There's a plate too many."

Borja, obviously. Lola had invited him. Merche would be eating grapes with her husband, to keep up appearances, so Borja was free. On the one hand, I was happy to see in the New Year at home with my brother, but on the other I worried about my sister-in-law's reaction. Borja didn't know, but Lola had renewed hopes regarding the feelings she aroused in my brother.

The two appeared, very elegantly dressed, at nine-thirty sharp. Borja seemed rather tense and had brought a bouquet for Montse; Lola was also on edge although there was a big smile on her face. She was less made up than usual and looked really pretty.

"At least take off your slippers and put your shoes on! . . ." whispered Montse, who'd also dressed up for the occasion, while we headed to the kitchen to prepare the drinks.

I took off my cords and checked shirt and put on something more stylish – though still no tie – in order to please my wife. The dinner was delicious and we had a wonderful time. Thanks to the good offices of the cava I managed to forget the complicated tangle embroiling my brother and me, even with him sat there opposite me and next to Lola. After choking on our grapes as we watched the clock strike twelve on Channel 3, we all rehearsed our New Year good intentions: I was set to give up smoking and Montse (who doesn't smoke, or so she says) was going to be more patient and take life more philosophically. Borja declared that he would read the newspapers from time to time to find out what was going on in the world, and Lola promised she'd finally get round to throwing away all the clutter she'd accumulated at home (I don't know whether Borja realized, but I saw this as her way of insinuating she was making room for the new clutter about to arrive).

We enjoyed a peaceful soirée, the only moment of tension arising at four minutes past twelve when my brother's mobile rang and he got up and went into the lobby to answer the call discreetly. Lola tried to ignore him, and Montse gave me the evil eye, as if I were to blame. Borja came back after a couple of minutes and explained quite naturally that it was his aunt from Santander who always called to wish him a Happy New Year. Neither Lola nor Montse nor I believed a word of it, but it was thoughtful of him to invent an excuse so Lola would feel less upset. Merche's untimely call was all forgotten when Borja put his hand around her waist and said something to her that made her smile.

Lola and Borja disappeared around half past one. Montse's friends soon followed them. My mother-in-law was already asleep, and my wife and I went straight to bed. I slept like a log and the next day, when I woke up, it was gone twelve. Montse had been thoughtful enough not to wake me up.

I heard nothing from Borja or Lola for the whole day. It seemed like a welcome burst of normality after a month beset by sudden surprises. We listened to the usual New Year Vienna waltzes on television – while I breakfasted, Montse and my mother-in-law ironed and folded clothes –and, just before two we all put our coats on to go out for lunch (thanks to the generous payments courtesy of Lluís Font we could allow ourselves that luxury this year). Later in the afternoon, the twins, keen to stake their independence, went to a friend's house, while we accompanied my mother-in-law home and took Arnau to the cinema. On our return, Arnau soon fell asleep, and Montse and I frolicked on the sofa while we made plans for the Easter holidays, now that our finances seemed to be in a better state and the bills weren't piling up.

Only one episode with my mother-in-law slightly upset the New Year's Day peace. It was just before we went out to eat, when the issue of the painting in the passage re-entered our conversation (the previous day we'd told her the frame had broken and it was being repaired). Joana hadn't swallowed this and I could hear her fussing as she walked by the empty wall on her way to the kitchen. Hoping to avoid any awkwardness I mentioned casually the way her initials, J.M., happened to coincide with the famous painter's. I shouldn't have opened my mouth.

"Of course I knew!" she said, raising her voice in a mildly surprised tone. "Why do you think I sign my paintings like that?"

"What do you mean?" I asked not sure where this was all heading.

"Well, you know, I imitate Joaquim Mir's signature!" she said, as if it were obvious.

My heart almost gave up on me. I don't know if I went white or red, but I was baffled for a moment trying to pretend I'd not heard what I'd just heard. I had no desire to deal with the consequences of what my mother-in-law was insinuating, but finally I took a deep breath and asked her: "What do you mean 'I imitate Joaquim Mir's signature'? You aren't suggesting . . ."

"Well," she started, as if it were the most normal thing in the world, "I didn't know how to sign with a paint brush . . . And as our initials coincide and the picture I gave you is a copy of one of his . . ."

"The picture is what?!" I exclaimed.

"But I told you . . ." she protested. "You never listen to me . . ."

My mother-in-law sighed deeply and looked at me as if I wasn't right in the head.

"We once went to the museum in Montserrat with the people from the academy" – she was alluding to the art workshop in her neighbourhood, where she's been going twice a week ever since she was widowed – "and I bought a postcard of one of his pictures. Naturally, as the postcard was very small, I couldn't make an exact copy, but I got his signature from the big poster in the academy." And she added, "I did practise a bit though, you know, because I wanted it to look right."

"The last straw," I thought as I imagined the little scene there'd be when I recounted this surreal mess to the Honourable Lluís Font MP.

Nonetheless, after the initial shock and thinking it over for a few seconds, I decided not to give too much importance to my mother-in-law's confession. I reckoned that any art expert would realize that the canvas painted by Joana was no Mir, however well she'd imitated his signature. It was absurd: completely ridiculous. As I could do nothing about it right then, I put Joana's surprise revelation to the back of my mind and concentrated on celebrating New Year's Day like a normal human being, that is, by stuffing my gut in a good restaurant with my wife, my mother-in-law and the children. The following day I'd have to go to the funeral of a woman I didn't know, and that prospect hardly thrilled me, then on Tuesday we had to meet a Mosso d'Esquadra off the record following the instructions of an important politician who had perhaps done his wife in and who'd had a painting confiscated – a painting that bore the fake signature of a famous painter. I waxed nostalgic momentarily for the uncomplicated life I'd led as a boring bank clerk, until I observed Montse humming as she got ready to go out, and thought I'd not seen her looking so happy for years, with her plait down to her waist, her long skirt and first wrinkles, about which she had no great complexes. I asked Joana to look after Arnau for a while, went into our bedroom and drew the curtains. Before Montse had time to put her tights on, I slowly locked the door and slipped them off her, giving her no time to protest.

18

The rich are even lucky with the weather, I remember musing while I was eating breakfast and looking out of the window to see what kind of day was in store and deciding what clothes to put on.

The day had dawned with a cloudy sky the morning of Lídia Font's funeral, but it was a light grey that didn't threaten to unleash a storm. It drizzled from time to time, enough to persuade people to take their umbrellas out, but not enough to spoil anyone's hair. It was a sad, tranquil day, the weather best suited to funerals, I reckon. A sun-scorched day doesn't really go with this kind of ceremony and a black stormy sky can transform a burial into a much more macabre ceremony than is reasonable. The day we buried my father-in-law, may he rest in peace, it chucked it down and there was thunder, lightning and a hurricane that turned the procession to the Montjuïc cemetery into a grim queue of cars and taxis in which the mourners cowered, sheltering from the ravages of the blackened sky. The day we buried Aunt Júlia, on the other hand, fell in August, the sun shone very brightly and the ceremony was rather lacklustre because as soon as it was over we all rushed to the nearest bar for drinks to avoid dehydrating and ended up having aperitifs, with olives and tapas. That's why I reckon wintry weather is much more appropriate: a solemn image of black umbrellas being raised over dark suits, but not a violent downpour forcing people to run hither and thither, and no bearers rushing to place the bier in the hearse as a curtain of water descended, afraid the coffin might slip from their hands and slide along the ground (which must have happened more than once).

Mass was at five sharp, the bull-fighting hour. I ate lunch at home with Montse and the children, and my brother picked me up just before four. This time he wasn't driving the Smart, as he didn't think it was the car for a funeral.

At four thirty, the square was a mass of umbrellas waiting for the priest to open the church doors. I'd followed Borja's advice and wore a black tie. My suit was the usual dark grey Armani that I'd worn so much of late it needed dry-cleaning, and I had on some new shoes. My brother also wore a dark suit, a white shirt and black tie, a little over the top if you ask me. My sky blue shirt was quite restrained enough and thankfully didn't jar with the sober dress of the mourners. Nonetheless, I did notice the quite extreme black numbers some bejewelled ladies were flaunting under their half unbuttoned mink coats.

As it was Monday and the Christmas holidays, there was hardly any traffic for that time of day. My brother and I had opened our umbrellas, not so much to fend off the fine drizzle as to shield us from the curious gazes of the people there. At this kind of funeral, which involves a famous or public figure, one diversion people enjoy is watching and commenting on who has come and who hasn't. That final farewell, in certain echelons of society, still indicates the relative importance of the deceased and the social position occupied by their nearest and dearest.

Obviously it wasn't a good day because it fell in the middle of the holidays, but I'm sure more than one person had driven down to Barcelona from a ski resort to be present at

Lídia Font's final rites. Our client was sufficiently important for some individuals to feel obliged to attend. The President of the Generalitat and the Mayor of the city, however, were not in the funeral cortège. They had sent apologies claiming they hadn't wanted their institutional presence to disrupt the family nature of the ceremony, likewise the national leader of the MP's party. This was clearly an excuse, because there were some three hundred people crowded into the square, and, as far as I know, only kings and sultans have that many relatives. I imagine that none of the distinguished absentees wanted to be in a photograph that might connect him, albeit indirectly, to the unresolved matter of the murder. Logically enough, there were lots of journalists.

The ceremony, mass included, was moving, but above all it was drawn-out. As not everyone could find a seat in church, the ladies sat and the men stood. My new shoes were hurting and the funeral felt like an eternity. At the end, those in attendance filed past to give their condolences to the family, who stood in a row by the altar: the MP was first in the retinue with his daughter on his right. Next to her stood a cohort of relatives in mourning who all looked on impassively. I recognized Sílvia Vilalta, and didn't think she looked exactly grief-stricken.

I stayed the course rather well until I had to offer my hand to Núria Font, the daughter of the deceased. She was a fair-haired, scrawny fifteen year-old who kept drying her tears. She seemed very upset and leaned on her father, who was holding her arm. She was as pallid as her mother must have been, and although she wasn't crying when I gave her my hand, her eyes and nose were red and sore. Her hand was icy, and when I offered her my condolences quite timidly

211

she thanked me like a robot. She seemed about to faint and the sudden memory of my own parents' death hit me like a lumbar punch and made my eyes moisten.

I was thirteen years old and I didn't go to the funeral. Borja was still in hospital recovering from concussion. Although I'd only a broken arm and a couple of cracked ribs, I was forced to stay at home with my relatives from Soria. Aunt Teresa, Uncle Faustino and I, dressed in obligatory black, waited sorrowfully for the other relatives who'd gone to the cemetery. My aunt sobbed silently and dried her tears on a cotton handkerchief, muttering from time to time between sobs: "It was God's will."

He could stick his will you know where, I'd have retorted now, but at the time, obviously, I said nothing. Uncle Faustino, sturdy and taciturn, simply looked at his watch, stared at the ground and said nothing. He was my father's brother and was completely distraught. I swallowed my tears, devastated and in a rage because I'd not been allowed to go to the cemetery and bid farewell to my parents. The hospitalized Borja was still unaware of what had happened.

Uncle Faustino suddenly got up: "Fuck bloody God! . . . If I catch the bastard driving that car, I'll kill him!" he exclaimed in his Aragonese accent.

He hid his head in his hands and began to cry disconsolately. After a while, he got up again and said: "It's much better if things don't stay pent up here," he said tapping his chest. "You've got to get over these blows, what ever it takes . . ." And he went straight to the kitchen and came back with a bottle of cognac and three small glasses.

It was the first time I'd tasted real alcohol (wine and fizzy pop and the half a glass of champagne we were allowed to drink on special occasions hardly counted). I felt queasy and started to cry as disconsolately as Uncle Faustino had a few moments earlier. It was the first time I'd managed to cry like that from the time they told me in hospital that both parents had died instantaneously in the accident.

In the months to come I spent each night trying to relive that funeral I hadn't attended. I imagined the priest, the coffins, the people dressed in black and the laments. I saw my brother and myself receiving condolences, and also the biers being dropped deep inside the dark niche while we all wept miserably. Before falling asleep exhausted, I'd remember what Uncle Faustino had said – "You've got to get over these blows" – and cried and cried until I fell asleep. The idea of doing in the pisshead who'd forced my parents over a precipice on the Garraf corniche also went round my head. I ate almost nothing, refused to go to school and spent every day crying and sleeping.

Once again it was my brother who took hold of the situation. Initially, when he recovered from concussion and was allowed home, he behaved the same way as me. He cried all the time, went round in a sleepwalking daze and wanted to be by himself. Seeing Pep in such a state upset me as much as remembering my parents were dead and would never come back. We were both distraught, but I knew that if my brother, who was the more resilient of the two of us, didn't recover from this blow, I never would. Finally I fell ill and a raging temperature kept me delirious in bed for three days. When I came round, Pep was his old self and assumed, as usual, the role of elder brother. For a few months we dedicated body and soul to trying to find out – quite unsuccessfully – the identity of the drink driver so we could beat him up and return him to his Maker. I suppose that was our first job as detectives, although it was a disastrous failure. Over time my brother and I managed somehow to overcome the tragedy and get on with our lives, but I've always wondered if that concussion did any lasting damage and what went through Borja's head the three days I was so ill.

He never goes to funerals, he admitted to me one day. Apparently it's the only thing he doesn't feel able to face. This was why he stayed outside the church, a move no one could misinterpret because there simply wasn't room for everyone inside and he wasn't the only one stood in the square during the ceremony. Consequently, when I spotted the man with whom Lídia Font had conversed in the Zurich among the crowds filling the church, I couldn't alert my brother.

It happened right at the end, while I was queuing up to offer the family my condolences. When I spotted him, four or five people were in front of me and I could hardly rush off in hot pursuit in full view of everybody. I waited patiently and enacted the ritual handshake and condolences, hoping I'd be able to catch the man when I left the church. It was my bad luck that the person in front lingered at least a couple of minutes with the MP while I became increasingly agitated, as I saw the man I'd seen in the Zurich slip away into the crowd.

When I emerged, the memory of my parents still churning round my brain, I tried unsuccessfully to locate him among the crowds packing the square. I walked despairingly over to where my brother stood. He was chatting in relaxed fashion to Mariona Castany, but I had no qualms about interrupting their conversation to tell Borja what had happened.

"He's here! I saw him in church!" I said excitedly.

"Hello, Eduard. It's such a tragedy, isn't it? We were just saying to Borja . . ." Mariona seemed put out by my impertinent interjection.

I greeted her properly and apologized for my rudeness. Our little group was joined by another of the acquaintances of Mariona, who embarked on the introductions *comme il faut* while I got more and more stressed. In the meantime men in grey loaded the coffin and wreaths into the hearse. People started to drift off and the square soon emptied out.

"But how could you let him get away!" Borja sighed angrily when I finally managed to explain whom I'd spotted. "He's the only lead we have! . . ."

"It was just that I was in the queue, and thought it would look rude . . ."

"Lluís Font would have understood."

"Yes, but the other people . . ."

"What the hell! You don't even know them! . . ." And he was right.

I don't know why I was being such a stickler for decorum. I suppose it's because when I'm in this kind of company I get nervous and try to imitate the way Borja behaves so as not to put my foot in it, which is far from easy when you consider the stacks of unspoken codes at play that are totally alien to me. But I can't deny I'd let our only lead get away and I felt like a real dumbo.

"Well, at least we know he came to the funeral. Someone here must know the guy!" said Borja.

"I expect only Lídia Font knew him. He's probably a nobody . . ." I said half-heartedly.

"If he were a nobody, Mrs Font wouldn't have bothered to go down to the plaça de Catalunya to talk to him on a Friday evening, right?" he argued bad-temperedly.

"I suppose you're right," I conceded. "I'm really sorry, you know."

"OK, let's forget it. It's history now. And we've got work to do."

My brother may not have any other virtues, but he never bears a grudge. When I make a mistake, which is more often than I would like, he'll first react like a harpy but he doesn't let it smoulder on. As far as I can recall, he's never really rubbed my face in my mistakes, and some have been quite scandalous.

While I'd been acting the fool in church and letting our main suspect escape, my brother hadn't wasted his time. At nine, after we'd been home for a change of clothes, we met Mariona in Flash Flash, a laid-back restaurant that's managed to retain its Seventies Pop-Art style without seeming old-fashioned. It's near the centre of town and specializes in omelettes, hamburgers and salads. It's a haunt of the well-heeled classes of Barcelona and has the advantage that you can't book a table. Borja wasn't sure whether Mariona had made an rendezvous with him there in order to confide some juicy titbit or to extract one from him, but he insisted I should accompany him and use the opportunity to give him a detailed description of the man I'd seen in the Zurich and now at the funeral.

"Poor Lídia, what a coincidence!" Mariona opened fire. "It's less than a month since we were talking about her. Do you remember?"

"Yes, of course. A real coincidence! The world's going from bad to worse . . ." said Borja trying to handle the situation without showing his cards. "There are so many lunatics out there! . . ."

"She ate some poisoned sweets apparently . . ." Mariona let slip casually.

216

The police had told journalists they were sweets not *marrons glacés*.

"So the newspapers said," I said, knowing full well my brother's tactics when he felt like taking people on a wild goose chase.

"It's rather strange, you know . . ." continued Mariona. "I mean it must have been a lunatic . . ." And she added sarcastically, "I didn't know nutcases were that sophisticated."

"Yes, it is very peculiar," Borja allowed.

By that time there was only one table free in Flash Flash and it was quite noisy. Even so, Mariona lowered her voice.

"So? How did it all turn out? Did or didn't she have a lover-boy?"

She'd finally decided to ask the question that was burning her lips.

"You were right, Mariona," said Borja as he tucked into an aubergine omelette. "Lídia had nothing going on. Her husband dreamt up that little drama all by himself."

"I reckon it wasn't quite a drama, you know, more a . . . I suppose you found out. As I see you're on such good terms with Lluís . . ."

"What do you mean?" he asked feigning surprise.

"Shall we ask for another bottle of wine?" suggested my brother's friend rather than replying to his question. "I don't know why," she smiled regally, "but funerals always make me thirsty."

As the model gentleman, Borja asked the waiter to bring a second bottle of vintage wine with a price tag to stand your hair on end. It was delicious. My brother waited patiently for the wine to be poured before resuming the conversation. He didn't want to appear impatient.

"I don't know what you meant by whether we knew . . ." Borja returned gently to the matter in hand.

"Well, just that Lluís is seeing Sílvia, his sister-in-law. But that's not news to anyone, of course. It's common knowledge."

This was totally unexpected. Our client's confused confession had led us to think that the affair was still a well-kept secret and that, except for those involved (and obviously more recently the police) nobody was aware of the MP's incestuous little fling. Mariona Castany's revelation – a woman who never ceased to astonish – changed everything.

"He doesn't seem to think that," Borja ventured boldly. "In fact, he's convinced nobody knows he and his sister-in-law . . ."

"Poor Lluís is a little ingenuous at times! . . ." she smiled. "Sílvia made sure she broadcast it to all and sundry. That's why she fell in with him, so she could spread the good tidings and undermine Lídia. Sílvia knew full well what an interest Lídia took in her husband's career."

When she saw the dumbfounded looks on our faces, she added: "Sílvia's had it in for her sister for years. I reckon she's never forgotten the nasty trick she played on her over Carlitos Carbonell. The poor girl must be very much in love, but fancy having the patience to wait all these years . . ."

"Now I really don't know what you're talking about, Mariona. I've been living abroad for so long . . ." whispered Borja.

"I'm referring to Sílvia and Carlitos, the heir to the Carbonells. Of course the Carbonells were practically bankrupt, so 'heir' is purely metaphorical. The fact is Sílvia Vilalta and Carlitos were about to get married. There'd not been any formal engagement, but everyone thought it was serious and they'd soon be officially betrothed. The Vilaltas were pleased enough, because although Carlitos wouldn't come into money he was a nice young man and his family was still well connected, particularly in Madrid. And as Sílvia had always been a rather strange girl . . ."

"That's right," I said, remembering the incident with the Cuban.

"Lídia carried on until silly Carlitos became completely besotted, broke up with Sílvia and began going out with her. Sílvia couldn't compete with a stunningly beautiful woman like Lídia. Not that Sílvia was ugly, but, of course, Lídia was much cleverer and far more scheming."

"But that's ancient history," I said. "Besides, Mrs Font and this Carlitos never married."

"Of course they didn't! They lasted a couple of months. She sent him packing without even a goodbye. But naturally after Carlitos had treated Sílvia so badly, it was impossible for them to get back on speaking terms."

"Sílvia must have really flipped," Borja suggested.

"Apparently," she said almost whispering, "she tried to commit suicide by swallowing her mother's sleeping pills. The family covered it up, of course, and she's had it in for her sister ever since. I don't suppose for one minute that she was the only one."

"In other words, Lídia Font has her enemies," concluded Borja.

"As many as she has admirers."

When we were eating our desserts, Borja asked me to describe to Mariona the man I'd seen in the Zurich. I did as I was told, but she didn't seem to recognize him. The initials "S.M." didn't mean anything to her either.

"I'll give it some thought. You two are obviously on to something, aren't you," she asked inviting us to let her in on our secrets.

"I'll let you know one of these days," Borja replied with a wink, "but not right now. Trust me."

Mariona seemed disappointed but didn't persist. She wasn't the kind of woman who goes around prying into everyone's secrets, although she made it known that we owed her a favour. We'd clearly aroused her curiosity.

As it was getting late and we were tired, we asked for the bill. Mariona went as if to search her bag for her elegant Hermès wallet where she keeps a single exclusive card with no limit. Borja stopped her and quickly took out his wallet, which was thicker than usual that night.

"No, no, Mariona. This one's mine." And he put several notes on the table. "And to change the subject to something that has nothing to do with your cousin, do you know a painter by the name of Pau Ferrer? I've been told his paintings are a good investment."

I assumed Borja wanted to find out if by any chance Mariona was up to speed on the portrait and the MP's suspicions.

"Pau Ferrer? Well, naturally . . . I was introduced to him once at an exhibition. But I didn't buy anything. I suppose because I didn't really like his work."

"And what's your opinion of him?"

"Ugh, middle class! . . ."

And she looked at me rather embarrassed, knowing she could never go back and amend that ever so sincere, spontaneous answer.

19

Eudald Masoliver, Lluís Font's contact, was a Mosso
d'Esquadra, one of our very own home-grown Catalan
policemen. Borja had phoned him, and, after deliberating
and trying to put him off, he'd finally agreed to meet us on
Tuesday at 8 p.m. He didn't seem overenthusiastic about
spying for Lluís Font, and even less so about having to do
so through us.

Masoliver was waiting for us at the time agreed in the
cafeteria in the Corte Inglés on the plaça de Catalunya. My
brother had refused point blank to go in the Smart because
it's always impossible to park in the centre and so we'd
taken a taxi. It was only three days to January 6 and that part
of the city was crammed with people buying presents and
with gawping tourists in shorts clogging up the pavements.
There wasn't room to swing a cat in the Corte Inglés and
not a single empty table in the cafeteria on the top floor.
A few years ago, while the champions of independence
burned buses in the square and fought it out with the riot
police, that cafeteria had turned into an improvised box at
the opera from which bystanders – and I suppose the secret
police – gazed down on the spectacle.

As we didn't know one another and we had no idea what
Masoliver looked like, he'd agreed with Borja to put a copy
of *La plaça del diamant* on his table. It was unlikely that two
people would coincide on the same day at the same time
with that novel in that big department store cafeteria. We

saw lots of shopping bags around, but no books, except for the one our contact had brought with him. Borja reckoned that three men seated at a table amid the noise and bustle wouldn't stand out if they didn't stay too long.

Thanks to the lack of interest people in this country have in reading books ever since the censors disappeared, we located him very easily. Masoliver must have been about thirty and was tall and broad, as befits a policeman, although he also looked as if he could be a university student. We were beginning to be shocked by the fact that all the policemen we came across looked like students rather than famous boxers.

The young man appeared ill at ease, but he was handsome and all the girls looked at him out of the corner of their eyes. After we'd done the introductions, he took a black folder out of a plastic FNAC bag and asked us to open it. He said the file inside was for us. He immediately put the folder back into the bag.

"I've photocopied the main documentation on the case," he said rather brusquely. "You won't find my fingerprints on any of these papers. And should you decide to start putting it around that I was the one who gave you this information . . ."

"No need to worry on that count. We'll be most careful. Besides, we're all in this together . . ." said Borja putting him at his ease.

The policeman sighed and glanced around.

"I owed Mr Font this favour. As I expect you know, he gave me a hand when I needed one," he said sounding rather embarrassed. He too seemed stressed.

You could understand why. If his superiors found out what he was up to, Eudald Masoliver would have to face serious consequences. The other side of the coin was that they could accuse us of bribing a man of the law, even though we were doing so as intermediaries for a third party. Despite the risk we were running, we were thrilled to see such a fat dossier, the contents of which would reveal where the suspicions of the police were pointing.

"Right, I must be off," said Masoliver. "You have to keep these papers somewhere secure. Or better still: burn them once you've read them." And he added, looking very worried, "My wife's pregnant . . . Please don't get me into any trouble."

"You don't need to worry in the slightest," pronounced Borja in the confident tone of a man of integrity. "Congratulations, by the way."

"Do you know whether it's a boy or a girl?" I asked trying to be pleasant.

"Goodbye, gentlemen." Masoliver scarpered as quickly as he could.

Borja and I decided to take a peek at the papers there and then. Surrounded as we were by tourists and teenagers licking ice creams and sending text messages, it certainly wasn't prudent to start reading the police dossier in that busy cafeteria. However, neither my brother nor I could resist the temptation.

We started on the autopsy report. It explained how Lídia Font had died from cardio-respiratory arrest after ingesting a poison made from *Amanita phalloides*, a highly poisonous variety of mushroom. The huge amount of poison in her blood had led the forensics to conclude that the mushrooms had been processed in such a way as to distil a high concentration of poison, the reason why death had been almost instantaneous. In its natural state, this kind of

223

mushroom, although lethal, took several hours to make an impact and lead to a fatal outcome.

The poison had been found in the *marrons glacés* and not in the bottle of cognac, as the MP had already revealed to us, but not all the titbits were poisoned. The forensic report included a sketch showing how the *marrons glacés* had been distributed in the box. Two places in the drawing contained question marks. We presumed that one belonged to the chestnut Mrs Font had eaten, and the other to the one my brother had swallowed shortly afterwards.

x			?	x
	?		x	
		x		

"Don't you remember which you chose?"

"I think it was the one in the top row, but I'm not sure. You can appreciate I didn't look too closely . . ."

"All right, in any case only five out of a box of fifteen were poisoned," I continued. "That's odd, isn't it? Why not poison the lot?"

"I expect the murderer didn't have enough poison," reflected Borja.

"Maybe, but they don't seem to have been placed randomly. The poisoned ones make a shape. If you ate the one at the top . . ."

"It's in the form of a V," observed Borja.

"The murderer's initial?" I suggested half-heartedly. "Perhaps he's a Víctor, or a Valentín . . ."

"Or a Valèria, or a Vicky . . ." Borja continued.

"Vicky sounds ridiculous for a murderer's name. At the very least Victòria . . ." I retorted.

"Whatever," he allowed. "And talking of initial letters, let's see what's in those compromising reports that the woman we're concerned about commissioned!" he said, searching among the photocopies.

Fortunately, Masoliver had photocopied the three documents that the police had requisitioned from the Fonts' house. In fact, the three reports were very short, as if sparing us the detail. The one with the initials "L.F." (Lluís Font) merely recounted that L.F. and S.V. (Sílvia Vilalta) met up repeatedly in a flat that L.F. owned above his office. It also said that they had once had dinner together in a restaurant in the Port Olímpic and that sometimes the woman left the flat with wet hair. There was no photograph or hypothesis, as if no further explanation were called for.

The dossier with the initials "N.D." (Nieves Dalmau) explained that N.D.'s mother was a single mother and had worked various Barcelona clip-joints in the Sixties and Seventies, including a very famous one on the carrer Ríos Rosas, and that nothing was known about her father. Nieves herself had worked some of those clubs, but only for a few months, before she married E.D. (Enrique Dalmau), who at the time fancied himself as a poet and was rather leftwing. The third dossier, with the mysterious initials "S.M.", merely said that nothing abnormal or scandalous had been discovered in the subject's behaviour or life, and gave no lead as to whether it was a man or a woman. None of the reports were dated.

We then glanced at the statements made by witnesses: by Lluís Font, his daughter and Yanbin, their maid. The police had also taken statements from the staff in the Foix patisserie and from the relatives who came for Christmas dinner. Unfortunately, nothing in those statements added anything to what we already knew, but I was reassured to see that none contained any mention of the painting or of us, except for the brief note to the effect that one of Lluís Font's consultants had accidentally eaten one of the titbits from the box. Borja gave a sigh of relief when he saw his name didn't appear: he was worried that blunder might have thrown up his fake identity.

Someone had handwritten a list of names and we presumed this was the provisional list of suspects. The order of appearance was as follows:

- Lluís Font (the victim's husband)
- Sílvia Vilalta (the victim's sister)
- Carlos Carbonell (Sílvia Vilalta's former fiancé)
- Nieves Dalmau (née Gómez, Enrique Dalmau's wife)
- Enrique Dalmau (MP)
- Mariona Castany

"What the hell is Mariona's name doing here?" asked Borja taken aback.

We looked at the list again, in case we'd read it wrongly. But there it was, without any explanatory note next to it.

"This is a turn up for the books . . ." I whispered, smiling wanly. "Perhaps your friend had a reason to get rid of her cousin."

"Mariona is a real lady!" my brother protested.

"So was Lucrezia, Borja," I replied ironically.

"Don't be so stupid . . ."

But I realized the fact he'd found that name on the list had shocked and worried him.

With the one exception of Mariona Castany, it wasn't difficult to imagine the motives the other individuals had for eliminating the illustrious, if devious Mrs Font. I expect the MP had fallen in love with his sister-in-law and decided to remove his wife from the scene, whom he anyway suspected was carrying on with an eccentric artist. He'd told us "*we* do not divorce just like that" and perhaps he was right. Perhaps he found it easier to get rid of his wife than to send her packing, to endure an acceptable period of mourning and then discreetly marry his sister-in-law. On the other hand, perhaps Sílvia Vilalta was also in love with her brother-in-law (although the incident with the Cuban would belie that) and aspired to become the next Mrs Font. Or perhaps she'd simply poisoned her sister in order to take her revenge on the nasty trick Lídia had played on her years before when she'd stolen her boyfriend.

As for Carlos Carbonell, who'd been Sílvia Vilalta's boyfriend and then Lídia Font's, he could have had the same motive: to take revenge on the woman who'd ruined any chance he ever had of marrying a wealthy heiress. As for Nieves and Enrique Dalmau it was obvious that if the news got around that the presidential candidate's mother-in-law had been a prostitute and that Nieves herself had worked in a clip-joint as a young woman, the scandal would put an end to his political career. However, what Mrs Font – who was no fool – was really after wasn't so much to drive Enrique Dalmau definitively out of politics as to force him to withdraw from the race to become secretary-general and back her husband one hundred percent. She had him by the scruff of his neck . . .

We were totally bemused to see Mariona Castany's name on that list. The only evidence linking her to the whole malarkey was the fact we'd seen Enrique Dalmau leave her house a few weeks before the dismal deed was done.

"It would hardly do for us to turn up at her house and ask her if she had any reason to get rid of her cousin," I commented.

"Hardly. But if her name appears in these police papers, there must be something in it," said Borja anxiously.

After scrutinizing every single one of the photocopies, we decided to see our client the following day and ask him about his friend's possible implication in his wife's murder. Borja suggested we should also talk to his daughter, if she felt strong enough to see us.

"The girl probably knows something. Her mother may have confided in her," said Borja.

"I doubt it."

"We can't lose anything by asking," my brother insisted.

"I'm not sure her father will agree. She's only a girl . . ." I objected.

"A fifteen-year old, Eduard. Perhaps she'll recognize the man in the Zurich."

"You're right," I said, less than convinced. "To change the subject, what are we going to do with these papers?" I asked as I put them away in the bag.

I wasn't at all happy about being in possession of those stolen photocopies. If the police happened to find them (a circumstance that might arise given that Borja had swallowed one of those *marrons glacés*, that they'd caught us in the MP's office on Boxing Day and that the painting now in the hands of the police had been painted by my mother-in-law and not by a party loyalist), my brother and I could end up locked in the Modelo facing serious charges. Where could we hide them? At my place? At Borja's where Lídia Font's portrait was already tucked away? Given the way our client had reacted so gingerly to the no longer so mysterious picture, it was unlikely he'd be prepared to hide them in his house or office.

I mentioned my worries to Borja and he immediately agreed it was a risk we couldn't afford to run. He said he'd take the photocopies to his place, scrutinize them again in case we'd missed some detail and would then do exactly what the policeman had suggested.

"By the way . . . I ought tell you something about the painting by my mother-in-law we took from my place . . ." I said as I was leaving.

I explained the convoluted story about my mother-in-law being inspired by a Joaquim Mir painting and how she'd faithfully copied his signature. After listening to me attentively and looking rather shocked, my brother laughed it off. He said any expert would see the painting wasn't genuine.

"Don't worry. It will soon all seem like one big joke," he smiled reassuringly.

A joke that would end up costing me 2,000 euros.

20

"I don't understand, Montse. It's not like Borja," I fretted.

"Perhaps he stayed with his girlfriend yesterday and slept in this morning," Montse replied provocatively.

"No, she's off skiing with her husband in the Alps . . ." I countered.

"Well, well, so now we know! . . ."

I wasn't in the mood for sly digs. I'd agreed with Borja that I'd pass by his place at around eleven and we'd go together to see the MP. It was gone twelve and Borja was giving no signs of life, so I was starting to get worried. I called him on his mobile several times, but he'd either switched it off or was out of range. No, it wasn't at all like Borja. Lack of punctuality was not one of his shortcomings.

"You know what? I might as well head over to his place."

"Will you be back for lunch today?" grunted Montse.

"Hmm . . . I'll call you later."

I caught a taxi and when I arrived, my heart gave a turn. Two fire engines, a city police car and an ambulance were parked outside the entrance to the building where my brother lives. The street smelled vaguely of burning.

I looked up and saw smoke coming out from one window and that some bits of the façade were sooty. The window belonged to Borja's flat.

"Take it easy, Eduard. It's OK . . ." he said putting his hand on my shoulder before I realized he was standing next to me.

I felt relieved to see that my brother, although looking pallid, was safe and sound. He was in his dressing gown and slippers and also smelled of smoke. I hugged him, and began to calm down. My heart gradually resumed its normal rhythm.

"God! What's happened?" I whispered.

"OK, all clear. We're off," said one of the firemen. "Wait for all the smoke to go, right? And next time be a bit more careful . . . Tell your girlfriend to e-mail her letters to you. And then you won't need to burn them . . ."

"Don't worry, it won't happen again. And many, many thanks!" exclaimed Borja shaking the fireman's hand warmly.

The ambulance and fire engines disappeared in a flash, unlike the small group of onlookers that had gathered around us. Smoke was no longer coming out of the window.

"What the hell happened?" I repeated.

"Let's go for a coffee and I'll tell all. You heard what the man said. We've got to wait a bit before going back up," said Borja.

"But you're wearing your dressing-gown and slippers!"

"So what, half the neighbourhood has seen me in this state," he replied resignedly. "At least it's all Calvin Klein!" he said as if that detail made all the difference.

I said nothing and we went into the bar on the corner. Rather than straight espressos, we ordered two laced with cognac to help get us over our fright.

"It was a stupid accident," Borja started. "This morning I took the photocopies Masoliver gave us into the bathroom, to burn them, but when I lit them, the paper started shooting off in all directions, including into the wastepaper basket. The tissues and plastic bag there caught fire, then the curtain . . . I tried to put the fire out, but only made it worse because I poured on the bottle of massage oils and the silk dressing gown hanging behind the door flared up . . ." He sighed. "In the end, the firemen had to come to sort it out."

"But are you OK? You haven't hurt yourself?"

"I think I've singed a few hairs," he said, touching his locks. "I'll have to pay my hairdresser a visit."

"What about those papers? What did the firemen say?" I asked, rather alarmed. "Did they realize what you were up to?"

"I told them I was getting rid of some very compromising private letters . . . That my fiancée would be back in the morning, and that she's very jealous, and as she'd not written them . . ."

"Did they believe you?"

"The papers all went up in smoke. Besides, what else could I say?"

"You tell me. The scrapes you get into . . . You didn't have to take Masoliver's words so literally. You could just have torn the papers into little bits and thrown them in the rubbish," I retorted.

"Anyway, what's done is done. It was nothing serious in the end . . . Just a scare. Come on, drink up your coffee."

We waited a quarter of an hour before going to see what state the flat was in. Luckily only the bathroom had been ravaged. The rest of the flat was intact although the parquet floor was still swimming in the foam the firemen had used to put the fire out. Borja got dressed and, as it was lunchtime, I suggested he come to my place to have a shower and some lunch. We could see Lluís Font later.

"What are you going to say to Merche about the fire?"

"I don't know. How about I was running a bath and lit one of the candles she gave me as a present . . ." he said brazenly.

"Don't make her feel guilty into the bargain . . ."

"No need to worry on that count. Merche is no cherub."

Montse looked pleased to see us and, predictably, the small matter of the fire took up most of the conversation. We ate macaroni and pork escalope, and for dessert, a lemon cake that Borja had insisted on buying in order not to appear empty-handed. Lola wasn't around and Montse took the opportunity to drop a few hints to my brother.

"So your fiancée is skiing in the Alps . . ." she dropped casually into the conversation.

"What fiancée? You mean Merche?" he said, ignoring the thrust of the word "fiancée". "We're just friends . . ."

I bet Borja had got that response ready days ago.

"Just good friends, you mean?"

"By the way, Montse, as Lola's not here now, I'd like to ask you something. How come such a fantastic woman like your sister is single? Why did she get divorced?" enquired Borja, as if he had a real interest in my sister-in-law's amorous past.

Montse wasn't expecting such an outburst. Nor was I. But it meant Montse forgot all about Merche and rattled on to Borja about her sister's virtues. Lola was sensitive, intelligent and self-confident, was besieged by a host of suitors and had a brilliant professional career. Listening to her, even I'd have fallen for her sister.

"So how's it going between you two?" asked Montse. "You've been seeing a lot of each other recently . . ."

"Well, I think we hit it off . . . Heavens. Look at the time!"

Borja glanced opportunely at his watch. "Eduard, I think we should be getting a move on . . ."

"Come on then!" I said, standing up. "We've got a meeting and people will be expecting you, you know?" I explained.

The moment had come to scarper. Though it was true the MP was expecting us. Montse wrinkled her nose but said nothing. She was in a hurry too: it was anti-tobacco therapy day and she still had to shower and wash her hair to remove all trace of the smell of nicotine.

Lluís Font ushered us into his drawing room. Someone had changed the layout: a glass-topped table with a vase of yellow roses and a new carpet now occupied the space where his wife's body had once lain. The Christmas tree had disappeared and large, flowery cushions were scattered over the settees and armchairs. Various pots with tropical plants stood by the windows.

We told him about our meeting with Masoliver and the information his friend had handed on, which was all the police had to go on. There was nothing new of any substance in it except perhaps for the presence of Mariona Castany's name on the list of suspects. We asked him what motive Mariona might have to murder his wife, but he assured us he didn't have a clue.

"So I am the first on the list . . ." he said shaking his head. "I expect that was inevitable."

"Well, someone has to be first. But that doesn't mean they have any proof," said my brother. "It's normal for the husband to be the main suspect in a case like this."

"Particularly if he's also the will's main beneficiary . . ." I added.

"They can have no evidence because I didn't kill my wife!" he shouted visibly angry. "And as for the money, I

235

don't need it. What do the police think? That I'm some upstart living on his wife's income? Please, don't make me laugh! . . ."

"If your wife had asked for a divorce, that would have changed your financial situation . . ." I insisted.

Borja glared at me and I gathered it was better not to pursue that line. On the other hand, the MP had barely reacted to my comment. I don't know if he was refusing to condescend to answer or was at a loss for words.

"We'd like to ask you something," said Borja, changing the subject. "We'd like to speak to your daughter for a moment, if you'll allow us. I'm not sure, but we thought she might know something . . ."

"Núria?" asked our client rather surprised. "I don't think so . . ."

"The fact is that just before Mrs Font spoke to that man in the Zurich" – Borja preferred not to mention we'd also seem him on the day of the funeral – "they spent the afternoon together shopping. Perhaps she confided in her, told her something . . . That's if you want us to continue on the case, naturally," my brother added.

"Of course," the MP replied hurriedly. "Núria is in her room. She's still not got over it."

"Would you let us talk to her by herself for a few minutes?" Borja insisted.

"I'm not sure . . . If you think it's important and she's in the mood . . . But I hope you will be tactful. I mean there are things my daughter doesn't know and it's better if it stays that way."

He was probably referring to her father's affair with her aunt and the fact that her mother used to go around bribing all and sundry in order to get her own way.

236

"Don't worry. We only need to ask her about two very small matters. Whether your wife had mentioned she was afraid of anyone, and whether she was worried by anything . . ." Borja continued.

"Very well, I'll tell Yanbin to inform her, although she's probably asleep . . . She's been shutting herself up in her room of late."

Núria Vilalta soon appeared leaning on Yanbin's arm. She was pale and wan. She wore flared jeans and a sky-blue T-shirt that exposed her navel and didn't seem the most appropriate garment for this time of year. She was also very thin. A bag of bones, I mean.

"Núria, these gentlemen want to speak to you for a few minutes. They are trying to find out what happened to Mummy."

"All right," she replied.

The girl and the maid whispered a few words to each other in a language I couldn't identify but which I didn't think was European. Then Yanbin kissed her on the cheek and stroked her hair like a loving mother before making a discreet exit.

"If you like, you can use the time to make those calls . . ." Borja suggested to Lluís Font.

"Yes, of course. I'll be back shortly."

Núria Font eyed us unenthusiastically and flopped on the settee. She looked pretty out of it.

"You are the detectives Papa contracted," she said.

"More or less," I answered.

"And how can I help you?"

"We want to know," Borja took the initiative, "if your mother told you anything that might relate to what has happened. Whether she was afraid, or worried about anything . . . Do you know if somebody wanted to hurt her?"

237

"The police have already asked me all this," she said forlornly. "I don't know anything. Nobody ever tells me anything . . ."

She suddenly lost control and began to sob her heart out. I felt wretched making her suffer like that.

"I can't stand any more. I can't stand any more . . ." she muttered between sobs.

"Don't worry," I said genuinely moved. "We won't bother you now. Do you want us to call your father?"

"You don't understand . . . Nobody does! . . . I hated her! I wanted her to die! . . ." she said shaking and crying. "And she did!"

With two daughters around her age, I'm more used than Borja is to this kind of adolescent outburst and attack of rage and sincerity. I decided to take control of the situation before Yanbin appeared and chased us out with her broom.

"All girls of your age hate their mothers and think like that," I said, remembering the rows Montse and the twins used to have sometimes. "It's normal," I said trying to look like an understanding doctor. "You mustn't feel guilty."

"I hated her . . . And now I hate the fact she's not here!" she confessed falteringly.

It can't have been easy being Lídia Font's daughter, I thought to myself. That girl hadn't inherited her mother's natural charms or her personality. Though who knows what Lídia Font was like as a fifteen-year old and before she'd passed through the operating theatre? She was probably as insecure and wilting as her daughter.

"At least now I won't have to study at Oxford," she said, drying her tears.

"Were you thinking of going to Oxford to do a summer English course?" Borja asked affably.

"No . . ."

"You know in a few months this . . . Of course now everything seems like a new mountain to climb, but in time . . ." Borja insisted sympathetically.

"Mama wanted me to *study* at Oxford University . . . Three or four years." And she added, "Literature or something similar . . ."

"*Caramba*, not everybody can get into Oxford . . ." I said. "That's really good."

The Fonts' offspring looked at Borja and me as if we were two old fogeys from another galaxy. The generation gap is doubtless one of the most difficult to straddle, even more so if it goes with the social abyss between the classes that some reckon no longer exists.

"It's a load of shit!" she grimaced. "This Oxford business was all down to Mummy. Papa couldn't care less . . . She was the one who had set her heart on me studying *there.*" From her tone of voice it was obvious that going to Oxford appealed more to the mother than to her daughter. "I had to spend every day shut up at home studying in order to get high marks. They all hate me at school . . ."

"Bah, don't take any notice! It's not such a bad idea to get high marks, I can tell you," I said thinking of our twins.

"They hate me," she said moving from grief to rage, "because Mummy spent her time bribing my teachers to give me high marks . . . As if I didn't know! Everybody knows about it at school, and everybody hates Mummy, and I do too, of course. It's horrible. Horrible! I don't want to set foot there ever again! . . ." And she burst into tears yet again.

A small light flashed at the back of our heads. Perhaps it had been a good idea to talk to the daughter of the deceased after all.

"What do you mean exactly when you say she bribed your teachers?" asked Borja tactfully. "Do you mean she gave them money or presents? That she made generous donations?"

"I don't know how she did it. I expect she gave them money . . . I don't know. All I do know is that my marks were far too high. I'm not that clever . . . but not that stupid either."

"I'm sure she only wanted the best for you," I said trying to console her. "I don't think she wanted to upset you. She wanted you to study in one of the best universities in the world. Lots of people would like to go there."

"You know," she said rather woefully, "she liked all that business of gowns and ceremonies, and being able to put on those ridiculous hats . . . She thought Oxford was full of aristocrats and dreamed I would land one and we'd go to live in a castle, with butlers and all that. I could just see her bowing and curtseying to that old bag" – I assumed she was referring to Elizabeth Regina. "And she was obsessed by my accent, which she said was awful. I hate English!"

"Couldn't agree more!" Borja confessed. "Between ourselves, it's a language of savages. Wherever French exists . . ."

"Ugh, no way! I'd rather continue with English than have to study French," she retorted. "At least it helps me understand my favourite song lyrics."

I thought of the brilliant students, children of less well off families, who'd give their right hand to study at a university like Oxford. What was a dream beyond the realms of possibility for some, was a nightmare that this young woman had just shaken off. You couldn't reproach her in any way. Who'd brought up that skinny girl? I wondered.

Her extremely busy, important parents or a set of foreign maids to whom they'd paid a pittance?

"Do you know whether your mother had a really close friend? A woman she might have confided in?" asked Borja, returning to our concerns now Núria seemed to have calmed down.

"Mummy had no women friends. Last year she befriended our philosophy teacher, but I think she screwed that up."

"Really?" I said encouraging her to continue.

"She even came to spend a weekend with us in Cadaqués," she explained, "but I don't know what happened after that. Mummy must have bribed her. She gave me an A star for her course, but never liked me. My exam was a disaster . . ."

"And what's that teacher's name?"

Perhaps we'd be lucky and her initials would match those on the file we'd still not identified.

"Elisenda. Elisenda something or other . . ." She paused, straining to remember. "That's right, Rourell, I remember now! Elisenda Rourell. As far as we were concerned she was *a complete slag*." And she added. "They reckon she's had it off with every single teacher."

Our bad luck. The initials didn't match, but if all that blackmailing and bribing was right and Lídia had bullied the teacher into passing her daughter with top honours, perhaps her victim had decided to take her revenge by sending her a box of poisoned chestnuts. The idea seemed, nonetheless, slightly over the top.

"So, your mother was always around at school . . ." I insisted.

"She was always on my teachers' backs. My tutor was fed up with her."

"What was her name?"

"Vilardell. Assumpta Vilardell. We call her . . ."

"Yes, I can imagine what you call her," interjected Borja, pre-empting the joke about that famous brand of suppositories.

Lluís Font came in just then. We'd been talking to his daughter for twenty minutes and he must have considered that was time enough. Núria went back to her room with Yanbin and we told our client what her daughter had confessed to us.

"Yes, Lídia had got it into her head that the girl should study for a degree there," he confirmed, "and she may have put too much pressure on her about her studies. Some of our friends' children are studying at Oxford . . ."

"If your wife put pressure on the teachers to give your daughter top marks . . . there may be other things we don't know."

Borja was referring to the fact that other files might exist.

"Are you insinuating one of Núria's teachers preferred to kill Lídia rather than accept an envelope and give my daughter a high mark?" He smiled, "You clearly don't know what these teachers earn! . . ."

I did know, and also how most were too disillusioned to act heroically in the presence of all-powerful, fawning parents. The most likely scenario was that the teacher concerned accepted the bribe and thanked her.

"Yes, if she had one backed into a corner . . ." agreed Borja. "We still haven't identified the mysterious man your wife met in the Zurich. And we must take into account that he didn't seem like anyone belonging to your circle, judging by his appearance."

"Frankly I don't know what to think," our client said. "But as things stand, with me as suspect number one, it wouldn't be a bad idea if you did identify this man and talk to him. I give you *carte blanche*."

"I'd just like to say that we've run up considerable expenses these last few days. You must understand we've had to put other cases to one side, and obviously . . ."

"I'd imagined as much." He took an envelope from his pocket that, as ever, Borja put away unopened.

"Thank you. Are you sure you can't think of any reason to link Mariona Castany with your wife's murder? She's the only name on the list that doesn't fit," Borja insisted.

"I really can't. I have no idea at all. It's very strange. Mariona is an old friend . . ." And he added with a smile, "She's a peculiar woman. Of course with the current account she enjoys she can allow herself the luxury of being whatever she feels like."

"That's all right, then. We'd better be off," said Borja bringing the conversation to an end. "We won't take up any more of your time."

Once we were in the street, I asked Borja if he'd considered the likelihood that the girl was implicated in her mother's murder. Perhaps she'd done something stupid because she couldn't stand the idea of having to go to Oxford. There are adolescents who commit suicide over all sorts of things that appear ridiculous to adults, such as getting bad marks, a romantic upset or not having many friends. Behind that bereft exterior, perhaps Núria Font was one of those who chose to act rather than to suffer.

"You can rule that out," declared Borja confidently. "If this girl had been intelligent enough with the knowledge necessary to plan and carry out such a thing, her mother wouldn't have had to bribe her teachers to give her top marks."

"I'd not thought of that," I admitted. "Maybe we can discount that possibility then!"

I couldn't help feeling sorry for that unhappy, abandoned girl, and was pleased that my twins, for all their defects, didn't resemble her in the slightest.

21

It was still early, so when we left the MP we decided to go straight to see Mariona Castany. We knew she would be in Barcelona until after the Day of the Kings, because she belongs to that tiny cluster of privileged beings who don't have to wait for Christmas or August in order to go on holiday. She'd mentioned that, once the festivities were over, she intended to go to the Caribbean for a month, to one of those places that don't appear in travel agencies' bargain offers. Since we couldn't think of any other way to clear up her possible involvement in the case, we decided to take the bull by the horns and tell her what we'd found in the police reports.

"What a surprise! I wasn't expecting to see you today!" she smiled when Marcelo announced we were paying her a visit.

"Do forgive us for appearing like this, Mariona, but it's urgent. Can you spare us a moment?" said Borja pretending to be very upset.

"Martini or whisky?" asked Mariona. "Better a whisky at this time of day, I should say."

And before we could say no, she'd started to pour the drinks.

Without more ado, we confirmed we were unofficially investigating Lídia Font's death on instructions from her husband, as she'd suspected the night we'd had dinner together at Flash Flash. Although we'd no idea as to what had really happened, we'd been shocked to discover she was one of those suspected by the police, even though, Borja added prudently, her name wasn't among the first on the list.

Mariona Castany didn't flinch. What's more, she smiled half coquettishly and half mischievously like the self confident, self-possessed woman she was. In fact, she seemed to find it amusing, as if at heart she was flattered by the idea she might be suspected of murdering her cousin.

"And you'd like me to tell you why I'm on that list? . . ." she responded, as if it were the most natural thing in the world, while savouring a generous gulp of scotch.

"Well, sooner or later we're bound to find out," said Borja. "We only want to help as much as we can. The police are a bit slow on the uptake, obviously. We thought it better you knew, and that if there is anything that justifies their suspicions . . ."

"I see now. You've come to give me a helping hand," her tone couldn't have been more ironic.

"It's the least we could do," I interjected playing her at her own game.

She lit a cigarette and sat back. She was dressed in white, which made her eyes seem an even deeper shade of blue.

"Well, if someone has told the police (I can imagine who it may have been), it's of no matter. It's hardly a secret. Half Barcelona must be in the know."

The half of Barcelona that is north of the Diagonal, I thought, because once you cross that frontier I don't think many people are aware of the subtle scheming the city's wealthy ladies are so fond of. In fact, I doubt most of my fellow citizens have even heard of Mariona Castany.

"There was an incident in the club," Mariona began, "about a year ago. Lídia was annoyed with me because

I didn't commission her to refurbish my house in the Empordá. Only a few small changes . . . She was furious because everybody had assumed that she'd redecorated my country house, and naturally when someone congratulated her, she was forced to admit it wasn't her work . . ." She failed to suppress a catty grin.

"I understand," said Borja.

"So, we were in the club one day and Lídia started to make uncalled for remarks about my friendship with Isidre Vidal in front of other members, without mentioning his name, naturally." She was referring to the well-known architect who'd been Mariona's lover for years. "Isidre's wife, who was with another little group, heard what she said, because Lídia made sure she did. That would have been the end of the matter if that dimwit Sonsoles Pallarés, who never remembers the gossip she hears or considers who's in the vicinity, hadn't started to crack jokes about him. Roser, Isidre's wife (with whom, by the way, I'd always been on the best of terms), got up and strode out in a huff, hugely insulted. Lídia and silly Sonsoles had humiliated her. There are things nobody likes having rubbed in their faces. I was livid and I warned Lídia that a fellow from Marseille might come knocking on her door. And added, for good measure, that Marseille was a fascinating place where I had several good friends."

I didn't have a clue what she meant but my brother got it straight away.

"My God! . . . You publicly threatened her with murder!" he exclaimed.

Apparently, the reference to the "fellow from Marseille" was a euphemism for a contract killer.

"Bah, I heard that in a film! Obviously everybody knows that if I wanted to . . . But I only said it for the sake of it."

"The police must have taken you at your word, although apparently you aren't the only person who wanted to take revenge on your cousin," Borja went on. "People were queuing up."

"I'd told you so. Although, in fact," she purred mysteriously, "I'd already had the pleasure."

"You're not suggesting . . ." he said rather taken aback.

All we needed was for the mighty Mariona Castany to confess she was involved in Lídia Font's death.

"That I sent her a box of poisoned sweeties! For Christ's sake, of course not! What happened was that after the episode in the club that day, poor Lídia got very few commissions." Out slipped another self-satisfied feline smile. "Lots of my very rich, very close friends decided to go elsewhere to contract their interior designers . . . and she suddenly dropped out of fashion. In the end she was forced stoop to the middle classes. Can you imagine?"

"She bloody deserved it," said Borja, ever the gentleman.

"And, obviously she didn't get an invite to the Prince's wedding either. Although she and Lluís were originally on the list . . ."

"You are devious, Aunt Mariona," quipped Borja in the most fawning of tones.

You don't play around with a woman like Mariona Castany. Borja and I were confident after that exchange that it was highly unlikely Mariona would have bothered to take Lídia Font out of circulation. If what she wanted was revenge, Mariona had no need to go to Marseille for a solution. She only had to trip her up from time to time and shut a few doors in her face. Mariona held lots of keys and she used them at will.

"What about Enrique Dalmau? Are you very close friends?" Borja asked, remembering we'd seen him leaving her house just before Mrs Font was murdered.

"So you know about that too? Well, well . . ." Mariona replied clearly taken aback.

"Lídia was blackmailing him so he would support her husband," my brother blurted out rather rashly. "He's on the police list of suspects as well."

"He came to me for advice," Mariona acknowledged, rather averse to having to tell us so much. "I told him that the best he could do would be to find another hobby away from the world of politics. It could have turned into rather a nasty scandal."

"Thanks again and sorry we barged in so," said Borja as we bid her goodbye.

"You're always welcome here. Goodbye, my friends. I do hope one of these days you'll fill me in . . ."

As we were leaving we saw it was starting to drizzle. It had been a long day and we were tired. We needed time to digest all we'd found out, so we decided to have the rest of the day off and go home. Borja had to clean the parquet and sort out the bathroom, and I'd agreed to run a few errands for Montse, not to mention buying the presents for the Day of the Kings. Besides, I was beginning to be rather sick of the woes of the wealthy and needed to disconnect, even if only for a few hours. The 3,000 euros in the envelope allowed me to forget about my bank account for a while, which was comforting after so many months of financial penury. It was January 4, very cold and, despite the flocks of urbanites off skiing, the city raced along at its usual noisy pace. They were getting the streets in the centre ready for Their Majesties from the Orient, who, according to the locals, always got a much warmer, more magnificent welcome in Barcelona than they did in Madrid.

22

We made little, that is to say, no headway in our investigations over the next few days. Nobody knew who the mysterious man in the Zurich was, though one of the girls in the Foix patisserie, the source of the *marrons glacés*, did tell us rather nervously that she thought she remembered selling a box of something to a helmeted motorcyclist in dark glasses one day when the shop was packed. According to this sales assistant, the man didn't remove his helmet at any point, so she wouldn't be able to identify him, if the occasion ever arose.

Lluís Font had to go to the police station a couple of times to answer questions. In the meantime, the newspapers were full of speculation as to the hand lurking behind this elegant crime. Some, particularly those on the left, pointed to her husband, while feminists licked their lips over the prospect of a case of male violence in the city's upper reaches; others favoured personal revenge or a calculated mistake made by the would-be murderer. One paper signalled the possibility it might be a classic suicide, and another even championed the hypothesis that the murder was part of a macabre role-play exercise.

Thanks to the information provided by Eudald Masoliver we learned that Carlos Carbonell had been living in Brussels for years. He worked as an interpreter for the European Commission and was married to a Belgian woman from a highly respected family who also toiled at the Commission.

He'd not been to Spain for years, and at this point it was unlikely he could be at all interested in taking revenge on his old girlfriend. And it didn't make much sense for the Dalmaus to get rid of Lídia Font. It was reasonable for them to suspect someone else might be aware of the information that Lídia possessed, so the most prudent path for them to take, as Mariona had suggested, would seem to be to retreat gracefully and accept defeat.

All in all, Borja and I were stumped about how to proceed. If the police, with all the latest forensic techniques at their disposal, weren't able to find an obvious suspect, what could we hope to do? On the off chance, after the school term had restarted, we decided to pursue our "Oxford trail" as Borja had baptised it, and we arranged to meet Núria Font's tutor. What we were really after was an exchange with Elisenda Rourell, Núria's old philosophy teacher. If they'd been close friends, my brother thought, perhaps in a moment of weakness Mrs Font had let her in on a secret or two that could cast some light on her death. We were so in the dark that any small clue would be welcome.

Núria Font was a pupil at one of those exclusive all-girl schools on Barcelona's Upper Side that are expensive, prestigious and ideologically conservative, though not necessarily Catholic. This home of juvenile learning occupied a splendid mansion looking down on the Bonanova and was surrounded by a garden that gave it the air of a mini-university campus. Around midday, once classes had finished, we showed up at the school and asked to see Assumpta Vilardell. The teacher received us in her office as if the Pope himself were deigning to grant us an audience. As well as being Núria Font's tutor, Miss Vilardell was also the director of studies, and the first thing she told us was how much work she had and that she could only see us for a few minutes. She was stiff, efficient and unpleasant and didn't wear her fifty-plus years at all gracefully – perhaps she was embittered by work, like so many teachers. She became very uptight when we showed an interest in her tutee's academic profile and the parental plan to send her to Oxford.

"This is a very proper school," she assured us, grimacing in disgust, "and I can tell you that the social or economic position of parents has no influence whatsoever on pupils' marks."

She said this so emphatically that the phrase *excusatio non petita* immediately came to mind . . . When we hinted at the rumour that Lídia Font had tried to influence her daughter's teachers into giving her high marks, she threw us out of her office.

Our exchange with Elisenda, Núria's philosophy teacher, wasn't any more enlightening, although we saw at once why there'd been an affinity between her and Lídia Font. She was in her forties, blonde thanks to her hairstylist, and wore pearl necklaces and countless little gilt chains round her neck and wrists. Her tan was care of ultra-violet rays and her attire was the snobs' uniform: designer jeans, and a sky-blue blouse under a navy blue sweater. The last thing she resembled was a philosopher, but then I remembered from my student days that although Pythagoras was a longhaired eccentric, Aristotle was definitely a Greek who liked the good life.

Nor was it difficult to imagine the scenario in which the philosopher and the MP's wife had become the bosom friends Núria had described to us. I expect Lídia Font had whetted the teacher's appetite by opening the doors to her exclusive world, and, once she'd got the A star for her daughter, lost interest in her new friend. Elisenda Rourell didn't give us any useful information, but we deduced that she was sufficiently annoyed with her former friend not to defend her against our insinuations. It was clear our conversation had put her on edge and that she was afraid a parent or an inspector would denounce her for that fraudulent A star. As we weren't policemen, we couldn't ask directly whether she'd sent a box of *marrons glacés* to Lídia Font, which anyway didn't make much sense given that Mrs Font had already got what she wanted from her. The "Oxford trail" seemed to have dried up so we called it a day.

Disappointed by our fruitless morning we decided to head off to eat in the Vell de Sarrià and draw up a balance sheet of the progress of our investigations. We were just getting into the Smart when I saw a man carrying a motorcyclist's helmet leave the school buildings. It was a black helmet.

"Borja, that's him!" I exclaimed nervously. "It's the man from the Zurich!"

"Are you sure?"

"Absolutely. I'm one hundred percent sure it's him," I replied excitedly.

The stranger stared at the ground as he walked and seemed totally self-engrossed. He didn't notice us. Suddenly, he frowned, swung round and went back into the school as if he'd just realized he'd forgotten something. Borja reacted quickly and accosted a huddle of four pupils who were chatting and laughing next to the wrought-iron fence that separated the school from the street.

"Hey, girls! Do you know that man with the black helmet who just went back into school?" he asked, smiling as seductively as he knew how.

254

"You mean Messegué?" replied one of the girls, who seemed decidedly unimpressed by my brother's charm. Although the pupils in that school wore a uniform, their manner betrayed the exclusive world to which they belonged.

"He's a Latin teacher," said another pupil who was the most Lolita-ish. "He's an oddball."

"Do you know what his Christian name is?" I asked in a flash.

His surname matched one of the initials in the files found at Lídia Font's place.

"How should I know!" the girl replied scornfully. Another shrugged her shoulders.

"It's Segimon," said the one wearing glasses.

She was the only one who looked like a student.

"In other words, Segimon Messegué," summed up Borja. "We call him . . ."

"Shut up, dude!" her friend interrupted. "Who are you gentlemen exactly? Are you selling encyclopaedias?" she added sarcastically looking us up and down.

"We work for a production company," said a deadpan Borja. "We're recce-ing scenarios for some American film-makers." The attitude of the four adolescents changed radically. "As a matter of interest, would you be prepared to work as extras if we shot some scenes in this school?"

"A film?!" all four chorused. "I want to be in it! I want to be in it!" And they all began to jump up and down, visibly thrilled.

"Well, we'll have to see what the producer thinks of this place," Borja went on. "You see the film is set in a school."

"Is it a horror film? Who's in it? Anyone famous?" asked one of the girls, getting all hot and bothered.

"Well, that's top secret and confidential. We can't spread it around . . . But if you promise not to tell anyone . . ." said Borja, who'd got them eating out of his hand.

"We promise! We promise!" the quartet pledged in unison, still jumping up and down, their eyes glittering.

"I can't tell you his name . . ." He paused, "But I will tell you that the lead actor was also the hero in *Titanic*." And he winked at them.

"Di Caprio! Di Caprio!"

They started to hi-five each other, clapping their hands ecstatically.

"Hey, it's a secret, right?" added Borja putting a finger on his lips.

The girls looked beside themselves. They couldn't stop grinning.

"Why did you say that your Latin teacher is an odd-ball?" I asked. "We thought we recognized him . . ."

"Last year he got into big trouble because he made us translate some dirty poem about a guy sucking off somebody or other . . ." one of them answered very matter-of-fact.

"It was Virgil," said the girl in glasses.

"I expect you mean Catullus," I corrected her hesitantly.

"No, because he writes in Latin," confirmed her friend knowingly. The other three nodded.

"So what happened?" interjected Borja.

"They were going to sack him, but he said sorry and they let him stay."

"Besides that," chimed in the girl in glasses very secretively, "he's not married and lives with his mother, who's handicapped. He's a real weirdo."

"You're not kidding," chimed in her mates.

Borja looked at me questioningly.

"I'll tell you later," I mumbled.

One of the advantages of living with two adolescents is that it keeps you a bit abreast of the language young people use.

"He's a perve," asserted the local Lolita. "He's always looking down my top."

It was really very hard not to stare at that girl's swooping neckline, as she wore her blouse unbuttoned down to her navel and had no need to envy the busty charms of a Marilyn Monroe, for example. Naturally, she didn't look a sweet sixteen.

The man with the helmet, whom we now knew was called Segimon Messegué, came back out of the building as self-engrossed as before carrying a sheaf of papers under his arm. He walked over to a motorbike, a rather battered old Vespa, and before he could put his helmet on Borja went over and accosted him.

"Mr Messegué? Segimon Messegué?" He nodded. "We'd like to talk to you for a moment. It's about Lídia Font."

When he heard that name, our suspect blanched and started to stammer. It looked like we'd hit the right trail this time.

"I . . . I don't . . . I have to . . ." was all he could mouth.

"Listen," said Borja not batting an eyelid. "We must speak to you right away. We know what happened to Lídia Font."

"My God!" he piped.

Borja had taken a shot in the dark and, apparently, hit the bull's eye. What that man didn't know is that we were as surprised as he was.

"You're policemen, aren't you?" he said shaking all over.

"No," Borja shook his head. "We aren't police. That's why we need to talk to you immediately."

I imagine Borja was afraid the fellow would take fright and disappear, or use precious time to destroy compromising evidence now he knew he'd been found out. Of course, we had no evidence to implicate him in the murder. It was all conjecture, but he wasn't to know.

"I . . . today . . . my . . . my mother is expecting me . . ." he answered, clearly bewildered. "The girl who looks after her has to leave early today . . . today . . . and I don't like leaving her by herself . . ." he tried to explain. "I must go home. You must . . . you must . . . understand me."

"Perhaps you'd prefer us to call the police . . ." Borja threatened.

"Perhaps you could . . . come home with me . . . it's my mother," he suggested. "I assure you . . . I can . . . explain everything."

"All right. We'll come with you," Borja agreed, given we had no alternative. "But you'd better leave the bike here and come with us."

"Yes . . . of course . . . whatever you . . ." he mumbled.

With no time to discuss our strategy, we walked silently down the Bonanova and hailed a taxi. For my part, I wasn't at all sure that this was a good idea, but it was too late now. I hoped my brother had something good in mind before things got completely out of control.

"My God! So you know . . ." he whispered despondently as we got into the taxi.

Right then, it was as if the whole world had come crashing down on the head of one Segimon Messegué.

23

Weren't we walking straight into the wolf's mouth, like two lambs to the slaughter, I remember thinking as the taxi drove off. Segimon Messegué , a man who was a complete unknown to us and who we now knew almost for certain had murdered Lídia Font, had asked us to accompany him to his den and we'd fallen into the trap.

He was a shy bachelor of nondescript appearance: a middle-aged man still living with his handicapped mother, or so his pupils said . . . Hadn't I seen it all before on celluloid? Right then, inside the taxi, I wished I were less of an unbeliever, and I could seek succour from a saint. I was gripped by an atavistic terror fed by gruesome scenes from so many films. We'd found the monster and were now staring it right in the eye.

While we drove down Muntaner I wondered what surprises awaited us in the home of this Catalan Norman Bates. Perhaps a torpid mother in a wheelchair in a gallery with modernist windows and geometrically patterned floor tiles? Prostitutes cut into little pieces and wrapped in plastic bags piled up in the pantry? Skeletons under beds or inside wardrobes? I was also extremely worried by what that man was intending to do with us once we were inside his house, because I didn't think he would just sit back and offer us a drink while we waited for the police to arrive. And even that depended on whether he was willing to let us use his phone to ring them, because to cap it all my mobile's battery had run out and Borja had left his mobile at home.

As we neared our destination, immersed in a sepulchral silence, I remember reproaching myself for not intuiting right from the start that a sadist or a lunatic hid beneath that appearance of a normal, very ordinary man, as any proper detective would have done. But when I'd seen him in the Zurich, arguing with Lídia Font, that wasn't the impression he'd given. He'd seemed harassed and worried rather than violent, although evidently these things aren't mutually exclusive. On the other hand, our murderer now seemed quite on edge. He was sweating and kept wringing his hands: he hadn't said anything since we got in.

Indeed nobody was saying anything inside that taxi, and the taxi driver must have guessed something was up because he didn't try to engage us in conversation either. He turned the radio up and forced us to listen to a programme dedicated to the menopause and different kinds of vaginal lubricants. I was praying my brother would have a change of heart and tell the taxi driver to take us straight to the police station: in the circumstances that seemed the sensible thing to do. What would happen, if once inside his house, the man pulled out a pistol and shot us to pieces? Or what if his speciality involved a butcher's knife? There were two of us, but I wasn't convinced Borja and I would be able to defend ourselves if that man did decide to attack us.

The taxi stopped in Mallorca on the corner of Muntaner. Segimon hurriedly paid what was on the meter and we all got out, heads down. I don't know about Borja, but my legs were shaking and my heart seemed about to leap out of my mouth.

"Pep, are you sure we should be doing this?" I whispered. "He could be dangerous . . ."

"We can't turn back now," my brother replied, his face panic-stricken.

Segimon Messegué walked a few steps and stopped in front of an ornate nineteenth-century building, its façade decorated with small red bricks. The wrought iron and glass front door was small and unimpressive, but altogether the building retained the modernist charm that had made this district so famous. Messegué took some keys out of his pocket and slowly opened the door. There wasn't a soul on stairs which were unlit and perfectly silent.

"I live on the third floor, flat 2," he whispered. "We can take the lift."

The lift was small and narrow, the original wooden model; once inside we couldn't prevent our bodies from touching. We went up silent and long-faced in keeping with the gravity of the situation. I was convinced my brother and the murderer could hear my heart thudding.

"We've arrived," announced Segimon Messegué haltingly when the lift stopped.

There was no light on the landing. He explained the bulb had gone several days ago but as the ceilings were so high it was difficult to replace because normal ladders didn't reach far enough. He also added that nobody lived in the flat opposite, and that made me even more frightened.

"Mother, it's me!" he shouted as soon as he'd opened the door.

He invited us in and strode off down the passage. We stayed in the lobby. The passage down which he disappeared was long and dark as they usually are in the Eixample district. Although our macabre host had switched the passage

261

lights on, the flat remained dim, perhaps because they still worked on forty-watt bulbs. Without hesitating, our murderer entered the room at the end of the dark corridor and shut the door behind him. Borja and I looked at each other completely at a loss.

Voices reached us in the lobby but we couldn't hear what they were saying. Norman Bates re-entered my thoughts and I almost fainted. I've never been keen on horror films, and felt panic coursing through me. Borja was gritting his teeth and didn't exactly seem to be in seventh heaven either. The good news was that the flat, though it smelled dank and needed a good spring clean, didn't reek of rotting corpses.

Segimon Messegué came back a minute later and said in trembling tones that his mother wanted to say hello. He asked us to follow his line and said we'd be able to speak at ease later. Disoriented by the fact we were in a strange flat and in a situation we'd not foreseen, Borja and I set off obediently along that dark passage like two criminals entering death row.

We stopped opposite that forbidding door which our host asked us to open. Borja, who was in front, gave it a gentle push and walked in warily. I followed him trembling and ready for the worst. Once inside, we both gave a deep sigh of relief and the adrenaline levels in our blood began to drop.

That bedroom faced the street and smelled sweetly of Heno de Pravia soap. The curtains were drawn back and let in sufficient light. Although the furniture was mahogany and antique, the wallpaper had a bright flowery motif and it wasn't the gloomy scenario we'd been dreading. A little white-haired old lady sat there in a wheelchair. She wore a sky-blue dressing gown and was watching television. When she saw us coming in, she greeted us cheerfully and asked us to come nearer.

"You must be the painters?" she asked lowering the volume with the remote control and smiling genuinely. She had only one thing she wanted to say: "Don't take any notice of my son. You have to listen to her. The house must be as she wants it." And convinced we knew what she was talking about, she added: "And this will be their bedroom, whatever my son says. It's the roomiest and looks on to the street, and I don't need so much space . . ."

"Don't worry, mother. We'll do whatever Lluïsa fancies," said Segimon Messegué trying to act normally. "These gentlemen and I need to talk figures now. We'll be in the dining room. Do you need anything?"

"No, I don't really. I'm fine. Don't worry about me. I think I'll have a nap . . . Listen, dear, offer them a coffee and a glass of something," she said hospitably. "I'm sorry, but as you see I can't . . ." she said touching her wheelchair.

My brother and I thanked her, half at a loss and half embarrassed. Maybe she was the one fond of serving arsenic to her guests, I thought, recalling how Lídia Font had died. Her sweet, inoffensive appearance certainly reinforced such a hypothesis.

Segimon Messegué led us silently down the passage to the other end of the flat. We entered a dining room stuffed with furniture that opened on to a gallery full of rather dusty plants.

"Lluïsa is my fiancée," he explained rather miserably as he invited us to sit down. "Her daughter is getting married in three month's time and we're thinking . . ." he hesitated for a few seconds and sighed bitterly, "we thought we'd modernize the flat a bit and come to live here. My mother,"

263

he added as if from habit, "wants it all to be done to Lluïsa's liking, so she feels at home."

Borja and I looked at each other, not knowing how to react. There was an antique wall clock in the dining room, the kind you have to wind up, and its monotonous tick-tock seemed to slow down the passage of time. I glanced around to check that there were no desiccated animals, but the shelves were crammed with books and there was a big glass cabinet full of cut-glass and a motley selection of objects: small coloured feathers like those used to decorate Easter cakes, a small Catalan flag, faded postcards, the odd statuette, china jug and souvenir. The walls in the passage were also full of shelves and books that smelled of dust, but nothing I could see betrayed an arsenal or the habits of a murderer or perverted lunatic.

"So, you've found me out . . ." he said softly, his eyes glued to the floor.

"It's not been easy, but we know what happened to Lídia Font," said Borja prudently, looking very serious.

I decided to keep quiet and let my brother do the talking. Barely an hour ago the mysterious death of the MP's wife had us completely stumped, but then the most unexpected of coincidences had led straight to the perpetrator. This nondescript man stood before us, as we now knew. We still had to find out why.

"And now I expect you'll want to inform the police . . ." he said, still looking at the floor. Apart from being upset he seemed embarrassed. "You did say you weren't police, didn't you?"

"That's right," nodded Borja. "We work for the husband of the deceased Mrs Font. He knows we're here." Ten out of ten for Borja! I thought. "But obviously we will have to inform the authorities . . ."

"I imagined as much . . ."

And with that the man hid his head in his hands and started to cry.

Borja had taken a second shot in the dark and hit the target again. In fact, the only thing that had led us to connect Segimon Messegué to the crime we were investigating was my chance sighting of his argument with the victim in a bar in the city-centre a few days before the murder, a coincidence he couldn't have foreseen. Apart from this circumstance, Borja and I still hadn't the faintest idea what had happened or why, although, by not denying he'd done it, our lead had indirectly confessed to the crime. Borja decided to get to the bottom of the case before ringing the police.

"I suppose," my brother began delicately, "Lídia Font was blackmailing you."

"Yes," Messegué acknowledged after drying his tears.

"It was over that Oxford business and her daughter's marks, wasn't it?" Borja continued gently.

"Yes."

"And you preferred to kill the mother rather than doctor her daughter's marks, right?" Borja hinted.

"Yes . . . No . . . Really," his voice was shaking, "it didn't really happen like that," he muttered.

"OK. Why don't you tell us what did happen?" my brother suggested, assuming the role of good cop.

Of the three files the police had found in Lídia Font's house it was precisely the one initialled "S.M." that stated that nothing had been found. That is, nothing to do with blackmail. It was very odd.

"It was self-defence," he muttered rather more calmly. "She," he added as if he regretted what had happened, "didn't give me any other option."

"So now you have the option of spending the rest of your life behind bars." I said not wanting to appear cruel, but bearing in mind that if Borja was playing good cop, the role of bad cop fell to me. "Perhaps you ought to have had second thoughts before acting as you did. After all, what's wrong with slightly doctoring a mark . . ."

"It was already too late. I . . . I'd not understood her, from the start." He paused. "To be quite honest," he said in a despondent, but dignified tone, "I'd rather go to prison. What Mrs Font wanted me to do was . . . monstrous. She'd have wrecked my life. Mine, my mother's, Lluïsa's . . . At least I can go to prison holding my head high."

Borja and I exchanged glances. What the hell had Lídia Font threatened to do to that poor devil who had preferred to go to jail on murder charges rather than accept a bribe? And when he said that bit about holding his head high, did he mean his professional integrity, the fact he'd refused to doctor Núria's marks? If that was all it was, that teacher had taken the defence of his dignity rather too far.

"Come on, anyone would think she'd asked you to give her daughter a doctor's or architect's qualifications on a plate. But we're talking year ten Latin," I argued, recalling how when translating Caesar I always got into a state about which armies were coming or going.

"Perhaps I should tell you what happened," he said with a sigh. "It would be a good idea to get it out of my system before I have to tell the police. It's the first time I've told anyone."

"Come on then," Borja encouraged him. "We're here to listen to your story. Get it off your chest."

24

The clock struck half past four with an antique timbre that reminded me of days spent at my grandparents. After our parents died, Borja and I spent lots of weekends in a flat like this one: old, dark and melancholy.

Segimon Messegué straightened slightly and tried to recover his composure. He wasn't crying now and seemed calmer, as if the prospect of telling us all was a form of liberation.

"In September, at the beginning of the school year, Mrs Font came to see me in my office and told me she wanted her daughter to get into Oxford. It was very important to her, for some reason or other. The girl" – he swayed his head – "wasn't a very good student, at least in Latin. After thinking it through later, I realized Mrs Font had offered me money, a financial reward or something like, but at the time I'd not really understood her and I thought all she wanted was for me to put pressure on her daughter to study harder. I told her I'd do all I could to ensure Núria got good marks, but, obviously, I meant I'd be on top of her, would pay particular attention to what she did, not that I'd give her a top mark for the fun of it. Núria only just passed when it came to her assessments. Her mother rang me at home in a rage and summoned me to meet her in a bar."

"And you met in the Zurich," I said.

"*Caramba!* You know that as well?" he said rather shocked.

"Please continue," said Borja looking daggers at me.

"She was very angry and insulted because I'd refused to take her money . . . and hadn't really understood what she'd been talking about. She said I was a nonentity, a shitty teacher, and demanded I change the mark and give her daughter an A. Then I got angry as well. I told her there was no way I'd do that, that if her daughter wanted to get the top mark, she'd have to earn it."

"But didn't you realize who you were dealing with?" Borja asked. "I mean Mrs Font was an important . . . influential person."

Segimon Messegué sighed and lowered his head. He looked exhausted.

"I know I'm nobody," he said, "but I don't deserve someone like Mrs Font coming and rubbing my face in it. I do my job well, and with the salary they pay me I can't live in the lap of luxury, as you see, but it's more than a lot of people can aspire to and I count my blessings. Maybe I've not done anything important in my life . . . compared to Mrs Font. But although you won't believe this in these circumstances," he paused, looked us in the eye and then stared back at the floor, "I am a good person."

"Good people don't sent boxes of poisoned sweets," I said gently.

"I told you it was in self-defence," he insisted.

"And what happened then? Did she offer you money again? Did she threaten you with something and you decided you had to poison her?" asked Borja.

"When I told her I wouldn't change Núria's mark, she got very angry and told me I'd regret it for the rest of my life. She said she'd spread it around that I abused my pupils and was a pervert . . . that she knew a couple of girls who'd be prepared to tell tales . . . indecent things. She also said she'd make sure I was thrown out of the school and would never find another teaching job." He paused, "You know? I thought she was quite capable of doing that."

"My, my, Mrs Font!" exclaimed Borja.

"And that's not all," the teacher continued. "She said she'd spread these terrible lies around the neighbourhood so everyone, my mother included, would find out . . ." And he burst into tears.

"What a bitch!" I shouted.

I don't know why, but I believed him. After seeing Lídia Font in action, I wasn't at all surprised by his revelation.

"But you'd already had problems last year when you got some girls to translate a racy Catullus poem in class."

Segimon Messegué sighed again.

"I don't know if you can imagine what an effort it is teaching Latin nowadays. The pupils don't take the slightest interest in anything. Do you know what they thought the Rubicon was after they'd spent three months doing Caesar to death? A disease . . . And do you know what they'd write in exams?" He sighed once more. "In the film *Gladiator* . . ."

"I understand," I said, thinking of our twins' apathetic attitude to their school work.

"I thought perhaps I'd motivate them with Catullus, connect with them . . ." he paused. "In fact anything Catullus wrote they've heard a thousand times on television with fully consenting parents. But it was a mistake on my part."

"You mean, Lídia Font trumped up those accusations," said Borja remembering nothing was on the file found in the Fonts' house.

"Of course she did!" he exclaimed very angrily, going red, whether from anger or embarrassment. "I've never, never, ever laid a hand on a pupil or done anything . . ."

"Calm down," said Borja, patting him on the arm. "Obviously, if as you say, none of this was true . . . I can understand you felt threatened, but you did have other options . . ."

Segimon Messegué looked at us as if we'd just touched down from the moon, a feeling that was beginning to feel familiar.

"You know what? I'm a bachelor, getting on in years, and still live with my mother. People think this isn't at all normal. Do you two never go to the cinema?"

"But you told us you have a fiancée?" I retorted.

"Her name's Lluïsa. We've been going out for a year and a half but nobody at school knows. She also teaches, although she works in another school. She's divorced with two children, a boy who's married and a girl who is on the brink. Lluïsa was going to live here after the wedding, but of course . . ." he said abjectly.

"So why didn't you tell anyone what Mrs Font was planning? Your headmistress, for example," Borja asked.

"You could have gone to the police and accused her of attempted blackmail," I added very professionally.

Segimon Messegué looked at us again, as if we were the freak show. He sighed, closed his eyes for a few seconds and slowly opened them again before resuming.

"I know what some people think, not just at school, but here too, in this neighbourhood: that I have a domineering mother and that's why I've never married, because I'm an only son and still cling to her skirts. That I'm a repressed homosexual . . . That I'm suffering from some kind of mental illness because my father left us . . . If you add to all this that I teach a subject as peculiar as Latin has become today . . . How do you think the police would have reacted if I'd told them this story?" He paused and added solemnly: "'And Brutus is an honourable man . . .'"

"Brutus? Who's this Brutus?" asked Borja alarmed.

"What I mean is that Mrs Font had the odds stacked in her favour. Who do you think they'd have believed? A wealthy, important wife of an MP, or a Latin teacher who's over fifty and does things people think are peculiar, like being a bachelor, reading books, not having much social life and living with his handicapped mother?"

Segimon Messegué was right. A few moments ago I'd put all those ingredients together and come up with the protagonist of *Psycho*. I felt ashamed of myself.

"I haven't offered you anything to drink," he said getting up. "I thought it might make you feel uncomfortable, given the circumstances . . . But I need a cognac."

He took three glasses from the cabinet and poured himself a glass of Magno. Just in case, we declined his offer.

"Do you know," he said, recovering slightly after his first sip, "films and all this psychoanalytical palaver have done a lot of harm to many people who don't lead what others consider a normal life. There are lots of neighbours on the staircase who look at me as if I am peculiar just because I live with my mother and never married. Whenever they put one of those films on telly, they look at me the day after as if they're trying to detect something . . ."

He went silent for a few moments, thinking what to say next. In the end he sighed and finished telling us his story: "When I was six, my father abandoned ship and left us just with the clothes we were wearing. He took the tiny amount saved in the bank, the jewels, cutlery and silver picture frames. He left us with the walls and furniture. Someone told us he went to Argentina, but we never heard any more of him. I don't even know whether my father is dead or alive . . ." He paused and took another sip of cognac. "My mother had to slave away to make ends meet and give me a decent schooling. She said she was working as a seamstress but was really cleaning houses. She was ashamed people might find out, you know? A maid doing the housework . . ."

Borja and I looked down, upset. We could still remember what things were like thirty or forty years ago.

"I'd finished my degree and was working as a teacher: I was about to get married. Suddenly my mother fell ill and, when she recovered, the doctor told us she'd have to spend the rest of her life in a wheelchair. It was a virus, one of those rare diseases that affect the spinal column . . . Carmen, the woman who was my fiancée at the time, insisted we put her into a home, and even found a very nice one on the outskirts of Barcelona. Carmen," he added even more miserably, "wasn't prepared to take responsibility for that kind of situation."

"Sometimes, when you're young, it's difficult to cope with this kind of misfortune," I said to console him.

"Do you know how old my mother was?" he stared at us. "Forty-three. Only forty-three," he repeated, "I couldn't sentence her to a life among the sick and deranged for the rest of her life. It wouldn't have been fair."

"So you decided to break off your engagement."

"Carmen forced me to choose between my mother and herself . . . And I chose. From then on I couldn't find any woman prepared to accept my situation, until I met Lluïsa, obviously. Whenever I got to know a young woman and told her I lived with my handicapped mother, she wouldn't even deign to come home and meet her . . . You can see I'm an average-looking man of modest means and as the years passed by, it got more difficult to get to meet women. But I've never felt so desperate that I wanted to propose to the first person who came along. Time has shown I was right because I did finally find the woman of my dreams."

The sky was starting to darken and we were almost engulfed by shadows, but Messegué showed no sign he was going to switch the light on. That penumbra, together with the clock's monotonous tick-tock, created a strange feeling of peace within me.

"I know it doesn't fit the stereotype," he went on, "but, despite her condition, my mother isn't domineering or embittered or one of those who always find fault with their potential daughters-in-law," he said, as if he'd read my thoughts. "On the contrary, she's always been very optimistic and notices people's good qualities rather than any defects. She tried to understand my father's decision from the beginning, and even today absolves him of any blame. She says that sometimes people take decisions they will later regret, but it's often difficult to retrace one's steps." He paused again. "I couldn't put her into a home. You do understand that, don't you?"

I suppose we are used to clutching to stereotypes as props to get us through life. They often work but not always. How often did I employ those same clichés day-in day-out to judge others? Just before that confession, I'd been feeling terrified at the thought that Borja and I had a disturbed criminal on our hands, simply because the man's life was slightly different from how people think things should be. I'd been unfair.

"Of course she doesn't know," he added, "that I didn't marry because I didn't want to consign her to a home, I mean. I've always told her that I couldn't find the right woman." He smiled. "Now she's delighted by the prospect of Lluïsa. They both are. If they," his voice fell despondently, "had ended up believing, even slightly, the evil slander that woman wanted to . . ."

"So you decided to send her a box with a few poisoned *marrons glacés* . . ." said Borja.

"Initially I thought that what Mrs Font had said was pure bluff, a ridiculous threat, and that would be that. In fact, I'd already decided that Núria's next mark would be an A star. But, one day, just before the start of the Christmas holidays, I had to go the headmistress's office and I overheard Maribel, her secretary, cancelling a lunch appointment that Mrs Font and the headmistress had arranged. The headmistress, Mrs Casas, was in hospital recovering from gastro-enteritis, the holidays were approaching, and Maribel was arranging for them to have lunch after the holidays. I remember she told me Mrs Font was always pursuing the headmistress and this time claimed she had something very important to tell her . . . I was alarmed. I thought nothing would stop that woman and that I had to do something."

"Take her out of circulation, for example . . ." I said.

"No . . . I never thought in such brutal terms," he said, embarrassed. "But what would you have done in my place?" he implored. "What could I do?"

I imagined the situation, with Montse and the children in the middle, and the truth is I couldn't think what to say. Borja lowered his eyes and said nothing.

"Naturally I was incapable of doing anything . . . physically, you understand. I . . . the most that I . . . that I can . . ." he avoided using the word "kill" ". . . I wouldn't hurt a fly, I swear. In fact, it was Suetonius who gave me the idea."

"So you had an accomplice," Borja rushed in.

"I think he means the Latin writer. He's been pushing up daisies for centuries," I pointed out.

My brother knows all there is to know about what kind of flowers you should take to a dinner, but zilch about classical literature.

"It was her name. As she was a Lídia, I immediately remembered the story according to which Livia killed Augustus by poisoning the figs he'd picked off the tree. At school all the teachers knew Mrs Font was partial to glazed chestnuts. I know nothing about poisons but I am a mushroom lover. One Sunday, after overhearing that conversation in the headmistress's office, I went to the countryside with Lluïsa to look for mushrooms, and by chance found some amanitas. That's when I thought of the idea."

"And why did you only poison some of the *marrons glacés*?" asked Borja. "Do you know I ate one by accident?"

"I'm so sorry . . ." he said genuinely upset. "But that's why I did it. In case somebody else ate them . . ."

"Did you never think you might poison the whole family?" It was obvious that if he'd intended to put an end to Mrs Font, he'd acted rashly.

"I knew Núria wouldn't eat them because she's anorexic. Mr Font, her father, suffers from diabetes and never eats sweets. Besides, Mrs Font was really crazy about them." He added, "I know all this thanks to Miss Rourell, a teacher who spent a weekend with them in Cadaqués and spent the next month gossiping about them in the staffroom."

"The poisoned sweets formed a 'V' in the box," I recalled. "That was no accident, I suppose?"

"I pledged myself to the goddess of Victory," he said head bowed. "By way of a small homage to the ancients who'd

275

inspired me . . . That may seem absurd, but, at the time it felt opportune." Then he insisted again, "What else do you think I could have done? Let her get on with destroying my life?"

"Why didn't you take her to court? . . ." my brother retorted.

"It may not seem that way, but I assure you I do believe in the legal system. Don't think I'm one of those people who argue you should take justice into your own hands or anything like that. Quite the contrary. But," he continued after a pause, "in this case the law couldn't help. Many things fall outside its realm: rumours, insinuations, rank, suspicions . . . Perhaps nobody would ever accuse me of anything formally, but you know what people say: where there's smoke . . . And I can tell you," he added conclusively, "Mrs Font was all geared up to ensure there was no shortage of smoke."

The three of us stayed silent for a moment. My brother and I were reflecting on the implications of his confession, and from time to time Messegué wiped away his tears. What should we do now? Tell the police what the man had confessed and let the law courts deal with him? It was clear that a legal-aid lawyer, the only kind that a modest schoolteacher would get, could never stand up to a practice like Font and Associates. They'd bankrupt him before any judge ever passed sentence.

"You must believe me: I do sometimes have regrets," he said sorrowfully. "I know what I did was wrong. I'll have to live with it for the rest of my life."

Borja and I looked at each other without saying anything. We were both in agreement. We wouldn't be the ones to ruin that poor fellow's life. Hunting down Lídia Font's murderer was a task for the police, not for us. At the end of the day, we're just a couple of dreamers trying to survive in a cruel world.

So we informed him our task was to protect Lluís Font, not to discover the identity of his wife's murderer. As long as the police didn't accuse our client or any other innocent, we'd say nothing, we assured him.

Initially Segimon Messegué didn't take in what we'd said. He listened very intently, dried his tears and asked: "You mean you're not going to call the police? You're not going to tell anyone?"

"Our lips are sealed," Borja assured him. "As long as no innocent soul takes the rap."

"I'd never allow that to happen. You have my word," he replied, his eyes welling with tears.

He showered us with thanks, in a trembling voice, and was so overwhelmed that he started to explain about the partition walls his fiancée wanted to pull down in order to extend the kitchen, and gabbled on about a thousand other details that weren't really relevant.

We were almost in darkness when Segimon Messegué switched on the lights in the dining room. The clock had just struck seven and the telephone rang. It was his fiancée. The teacher told her euphorically that he'd ring her back in a while, and that, if she was up for it, they could look at some furniture in the morning. It was if he'd been reborn.

"You're lucky," Borja said dramatically as we walked towards the lobby, "that God doesn't play dice."

"Truth be told," Messegué replied, rather put out by my brother's philosophical comment, "God is a hypothesis I put behind me long ago. But if I had to choose," he looked at the shelves full of bound classical volumes, "I'd go for the gods of Rome. They did play dice, and were fortunately too busy to bother about us." He added, "I expect if the gods of today left us alone a bit more, our lives would be all the better for it."

"I quite agree," I nodded. I couldn't have said it better myself.

While we were still on the landing waiting for the lift, Segimon Messegué took Borja's arm and whispered: "There was no alternative, was there?" he asked as if that question was going to torture him for the rest of his life. "Tell me you understand, that I couldn't do anything else. I couldn't allow that woman to destroy my family . . ."

One of the disadvantages of not believing in God is not being able to enjoy his forgiveness. After that long conversation, I was sure that doubt, even remorse, would pursue that teacher for the rest of his days. It would be his hell, a hell he'd live with, but a hell all the same. We couldn't absolve him, and although I didn't unreservedly approve of the crime the desperate man had committed, I thought he deserved some sympathy. That's why I finally muttered very softly, though loudly enough for him to be able to hear me: "No, I don't think you could . . ." And I pressed the button hoping my brother and I would never regret the difficult decision we had just taken.

25

From time to time I've tried to get Borja to understand that Einstein didn't mean that chance doesn't exist when he said God doesn't play dice. Rather, Einstein was referring to the fact that if there are still dark areas in the theories that try to explain the workings of the universe it is because the theories in question have yet to be refined sufficiently. But he doesn't seem at all convinced by this argument, and in the case of Lídia Font's murder, Borja was convinced both the circumstances by which we discovered her murderer and decided to keep our lips sealed were the culmination of a strange chain of events that in his view wasn't at all random.

"Don't you see, Eduard? If a painter hadn't photographed Lídia Font while she slept and then painted her portrait, and if, as a result of the painting, her jealous husband hadn't decided to contract us because he thought his wife was cheating on him . . . Segimon Messegué would have committed the perfect crime!" he tells me when we recall this adventure, adding, excitedly: "And we were the ones no less who tracked him down!"

As I already have something of a reputation as a spoilsport, I decided not to tell my brother that, by definition, the perfect crime does not exist, and that, in any case, perfect crimes are committed day-in day-out.

Unfortunately we've become quite accustomed to co-existing with them: doddery grandparents who receive an extra dose of medicine because the family's at the end of its tether; children starving to death in the Third World while representatives of the world's governments meet around a succulent banqueting table to justify not doing anything; civilians massacred in so-called legal wars or hijacked by governments who believe themselves to be exemplary . . . These are the perfect crimes and not the murder of Lídia Font. Conversely, in the case we investigated most of the rules as to what constitutes a would-be perfect crime, where chance should play no role, had been broken. However, as I said, I keep these thoughts to myself. It's always comforting to work with someone who has a more naïve – and hence more optimistic – vision of life. If we both thought the same way, we'd have to shut up shop.

A week after the exchange with Segimon Messegué, Borja and I went to see Lluís Font in his parliamentary office and put to him our interpretation of the facts: his wife had been the unfortunate victim of a macabre role play. Although the police were shuffling a number of suspects, himself included, the business of the poisoned *marrons glacés* and the fact nobody recognized the motorcyclist who'd delivered the parcel meant that Borja and I favoured this hypothesis, which had already been headlined by a couple of newspapers. At first Lluís Font looked at us incredulously, as if we were out of our minds, but he gradually came to appreciate the virtues of our explanation.

"If I were you," Borja concluded solemnly, not to say threateningly, "I'd forget the whole thing and persuade a journalist to back our analysis and publish a convincing report to that effect. And I'd also try," he added equally seriously, "to get the police to consider this hypothesis and close the case as soon as is possible."

"I can only assume there's something you don't want to tell me . . ." he responded rather gloomily.

"Do you want us open up a Pandora's box or would you rather become your party's secretary-general?" Borja asked coolly. "You know what these things are like: it's easy enough to crack an egg, but when it comes to getting it back in the shell . . ."

Our client hesitated for a few seconds, as he silently weighed up the advantages of a simple, banal explanation that ensured nobody would find any more skeletons in his cupboards. The Right Honourable Lluís Font must have known his wife well enough to anticipate there might be other time-bombs somewhere that might blow up in his face.

"Well, if you really think that's what happened . . ." he said finally, acting innocent. "You are the professionals . . . Perhaps the police will come to the same conclusion. As I understand it, they've found no other leads." And he added compliantly: "Luckily, they've left me in peace."

The searches and questioning had apparently been wound up, and once Mrs Font was six feet under, nobody seemed to be at all interested in finding out what had really happened, with the possible exception of a few sensationalist publications that were still devoting column inches to the most extravagant theories. The rumour that the *marrons glacés* weren't poisoned but past their consume-by-date, had also done the rounds, an idea the patisserie was quick to deny in a thunderous press statement. By that stage, the police must have been aware it would be very difficult to solve the case, while, on the other hand, the presiding judge must have been afraid that if he continued delving he might unearth a scandal that he could end up regretting.

"Best of luck with the secretary-generalship," Borja wished the MP as he said goodbye and pocketed the final envelope that signalled the end of our investigation.

In a variation on Einstein's famous saying, someone wrote that God doesn't play dice with the universe, but a game of his own invention. We are the gamblers and he's the croupier distributing the chips. We're forced to inhabit a room in darkness and play his game for eternity, ignorant of the rules, with a pack of blank cards and an infinite number of calls at our disposition. It's hardly a very optimistic vision of the human condition, but it comes in useful when we need to seek consolation for the idiocies, big or small, that sooner or later we all commit.

I expect some smart guy will think that Borja and I assumed a role of dispensing judgement that wasn't rightfully ours when we decided not to take Lídia Font's murderer to the police, and will be scandalized to think that by the same token some people claim a right to seize arms and take justice into their own hands. I don't think one should take things that far. It may be true that neither my brother nor I had the slightest right to decide who is above human justice and who isn't, and perhaps we'll be reproached because we behaved like those arrogant little gods who see fit to pull the strings of happiness and misfortune from a heaven that does accept wagers, as if life were a game of dice. For my part, if we do find ourselves sitting by a table, in the dark, playing a one-off game we never asked for, under the invisible smile of the croupier who dealt the cards, I prefer to think we'll attempt to play the hands we've been dealt as best we can.

Epilogue

About a month after our last conversation with Lluís Font, a couple of newspapers published extensive reports on role-plays and the murders perpetrated by adolescents addicted to this sinister entertainment. A handful of experts defended the hypothesis that the strange circumstances surrounding the death of Mrs Font made it more than probable it had been such a crime committed by one or more players. One of the specialists, who appeared on various television chat-shows airing the topic, forwarded the thesis that the criminals might be youths connected to gangs of Eastern European mafiosi, who tried their hands at this kind of macabre entertainment as a way of initiating themselves in the criminal business organized by their fathers.

In subsequent months, the newspapers ceased to raise the topic. Given the total, disconcerting lack of evidence, the police finally embraced the hypothesis forwarded in the press as a possible explanation of the murder. And since neither the police nor the courts are what you call overstaffed (and since no doubt they'd received a couple of decisive phone calls), the dossier was left to rot at the bottom of a cupboard and, to all intents and purposes, the case was relegated to the archives.

Lluís Font and Sílvia Font never married. In fact, after her sister's demise, Sílvia Vilalta lost all interest in her brother-in-law, to the extent that they never spoke another word to each other after the day of the funeral. Mrs Vilalta cut her hair very short, bought loose-fitting clothes and came out as a lesbian. Needless to say, quite soon after that, she grew back her hair and married a slick Madrid businessman whose bank accounts were infested with red digits. Mrs Vilalta, now Mrs Perales, has become a fan of bullfights, white *orujo* and Holy Week Processions. She spends her summers in Marbella and Majorca, not always accompanied by her husband, with what remains of the jet set.

In the end Núria Font didn't go to Oxford. She matriculated in an art and design school and now works for the Catalan Bank Foundation. She's put on weight, made several visits to the operating theatre and gets more and more like her mother. Her boyfriend is a young man from a wealthy household, who is a member of the youth organization of the party her father heads, and occasionally, when not skiing in Baqueira, Núria babysits for the Infanta Cristina.

Enrique Dalmau didn't stand as candidate for the party secretary-generalship and enthusiastically supported Lluís Font's candidacy. He works as a consultant for the Telefónica and enjoys semi-retirement in the Empordá with his wife, who is by the day more tanned, wrinkled and bored with country life.

Doña Mariona Castany continues to be bored and to cough. She stopped her membership of the club to which her cousin had also belonged and now devotes her time to literary *conversazione*. Spiteful tongues say she's writing her memoirs and more than one soul is shaking in his shoes.

Segimon Messegué still teaches in the same school and is now married. His mother is gradually fading away but not in great pain. The three live together in the flat that now has several fewer partition walls and a bigger kitchen. Apparently they lead a peaceful, harmonious life as a thoroughly well matched couple. Despite the remorse that sporadically hits him, Messegué the teacher is a happy man.

Lluís Font is his party's secretary-general and for a second time will stand as its candidate for the Presidency of the Generalitat, although there's not the slightest chance he will become its Right Honourable President. His new partner is a famous, wealthy antiquarian he will most likely marry, and his golf swing has improved considerably. He no longer collects paintings and now devotes himself to philately.

Pau Ferrer made a miraculous recovery from his attack of apoplexy. However, he passed away a few weeks later, following a tremendous overconsumption of pastis celebrating his recovery. The value of his work has gone through the roof and the Town Hall named a street after him in Barcelona, in Poble Nou to be precise.

Lola and Borja still meet secretively, although Borja continues to be Merche's official lover and to live in her flat, which now has a new feng-shui friendly bathroom. Lola still psychoanalyses herself, does yoga and contributes to the wellbeing of the economy of La Rioja, but she's become more of an optimist and has decided not to give up hope. She's convinced one day she'll hook my brother.

As for the business of the paintings, Lluís Font wanted to forget all about the portrait Pau Ferrer had painted of his late wife. Borja took it to Holland (fortunately, after the painter had gone to pastures new), where he sold it incognito for a goodly sum that, as loyal brothers, we divided up equally.

My mother-in-law's painting, on the other hand, didn't go away. A committee of experts declared it was a genuine Mir and valued it at an astronomical figure. To spare himself further headaches, Lluís Font decided to donate it to Montserrat, where it now hangs on the walls of the Museum next to other, genuine, Mirs. Before it was removed, a fine arts student made us a copy (for the modest sum of one thousand euros), which we've hung back in the corner of our passage to keep Joana happy. As for the other paintings my mother-in-law finally agreed to give to Borja, I haven't a clue what he's done with them.